The Market Place of Appleby

THE COUNTY GUIDES

WESTMORLAND ALONE

IAN SANSOM

Fully Illustrated Throughout

4th ESTATE • London

4th Estate
An imprint of HarperCollins*Publishers*
1 London Bridge Street
London SE1 9GF
www.4thEstate.co.uk

First published in Great Britain in 2016 by 4th Estate
This 4th Estate paperback edition published in 2017

1

Copyright © Ian Sansom 2016

A catalogue record for this book is available from the British Library

ISBN 978-0-00-812174-7

Printed and bound in Great Britain by Clays Ltd, St Ives plc

MIX
Paper from
responsible sources
FSC™ C007454

Find out more about HarperCollins and the environment at
www.harpercollins.co.uk

For the other Morley

Here we entered Westmoreland, a country eminent only for being the wildest, most barren and frightful of any that I have passed over in England.

DANIEL DEFOE,
A Tour Through the Whole Island of Great Britain

CHAPTER 1

THE INFERNAL STREETS
OF SOHO

LONDON WASN'T KILLING ME. The opposite.

We had returned from Devon in a low mood. Things had not gone at all according to plan. Miriam was no doubt distracting herself with some dubious engagement or other and Morley was probably working on some mad side project – a history of war, perhaps, or of the Machine Age, or of Russian literature, or indeed of Russia, or of fish, of friendship, of God, of the gold standard, goodness only knows what. (See, for example, *Morley's War – And its Enemies* (1938), *Morley's Forces of Nature in the Service of Man* (1932), *Morley's Fish, Flesh and Fowl: A History of Edible Animals* (1935), *Morley's Mighty Bear: A Children's History of Russia* (1930), *Morley's Studies in Christian Love* (1934), *Morley's God: His Story* (1936), and one of my favourites, published rather unfortunately in 1929, *Morley on Money: How to Make It, How to Spend It, How to Save*

It.) I was just glad that I'd been granted a few days' leave. I had been making the most of them.

I had been drinking late in the Fitzroy Tavern, and had then found myself at an after-hours club just off Marshall Street which was frequented by some of my old International Brigade chums. The club was run by a big Kerryman named Delaney who ran a number of places around Soho. Delaney self-consciously styled himself as a 'character' – all thick Irish charm, topped off with faux-aristo English manners. He wore a white tie and tails, carried a silver-topped cane with a snuff-pot handle and came across as everyone's friend, the debonair host, generous, witty and easy-going. He was not at all to be trusted. I had been introduced to him by a couple of lads from Spain, Mickey Gleason, a tough little Cockney with a beaten-up face, and a classically dour stick-thin Scotsman named MacDonald. Gleason liked to boast that he had saved my life in Spain, when in fact all he'd done was to cry a well-timed 'Get down!' when we had come under unexpected fire one evening near Figueras. And MacDonald had loaned me money – dourly – on my return. So I was in debt to them both, in different ways. Delaney had also been in Spain, apparently, though I hadn't met him there. It was said that he'd been working as some kind of fixer. I rather suspected that he had enjoyed as much business with Franco's forces as with the Republicans.

Delaney's places were famous for their wide range of entertainments and refreshments, and for the clientele. It used to be said that to meet everyone in England who really mattered one had only to stand for long enough at the foot of the stairs of the Athenaeum on Pall Mall: the same might just as truly be said of Delaney's basement bars and bottle parties. Poets, artists, lawyers, politicians, doctors, bishops and blackmailers, safebreakers and swindlers: in the end, everyone ended up at Delaney's.

I'd started out drinking champagne with one of Delaney's very friendly hostesses, a petite redhead with warm hands, cold blue eyes, sheer stockings and silk knickers, who seemed very keen for us to get to know one another better – but then they always do. She told me her name was Athena, which I rather doubted. Sitting on my lap, and several drinks in, she persuaded me into a card game where I soon found myself out of my depth and drinking a very particular kind of gin fizz, with a very particular kind of kick – a speciality of the house. My head was swimming, the room was thick with the scent of perfumes, smoke and powders, I had spent every penny of the money that Morley had paid me for our Devon adventure, I was in for money I didn't have – and Athena, needless to say, had disappeared. My old Brigade chums Gleason and MacDonald were watching me closely. Even through the haze I realised that if I didn't act soon I was going to be in serious trouble: Delaney was renowned for calling in his debts with terrible persuasion.

I excused myself and wandered through to the tiny court-yard out back. There were men and women in dark corners doing what men and women do in dark corners, while several of the hostesses stood around listlessly smoking and chatting, including Athena, who glanced coolly in my direction and ignored me. She was off-duty. Out here, there was no need to pretend.

I picked my way through the squalor, past beer crates and barrels, and went to use the old broken-down lavatory in the corner of the yard. When I tried to flush the damned thing I found it wasn't working. I stood pointlessly rattling the chain for a moment and then climbed drunkenly up onto the seat and quickly discovered the problem. There was no water in the cistern. And there was no water in the cistern for a very good reason: the lav served as Delaney's quartermaster's store. I had found myself a little treasure-trove. A honeypot. I glanced up and thanked the heavens above. Through the rotting makeshift roof of the lav I could see the starry blue sky. It was a beautiful warm autumn evening. Suddenly, everything seemed OK. And anything seemed possible. I seemed to have shaken off my torpor. Without hesitation – without thinking at all – I decided that this unlikely Aladdin's cave presented me with the perfect opportunity to make up for some of my losses inside. I dipped my hand in and helped myself to some supplies. I took only what I needed.

I felt revived and reinvigorated. I considered returning to the game. I had a feeling my luck had changed. Athena and the other women had gone back inside and there were only one or two couples remaining in the yard. It would have taken a dousing with a bucket of cold water to get their attention. In the opposite corner to the lav was a convenient big black door out into an alleyway. I realised I could probably disappear and no one would notice.

I unbolted the door, slipped into the alleyway, and started walking.

The infernal streets of Soho were unusually quiet and I found myself once again wandering that blessed one-mile square, from Oxford Street to the north and Shaftesbury Avenue to the south, from Regent Street to the west and Charing Cross Road to the east, that strange other-world –

or underworld – where so many of us come to escape, and where many of us find ourselves for ever trapped.

Unfortunately I wasn't able to return to my temporary lodgings, a place just off Wardour Street that generously, if inaccurately, described itself as a hotel. I doubted that the management would be willing to accept an IOU for payment and there was no way I was parting with my recently acquired pocketful of treasure and so, eventually, exhausted from my wandering and still trying to flush the various excitements of the evening out my system, I found myself lying down to nap on a bench outside Marlborough Street Magistrates' Court. This was ironic.

In his *Dictionary of Usage and Abusage* (1932) Morley writes at great length, and with utter despair, about the common misuse of the term 'irony' by both the ill-educated and the over-educated. 'An ironic statement,' he writes, 'is like a good lawyer or a politician. It says one thing but means another. An irony is not merely something odd or unusual. The word "ironic" should never be used to describe the merely unfortunate.' My laying my head down outside Marlborough Street Magistrates' Court was not therefore, perhaps, *strictly speaking*, an irony. It was, however, at the very least, extremely unfortunate.

Marlborough Street Magistrates' Court was the first court in which I ever appeared. It was shortly after I had returned from Spain. I had become involved with a woman who was involved with a man who had treated her badly. Fortunately at the time I had money and resources and was therefore able to employ a good lawyer who managed to get me off with only a fine on a charge of common assault. This encounter with the law was an experience I was determined not to repeat. Morley would probably have called this hubris.

It was 3 a.m., I was cold and tired, and as far as I recall my reasoning went something like this: if the safest place to sleep rough is a police cell then the next safest is probably on the steps of a court. On both counts, alas, I turned out to be wrong.

I found myself prodded awake by three varsity types who had clearly enjoyed a long night at the opera. They were all in evening dress. There was a fat blond buffoonish-looking one who wore a yellow gardenia in his buttonhole, a greasy-looking one, with brilliantined hair, and the other – the other might almost have been me, before everything that happened had happened.

The first thing I knew was the greasy one tapping his cigar ash into my eyes.

'Come on, man! Up! Up!' He was leaning over me, breathing his fumes into my face. 'Show some respect to your betters, you filthy swine!'

'Hey! Tramp!' called the fat blond, with an Old Etonian drawl. He ran his fingers through his unruly mop of hair. 'What's the matter with you! Have you no home to go to? Eh? Come on! Come on! Up! Up! Up! Queensberry Rules, old chap! I'll take you on!'

The greasy one grabbed me by my lapels. I feared that at any moment he might reach into my pockets.

I acted on instinct.

I raised my knee, catching him on the side of the head. I had been involved in enough brawls in Spain to know that the important thing was just to get away. That's all I was intending to do.

As he was falling back I hooked my foot around his ankle and then swung a punch at his head with the side of my fist. He twisted as he went down and it was his face that hit the pavement first. There was a sickening thud. The fat blond then came roaring at me, but I managed to push him off easily, and he too went down. The third man ran off.

The fat blond would be fine: he was just winded and shocked. But the greasy-looking one had gone down hard and had gone very quiet: there was a pool of blood haloed around his head. He did not look at all well.

To repeat, to be clear, and in case of confusion: I had been attacked; I had acted in self-defence; and what had happened was clearly an accident.

In his controversial pamphlet 'In Defence of Self-Defence' (1939), a much misunderstood little treatise, Morley sets out the criteria by which a person or nation might justly claim the right to defend themselves. Morley's criteria are clear, detailed and as follows: self-defence may be permissible only if and when '1) a culpable 2) aggressor 3) knowingly initiates 4) an unprovoked attack 5) on an innocent victim 6) who is unable to avoid or escape harm 7) without causing necessary 8) or proportionate harm 9) with the sole intention 10) of defending himself'. Morley then further clarifies the permissible conditions and circumstances with a sentence that subsequently caused him much pain and harm: 'Even when such conditions are met it is still debatable whether self-defence by a nation or person can ever be considered a moral good.' His timing was unfortunate. It was a misjudgement: everyone, it seems, even Morley, makes mistakes.

All I would have had to have done at that moment was to explain what had happened to the police. It was perfectly simple. I was an innocent man, admittedly an innocent man with a criminal record, who had recently returned from Spain, admittedly fighting with the communists, and who had found employment with one of the country's most revered and famous authors, admittedly on rather false pretences, and I had been enjoying a quiet evening in Soho, admittedly in an after-hours drinking establishment, from which I had fled, admittedly owing almost one hundred pounds in gambling debts, and with a pocketful of illegal and expensive powders, which were not, strictly speaking, my own . . . *whereupon* I had become the victim of an unprovoked attack by culpable aggressors and had acted with the sole intention of defending myself.

I did not in fact attempt to explain this to the police.

I owed it to Morley not to get him involved.

And, of course, I owed it to myself.

I did what anyone else would have done.

I ran.

CHAPTER 2

RISE AND SHINE AND GIVE GOD THE GLORY

As dawn broke I found myself wandering up Great Portland Street, onto the Euston Road and along towards St Pancras.

The arrangement had been to meet Miriam and Morley outside St Pancras at 7 a.m. in order to set off on our next adventure. The first of the *County Guides* – to Norfolk – had been published to a few lukewarm reviews by the sort of reviewers who regarded Morley's work as beneath contempt. 'Yet another pointless and whimsical outing from England's self-styled "People's Professor,"' wrote some pompous – anonymous – twit in the *Times Literary Supplement* (or the 'Times Literary Discontent', as Morley called it). 'A work of enthusiasm rather than of serious scholarship,' complained some frightful bluestocking in *The Times*. 'Essentially frivolous,' concluded the *Manchester Guardian*. But Morley was not discouraged. He was never discouraged. He was not, I believed at the time, discourageable. The Grand Project, *Le*

Grand Projet – The County Guides, a complete guide to the English counties, a people's history, forty or more volumes in all, a volume to be completed every three to four weeks, his mad modern Domesday Book – was not to be derailed by anyone, rich or poor, educated, uneducated, varsity, non-varsity, dead or alive.

During my time with Morley I did my best to share his enthusiasm, and his enthusiasms, but I was really always trying to escape, to get away and to start again. The work was not uninteresting, of course, and our adventures became renowned but I was never really anything more than a glorified secretary. Morley referred to me variously over the years as his amanuensis, his assistant, his apprentice, his accomplice, his aide and, alas, as his '*bo*. None of these descriptions were really adequate. For all my work and for all that the photographs featured in the books were mine I was only ever an acknowledgement buried among the many others, the page after endless page of Morley's super-scrupulous solicitudes. 'With thanks to the ever-accommodating British Library, to the staff of the London Library, to the University of London Library . . .' and to all the other libraries, *ad nauseam*. 'To H.G. Wells, and to Gilbert Chesterton, to James Hilton, to Nancy Cunard, to Dorothy Sayers, to Rosamond Lehmann, to Naomi Mitchison, and to dear Wystan Auden . . .' and to all of my other famous friends. 'To the dockers of east London, to the factory workers of Manchester . . .' and to the fried fish sellers, to the piemen and piewomen, and the dolls' eyes manufacturers of this great island nation. 'To the people of Rutland, of East Riding, of west Dorset . . .' and of everywhere else. 'And to Stephen Sefton, and the Society for the Protection of Accidents, without whom . . .' Etcetera, etcetera, etcetera.

Every time we finished a book I vowed never to return. Sometimes I dreamed of going back to Spain, or of going back to teaching, of worming my way into the BBC, of pursuing photography seriously as a profession, of starting again somewhere else. Anywhere else. Anywhere but England. And every time I failed. I was always drawn back, again and again. I never quite understood why.

With St Pancras up ahead and the prospect of another tiresome cross-country jaunt before me I was thinking that this time I might simply trail off into deepest darkest north London, to lick my wounds, clear my head and devise a plan.

And then I saw Miriam.

In one of his very strangest books, *Rise and Shine and Give God the Glory* (1930), part of his ill-fated Early Rising Campaign – hijacked by all sorts of odd bods and unsavoury characters – Morley advises the early riser not only to practise pranic breathing and vigorous exercise, but also to utter 'an ecumenical greeting to the dawn', a greeting which, he claimed, was 'suitable for use by Christians, Jews, Mohammedans, Hindoos, and peoples of all religions and none'. Borrowing words and phrases from Shakespeare, Donne, Thomas Nashe, Robert Herrick and doubtless all sorts of other bits and pieces culled from his beloved Quiller-Couch and elsewhere, the greeting begins with a gobbet from William Davenant: 'Awake! Awake! The morn will never rise / Till she can dress her beauty at your eyes.' I was never a great fan of this 'ecumenical aubade' of Morley's but this morning it seemed to fit the occasion.

Miriam sat outside St Pancras enthroned in the Lagonda

like the sun on the horizon: upright, commanding and incandescent. Her lips were red. She had dyed her hair a silvery gold. She wore a brilliant green dress trimmed with white satin. And she had about her, as usual, that air of making everyone and everything else seem somehow slow and soft and dull, while she alone appeared vivid and magnificent – and hard, and fast, and dangerous. *Une maîtresse femme*. For those who never met her, it is important to explain. Miriam was not merely glamorous, though she was of course glamorous. Miriam was beyond glamour. Hers was an entirely self-invented, self-made glamour – a self-fulfilling and self-excelling glamour. And on that morning she looked as though she had painted herself into existence, tiny deliberate brushstroke by tiny deliberate brushstroke, a perfectly lacquered Ingres wreathed in glory, the Lagonda wrapped around her like Cleopatra's barge, or Boadicea's chariot.

'Good morning, Miriam,' I said.

'Ah, Sefton.' She took a long draw on her cigarette in its ivory holder – one of her more tiresome affectations. She brought out the ivory holder, as far as I could tell, only on high days, holy days and for the purposes of posing. She looked at me with her darkened eyes. 'Early, eh? Up with the lark?'

'Indeed.'

'And the lark certainly seems to have left its mark upon you.' She indicated with a dismissive nod an unsightly stain on my blue serge suit – damage from my night outside Marlborough Street Magistrates' Court.

I did my best to rub it away.

'I'm rather reminded of Lytton Strachey's famous remark

on that stain on Vanessa Woolf's dress—' (This 'famous' remark is not something that one would wish to repeat in polite company: which is doubtless why Miriam enjoyed so often doing so.)

'Yes, Miriam. Anyway?'

'Yes. Well. Father's away for the papers, Sefton, so really it's very fortuitous.'

'Is it?'

'Yes. It means that you and I can have a little chat.' This sounded ominous. 'Why don't you climb up here beside me.' She patted the passenger seat of the Lagonda.

'I'm fine here, thank you,' I said. It was important to resist Miriam.

'Well, if you insist,' she said. 'I'm afraid I have bad news, Sefton.'

'Oh dear.'

'Yes. I'm afraid this is going to be the last of these little jaunts that I'll be joining you on.'

'Oh,' I said, and said no more.

'Well, aren't you going to ask me why?'

I paused for long enough to exert control. 'Why?'

'Because,' she said triumphantly, 'I, Sefton, am . . . engaged!'

'Oh.'

'I think you'll find it's traditional to offer congratulations.'

'Congratulations,' I said. 'Who's the lucky fellow?'

'No one you know!' She gave a toss of her head and looked away. 'He gave me this diamond bracelet.' She waved her elegant wrist at me. 'Isn't it marvellous!'

It was indeed a marvellous diamond bracelet, as marvellous diamond bracelets go. Men had a terrible habit of showering Miriam with marvellous gifts – diamonds, sapphires, furs and pearls, the kind of gifts they wouldn't dare to give their wives, for fear of raising suspicion.

'Isn't it more usual to exchange rings?' I asked.

'Oh, the ring is coming!' said Miriam.

When the poor chap had finalised his divorce, I thought, but didn't dare say.

The sound of the city was growing all around us: horse and carts, cars, charabancs, paperboys, and above it all, the sound of a woman nearby selling flowers. 'Fresh flowers! Fresh flowers! Buy my fresh flowers! Flowers for the ladies!'

Miriam smiled her smile at me and glanced nonchalantly away.

'Anyway, Sefton,' she continued, 'this means that I won't be joining you and Father on any more trips. And so I just wanted some sort of guarantee that you'd be around for as long as this damned project takes. Father has become terribly fond of you, Sefton, as I'm sure you know.'

There was in fact very little sign of Morley's having become very fond of me. Morley didn't really do 'fond'. I don't think he'd have known the meaning of 'fond', outside a dictionary definition.

'Sefton?'

I didn't answer.

'As you know, Father needs a certain amount of . . . looking after. After Mother died . . .'

Mrs Morley had died before I had started work with Morley; he and Miriam rarely spoke of her.

'He needs a certain amount of care and attention. I hope you can—'

We were disturbed by the sounds of what seemed to

be an argument – of an English voice uttering some low, strange, unfamiliar words, the sound of a woman shouting in response, either in distress or delight, of voices calling out, and of general confusion and hubbub.

'Thank you!' called the voice. '*Gestena! Danke schön. Grazie. Go raibh maith agat! Xie xie. Muchas gracias!*' It was a Babel of thanks-giving. It could only be one person: Morley.

He approached us, be-tweeded, bow-tied and brogued as ever, and carrying what appeared to be every single British daily newspaper, and very possibly every European paper as well. He appeared indeed like an emblem or a symbol of himself: Morley was, basically, a machine for turning piles of paper into yet more piles of paper. He was also carrying, rather incongruously, an enormous bunch of gaudy and distinctly unfresh-looking flowers.

'Ah, Sefton!' he said, thrusting the flowers at me, and the newspapers at Miriam.

'Flowers, Mr Morley?'

'Oh no, sorry, they're for Miriam. The papers are for us, Sefton, reading material on the way.'

I duly handed Miriam the flowers.

'For me, really?' she said. 'You shouldn't have, Sefton!' She handed me the papers in return, shaking her diamond bracelet at me unnecessarily as she did so. 'They're lovely, Father, thank you.'

'Well, I could hardly not buy any flowers from the woman, since she allowed me to practise my – admittedly rather rusty – Romani on her.'

I had no idea that Morley spoke Romani. But I wasn't surprised.

[15]

'Devilish sort of language. Do you know it at all, Sefton?'

'I can't say I do, Mr Morley, no.'

'Dozens of varieties and dialects. Indo-Aryan, of course, but quite unique in many of its features – tense patterns and what have you. And only two genders. Easy to slip up. I fear I may have said something to upset the poor woman. I remember I was in Albania once and I thought I was complimenting this very proud Romani gentleman about his pigs, when in fact I said something about defecating on him and his family! Terribly embarrassing.'

'Father,' said Miriam. 'That's enough. Get in the car.' This was one of Miriam's more successful methods of dealing with Morley: shutting him up and ordering him around.

We were beginning to attract a small crowd of onlookers. The Lagonda was by no means inconspicuous, and Morley was the closest thing to a celebrity that one could possibly be without appearing on the silver screen. I scanned the crowd, beginning to feel distinctly uncomfortable. I half expected to see Delaney, Mickey Gleason, MacDonald, the police, or indeed my old varsity chums from the steps of Marlborough Street Magistrates' Court. Morley of course was unaware and oblivious, as always.

'Anyway, Sefton, now you're here you can tell me, what do you think of the Great North Road?' He was shifting quickly and apparently senselessly from subject to subject – as was his habit.

'The Great North Road, Mr Morley?'

'Yes, indeed, *the* great English road, is it not? The spine of England! From which and to which everything is connected. Any thoughts at all at all at all?'

I had no thoughts about the Great North Road, and

Morley wasn't interested in my thoughts about the Great North Road. He was interested in using me as a sounding board.

'Do you know Harper's book on the road?'

'I can't say I do, Mr Morley, no.'

'Pity. Marvellous book. Rather romantic and sentimental perhaps – and outdated, actually, thinking about it.' His moustache twitched – the telltale sign of an idea forming. 'Miriam, don't you think we could perhaps produce our own little *homage* to the Great North Road on this trip? *Four Hundred Miles of England*?'

'I think our hands are rather full at the moment, Father,' said Miriam. She got out of the car, and ushered Morley into the back seat of the Lagonda, and began fitting his desk around him.

'Well, a slim volume perhaps? *Three Hundred and Forty Miles of England*? We could stop our tour at Berwick-upon-Tweed?'

'Yes, Father.' This was another of Miriam's techniques for dealing with Morley: humouring him. It seemed to work.

'A little preface or prologue, perhaps? A record of significant stops and sights along the way. A kind of investigation of the *meaning* of the road. You know, I rather have the notion that it might be possible to invent an entirely new kind of writing about places – a kind of chronicling not only of their physical but also their psychical history, as it were.'

'Psychical geography?' I said.

'Exactly!' said Morley.

'I don't think it would catch on, Father,' said Miriam.

'No?'

'No, Father.'

'Well, just a straightforward guide then, perhaps? Stilton. Stamford. Boroughbridge. Are you a fan of Stilton, Sefton?'

'Stilton, Mr Morley?'

'The cheese, man. Are you a Stiltonite? Lovely with a slice of apple, Stilton.'

'Where do you stand on Stilton, Sefton?' asked Miriam.

'The English Parmesan, Stilton,' said Morley. 'Or perhaps Parmesan is the Italian Stilton . . .'

'Sorry?'

I was no longer listening. I had spotted a policeman who had noticed the crowd and who was now walking briskly towards us. He seemed to be looking directly at me. I was still standing by the Lagonda. I checked quickly behind me; if I was quick I'd be able to make it across the Euston Road and disappear.

All was not lost.

And then it was.

I had spotted him too late.

The policeman blew his whistle: many people had now stopped and were staring. I had nowhere to go.

'Hey! You!' he called, reaching the Lagonda. 'You! What on earth are you doing?'

'Excellent whistle!' said Morley, from the back of the Lagonda.

'What?'

'Your whistle, Officer. I wonder, is it made by Messrs J. Egdon of Birmingham, by any chance?'

'I have no idea,' said the policeman.

'They're renowned for their whistles,' said Morley.

'Really? And you're a whistle expert, are you?'

'I wouldn't say that . . .' began Morley. He was a whistle expert, obviously.

'Who are you and what do you think you're doing?' demanded the policeman.

'Well, to answer your second question first, if I may,' said Miriam. 'I think you'll find that what we're currently doing is speaking with you.'

'You are blocking the entrance to the station, madam,' said the policeman, unamused.

It was true: Miriam had parked, as usual, without care or regard for other road-users, and our small gathering of onlookers had begun to cause a problem.

'Oh, that!' said Miriam. 'Are we? Really? I hadn't noticed. I'm terribly sorry.'

'I'm not looking for an apology, madam. You realise I could book you under the Road Traffic Act of 1930 for obstructing the king's highway?'

'Oh, I'm sure you could book us, Officer,' said Miriam, lowering her voice and fixing the poor policeman with her most glimmering smile. 'But the question is, would you?'

This threw the policeman rather, who obviously was not accustomed to being flirted with by a woman of Miriam's considerable expertise and world-class charms. He changed his line of questioning and turned to me.

'Is this man with you, madam?' He had clearly noted my rather rumpled appearance.

'Him?' said Miriam.

I could see that she was considering causing mischief. I prepared to sprint.

'Of course!' she said. 'He's my fiancé, aren't you, darling!' She leaned across the car and offered her cheek for me to kiss. I had no choice but to oblige. 'He's just bought me some flowers, Officer. Isn't he adorable?'

'Ha!' came a laugh from the back seat.

'And this gentleman?' asked the policeman, nodding towards Morley.

'This is my father, Officer.'

'And where are you all headed this morning, might I ask?' The policeman addressed his question to me.

'We are headed to . . .' I had no idea. Miriam and Morley usually didn't tell me where our next destination was until we were en route. I rather suspected that this was often because they didn't know themselves.

'We are headed, sir, to the very heart of the country!' said Morley. 'The hub! The centre! The cultural capital!'

'And where is that exactly?' asked the policeman, having extracted a notebook from his pocket and taken down the registration of the car.

'Westmorlandia!' said Morley. 'Westmoria! The western Moorish county.' He began whistling the Toreador Song from *Carmen*. (He had a recording of the Spanish mezzo-soprano Conchita Supervia singing the role of Carmen, which he claimed was one of the great cultural achievements of all time. He also claimed this, it should be said, for Caruso singing '*Bella figlia dell' amore*' in *Rigoletto*, Rosa Ponselle in *Tosca*, and John McCormack singing just about anything.)

'No. Still no wiser, sir. If you wouldn't mind spelling that for me?'

'Westmorlandia! One of the truly great English counties!' continued Morley. 'Home of the poets! Land of the great artists! We shall be visiting the mighty Kendal. Penrith – deep red Penrith! Ambleside. And we shall follow the River

Eden as she rises at Mallerstang and makes her majestic way to the Solway Firth—'

'We're visiting the Lake District, basically,' said Miriam.

'Ah,' said the policeman, writing in his notebook.

'Westmorland!' cried Morley. 'Do get it right, Miriam, please. Westmorland! Which – combined with Cumberland – might together accurately be described as "*the Lake District*", though of course the designation is rather misleading because—'

'And what is your business exactly in Westmorland, sir?'

'Our business? Our business, sir, is to do no less than justice and no more than to offer honest praise!'

'*Exactly* what is your business in Westmorland, sir?' The policeman was getting tired: I'd seen it before. Morley's eccentricities could be extremely wearing.

'We are writing a guidebook,' said Miriam. 'To the county and its—'

'Roofs!' cried Morley. 'The roofs of Westmorland are some of the finest in the land, Officer. Did you know?' Morley had a great enthusiasm for roofs. He began explaining the quality of the roofs of Westmorland to the policeman, who wisely decided at that point that it was time to give up.

'On you go then, please,' he said. 'If you don't mind. Move along now, people,' he told the crowd. 'There's nothing to see here.'

'Thank you, Officer,' said Miriam. 'Come on, darling,' she said to me.

I remained silent and did not breathe a sigh of relief until the policeman had plodded his way far enough from the car and the crowd had begun to disperse, and then I breathed a very big sigh of relief indeed.

'Let's go,' I said to Miriam, moving quickly around to the passenger side of the Lagonda.

'All aboard the Skylark!' cried Morley.

'You're keen all of a sudden,' said Miriam to me.

'Charming man,' said Morley. 'The British bobby – curious, steadfast, and yet always polite.'

'Indeed,' said Miriam. 'Now, gentlemen, shall we just check our route.' She produced a map and several of the boards onto which Morley had mounted his county maps. 'Our route. We begin in London, obviously.'

'Starting at the GPO?' said Morley. 'The traditional starting point of the Great North Road?'

'Starting here, Father. And then Herts, and Beds, and Cambridgeshire, Rutland, Lincs, Notts, West Riding—'

'And then a left turn at Scotch Corner?' said Morley.

'And then a left turn at Scotch Corner,' agreed Miriam.

I was half listening and had already begun opening the door when I saw him: MacDonald. He was perhaps a hundred yards away, across the other side of the Euston Road. I recalled him mentioning before that he lived somewhere up around King's Cross. When he saw me, as inevitably he would, he would doubtless want to raise the small matter with me of my having abandoned our card game, and possibly the no less small matter of my having departed with several packets of Delaney's precious 'snuff'.

I stood rooted to the spot.

'Scotch Corner,' continued Morley, 'being of course the junction of the traditional Brigantian trade routes in pre-Roman Britain, and the site where the Romans fought the Brigantes. The Brigantes being?'

'A Northern Celtic tribe, Father,' said Miriam wearily.

[22]

'Correct! And they fought the Romans at the Battle of?'

'Scotch Corner?' I said.

MacDonald had seen me. He stared for a moment in surprise and then smiled a dark smile and began making his way hurriedly through the traffic. I had less than two minutes. If I stayed with Miriam and Morley and the car we wouldn't be going anywhere fast.

I had a choice. I could either make a run for it or . . .

'The Battle of Scotch Corner is correct!' said Morley. 'You know, perhaps you're finally getting to grips with this stuff, Sefton. We'll also have a look at the Stanwick fortifications, which are about five miles north-west of Scotch Corner, and which I think I'm right in saying form the most extensive Celtic site in Britain—'

'I think I might get the train, actually, Mr Morley, and meet you there.'

'The train?' said Miriam.

'Ah!' said Morley. 'You're thinking of the Settle–Carlisle line, Sefton, are you not? Possibly the greatest railway line in the country. A sort of railway companion to our Great North Road journey?'

'Exactly,' I said. 'That's exactly what I'm thinking, Mr Morley.' MacDonald was twenty yards away and closing fast. 'I would just need some money, to—'

'Of course,' said Morley. 'Good thinking, Sefton. I think it would certainly add immeasurably to the book if you were to travel by train, we were to travel by car, and then we could compare notes when we arrive in Westmorland and—'

'I really need to go now though.'

Morley consulted his two watches – the luminous and the non-luminous dials.

'Yes, the seven fifteen, would that be it?' He had – naturally – memorised most of *Bradshaw's*. 'If you hurry you might just catch it.'

'I'm going to catch it.'

'Good, now let's give the man the means, Miriam, shall we?'

Miriam looked at me suspiciously but nonetheless began rooting around in her handbag.

'And the camera, Miriam, give him the camera. Come on, hurry!'

'The new Leica, Father? But I thought I might—'

'Now, now, Sefton is our photographer. We did buy the camera for him. It's the new Leica, Sefton. I was particularly impressed by the set-up we saw in Devon, and I thought perhaps you might enjoy using it. Give you something to play with on the train.'

'I'm sure Sefton will find something to play with on the train,' said Miriam, handing over the camera and a handful of cash. 'That should be enough to cover a third-class fare, Sefton. You'll be travelling third class, of course?' Miriam smiled at me.

'For colour?' said Morley. 'Yes, good thinking, Miriam. Travelling with the people. Ours is a people's history, after all.'

'Of course,' I said.

MacDonald was just five yards away. I could see the veins throbbing in his neck and his eyes bulging.

'I think we'll beat you to it,' said Miriam, but I didn't answer: I had already begun to run.

'Sefton!' shouted Miriam after me. 'Where will we see you?'

'Appleby!' cried Morley. 'The county town of Westmorland! We'll meet you at Appleby, Sefton!'

I ran into the station, shouting to the porters for the seven fifteen: they pointed me to platform 3. I ran past the ticket inspector and made it to the last carriage of the train, where a young mother was struggling to get on with a young girl and a baby. The guard was calling the departure as I managed to lift up the girl and slam the door behind us – and the train shuddered forward.

I stood for a long time at the window looking out for MacDonald, but there was no sign of him. I must have lost him in the crowd.

Satisfied, I made my way to a compartment, squeezing past fellow passengers and their luggage. There was the woman with the baby and the child.

'Mummy, Mummy,' said the little girl. 'It's the nice man, Mummy.'

The young woman smiled at me warmly.

'Do you mind if I join you?' I said.

'Of course,' she said. 'Thank you so much for helping.'

'The baby will cry,' said the little girl. 'But all babies cry. What's that?' she asked, pointing at the Leica.

'It's a camera,' I said.

'What's a camera?'

'It's something that you can take pictures with.'

'Like a drawing?'

'Yes, I suppose.'

'Is there a pencil inside it?'

'No,' I said. 'There's not a pencil.'

'Is there a pen?'

'No, there's not a pen either.'

'Is there paint?'

'Look,' I said. 'Do you want to see?'

The girl looked at her mother, her mother nodded, and the little girl came and sat close to me; as we left London I showed her how to open the camera, how to check the shutter and the focus and how to frame a photograph. I took her photograph and she took mine.

'Are you coming with us?' asked the girl. 'Mummy, can the man come with us?'

'The man is on his own journey,' said the mother. 'He'll be going somewhere himself.'

'We're going to Carlisle,' said the little girl. 'Where are you going?'

I looked at her. I felt suddenly exhausted. 'I don't know, actually,' I said. 'I don't know where I'm going.'

'You're funny,' said the girl. 'You're a funny man!'

'He's just tired,' said the mother. 'Let him rest now.'

CHAPTER 3

72 MILES, 1,728 YARDS

IT WOULD NOT BE an exaggeration to say that Morley was obsessed with the Settle–Carlisle line. He was obsessed with a lot of things, of course, but the Settle–Carlisle remained for him one of the great foundation stones – 'one of the canonical lines', he famously called it – of England. I have no doubt that if he could have seen the destruction later wrought upon the railways he would not have despaired: he simply would not have let it happen. There would have been campaigns, organisations, books, leaflets, marches on London, a popular uprising: Mr Beeching would have taken one hell of a beating.

After our trip to Westmorland, Morley revised and up-dated his famous book, *72 Miles, 1,728 Yards* (1935), in which he describes the route of the Settle–Carlisle line, mile by mile, yard by yard, tunnel by tunnel, viaduct by viaduct, every gradient, every ascent, every twist and every turn. I doubted that the new edition would sell a single copy. It became a bestseller. His most popular lecture series – by far – during our time together was on the Settle–Carlisle line, more popular than the 'World of Wonders' series and the 'Home Husbandry' series combined, more popular even than the infamous 'Communism, Fascism: What *Exactly* is the Difference?' lecture, which always drew a crowd (and which, indeed, on a number of occasions, caused a riot). In the Settle–Carlisle lectures he lovingly described the planning and construction of the line, its maintenance, and its day-to-day operations, beginning and ending with a sing-song recitation of the names of all the stations: Settle, Horton-in-Ribblesdale, Ribblehead, Dent, Garsdale, Kirkby Stephen, Crosby Garrett, Ormside, Appleby, Long Marton, Newbiggin, Culgaith, Langwathby, Little Salkeld, Lazonby and Kirkoswald, Armathwaite, Cotehill, Cumwhinton, Scotby, Carlisle. Anywhere north of Watford the recitation of the station names alone would often earn him a standing ovation. (Admittedly, the lectures tended to be less popular in the Home Counties, though they played surprisingly well in London.)

Indeed, in recognition of his work promoting the railway industry in general and the Settle–Carlisle line in particular the big four railway companies – the old LNER, and the GWR, the LMS and SR – awarded Morley in 1939 a fat little golden locket, inscribed with his name, on a chain. He needed only present the locket to a ticket inspector on board a train to be granted free first-class travel the length and breadth of the country. Morley cared almost nothing for awards and baubles: one bathroom at St George's was rather eccentrically papered with moulding black and white certificates and citations that might more usually have been proudly framed and displayed, and a crusty old armoire in a guest bedroom served as storage space for his various medals, statuettes and gifts 'in recognition of', many of them featuring depictions of pens and quills carved in marble, onyx, or, in one case – after our trip to Durham – made out of coal. Morley referred habitually to such awards and honours as 'chaff' and, occasionally, as his 'pointless paper empire'.* But the Big Four locket travelled with him everywhere until the day he died.

According to Morley in *72 Miles* the Ribblehead viaduct was one of the modern wonders of the world, and the route of the Settle–Carlisle line 'a journey into the heart of England and Englishness'. (He also made this claim, it should perhaps be conceded, about the west Norfolk coastal route, the GWR journey down to Devon, the Esk Valley line, and the all-electric Southern Belle route from Victoria to Brighton.) Describing the Settle–Carlisle line he rose to sweeping rhetorical heights:

---

* The only piece of paper I ever saw framed was Morley's school leaver's report, an extraordinary scrap of a document, yellow with age, which hung above his desk and which placed him unceremoniously in division 'D' among his classmates, numbered at number 30 out of 30. 'Morley's schoolwork this year, as in every other year,' the report reads in its entirety, 'has alas been far from satisfactory. His test work has been uniformly poor and his prepared work often worse. In mathematics a typical piece of prepared work scored 2 marks out of a possible 50. In other subjects his work is equally bad. He has often been in trouble because he will not listen but will insist on doing things in his own way. I believe he has ideas of becoming a journalist or a writer. On his present showing in English this is quite ridiculous. He is a boy in possession of eccentric ideas who does not respond to the usual disciplines. He may possibly be suited to employment as an apprentice in some trade that requires neither rote learning nor regular hours.' Fair comments.

There is perhaps not even in Switzerland, nor in India, nor indeed in our own green and pleasant land, a more magnificent journey than that through the great valley of the Ribble, and on round the broad shoulder of the mighty Whernside at Blea Moor, on through the valleys of the Dee and Garsdale, up and over the watershed to the summit at Aisgill, and then through the justly named Eden Valley towards Carlisle. If the good Lord Himself had been a railway engineer during the glory years of the mid- to late nineteenth century, he could not have plotted a finer route.

'The Settle–Carlisle line is not a journey by rail,' he famously concludes *72 Miles*. 'It is the journey of a soul.' There was perhaps a slight tendency in all his work for Morley to wax unnecessarily lyrical but in his great paean to the Settle–Carlisle line his prose found its proper subject. The book combined perfectly his poetic instincts with his obsessive practical concerns. He was an expert on every aspect of the line, from the 'long, tall' Douglas fir and Baltic pine sleepers, to the 'doughty' granite chipping ballast, the 'proud' stations, the tunnels, the viaducts and the signals. And of course, alas, he became an expert on its tragedies.

I can imagine the journey that Miriam and Morley enjoyed on the way to Westmorland, the same journey as all our journeys: Morley seated in the back of the Lagonda, among his books and writing requisites, Hermes typewriter wedged into position on the portable desk, sharp pencils at his elbow and paper conveniently to hand, pouring endlessly forth like some magic fountain. His voluminous notes on the journey – including a ton or more of notebooks and index cards and papers for the putative book on the Great North Road, never published – are housed now, along with all his other manuscripts, in Norwich. There, in his favourite county, the 'still centre', the reader might recreate that journey from London to the Lakes, from the Whittington Stone at Highgate Hill, 'memorial to Britain's most benevolent citizen', through the beauty of Welwyn village, home to Edward Young, author of *Night Thoughts*, and, according to Morley, echoing Dr Johnson, 'perhaps England's most defected genius', and on and up past the famous Folly Gateway at North Mimms, stopping off for refreshments at the Roebuck at Broadwater, past the Caxton Gibbet, and on and on past Retford, Bawtry and Doncaster. Morley has often been described – and dismissed – as a mere antiquarian, a provincialist, a dull draftsman, a 'topophiliac', in the words of one particularly patronising critic in the *Listener*, devoted to places rather than to people, but he was also interested in the everyday lives of men and women, and in the chronological as well as the chorological: indeed, a part of his research for the Great North Road book includes dozens of typed pages on the history of the St Leger race, held annually since 1776, when it was won by a brown-bay filly sired by the mighty Sampson; the notes, like Morley, go on and on, and range wide and deep, a complete portrait of people in a landscape, a Brueghel in words. He was, in all his books, and certainly during my time with him compiling *The County Guides*, a celebrant of all that was living – though in reality our business was often with death.

My guess – though I can't confirm it – is that it was probably Miriam who spotted the train in the distance. She wouldn't have wanted us to beat her to Appleby. I can imagine her tossing back her head and stamping her elegant foot hard on the pedal. *We must get there before him.* Thank goodness she didn't.

On the train I was showing the little girl how to work the camera. Her name was Lucy. She had a gap-toothed smile and freckles, little fat cheeks, and ringlets, and dark, dark eyes – a happy carefree face, the picture of innocence, a perfect Pears soap little girl. Her mother was dozing with the baby in her arms, the baby's head resting gently on her breast. Lucy and I sang songs together and played games, and took it in turns to take photographs of the scenery. I took a photograph of her. She took a photograph of me. We whistled with the train's whistle and knelt together on the seats as the world went rolling by, enjoying the freedom and the speed: the rocks, the stones, the trees, the farms, the sorry-looking Swaledale sheep.

Click.

Click.

Click.

It was one of those warm September days that seems like a bonus, that makes you believe that you still have another chance and that everything is not lost. We cheered as we reached Settle, laid out like a neat little pocket handkerchief under the pure blue sky. We passed a graveyard and then emerged into the vast Ribble Valley. We hollered our way through the long dark tunnel under Blea Moor and again as we reached the summit at Ais Gill, the vast cliffs opposite like something out of the American Wild West, the blazing heather and the dry-stone walls making everything appear as though it were wrapped and packaged and ready for presentation. Looking back, I wonder if that was perhaps the very last time I was truly happy: enjoying the golden stillness of the English countryside, mind and body relaxed and calm, moving inexorably forward and on and up towards the future and adventure. I had no thought then for London and what happened there. No thought for myself. I was moving on. I was in transit, a pilgrim journeying towards better things. Everything subsequently seems somehow darker, less good, lacking, broken and profane.

At a certain point, just before Appleby, the railway crosses the River Eden for the first time. I lifted Lucy up a little by the window, so that she could admire the river and the little viaduct with its piers and parapets and arches: twin wonders of nature and of human invention. A southerly wind blew the choking smoke away and we were granted a perfect view of Westmorland, 'perhaps the most scenic county in England', according to Morley. And so it is. I gave Lucy the camera and held her tight while she leaned out and took photographs.

The road swoops along and around from the railway approaching Appleby and in my mind's eye I can see Miriam in the Lagonda, staring in dismay as we speed away before her. None of us of course had any idea that anything was wrong until things went wrong.

One moment we were upright, and then the next the carriage tipped and everything changed. I remember there being absolute silence before the screaming began.

In his short book about the history of the railways and their impact on the people and landscape of England, *Morley's Ringing Grooves of Change* (1938), in a chapter entitled 'Thundering Towards Our Fate', he writes that 'In our Steam Age, humans are becoming incapable of recognising the everyday. We value only the extraordinary. Trains themselves, for example, those astonishing creatures of such recent invention, exist now only in our conscious-ness and in the public imagination when they become un-tameable, when they become beasts, when they do damage or become derailed . . . It seems that in our time the rail-way accident,' he concludes, 'matters more to us than the railway itself. The crash, so much an admitted matter of course in railway travel, is becoming the condition of our culture.'

What follows is perhaps the most difficult and painful recollection from all my time with Morley. I will be as brief but as accurate as I can: the official records are of course available.

CHAPTER 4

PANDAEMONIUM

It was the most violent collision. There was a moment's shudder and then a kind of cracking before the great spasm of movement and noise began. I fell forward and struck my head on the luggage rack. I was momentarily stunned and knocked unconscious.

When I came to I found we were all tilted together into a corner of the carriage – me, the mother and the baby. Our coach seemed to have tipped to the right, off the tracks, and become wedged against an embankment. What were once the sturdy walls of the carriage were now buckled and torn like the flimsiest material: the wood was splintered, the cloth of the carriage seats split, everything was broken. I remember I shook my head once, twice, three times: it was difficult to make sense of what had happened, the shock was so great. The first thing I recognised was that the mother and baby were both crying loudly – though thank goodness they appeared to be unharmed – and that the carriage was shuddering all around us, shaking and groaning as if it were wounded.

'Are you OK?' I said.

The woman continued crying. Her face was streaked with tears.

'Are you OK?' I repeated.

Again, she simply sobbed, the baby wailing with her.

'We must remain calm,' I said, as loudly and authoritatively as I could manage, above the sounds, trying to reassure both them and myself, willing them to be quiet.

'Where's Lucy?' she said.

Where was Lucy?

I stood up, still rather disorientated and confused.

'I don't know—' I began.

'You have to get us out!' said the woman, between sobs. 'I have to find Lucy.'

'OK,' I said. I was still gathering my thoughts, trying to work out what to do.

'GET US OUT!' yelled the woman, suddenly frantic. 'I have to find my daughter! You need to do something.'

I didn't know what to do.

'You need to do something!' yelled the woman again. 'Help us!'

The carriage continued to rock and sway all around us; clearly, we had to get out.

I looked around: the window was open to darkness and the tracks beneath us.

'What's under there?' cried the woman. 'Is Lucy under there? Lucy! Lucy!' She did not wait for a response – she was hysterical. 'Lucy! Lucy! Lucy!'

'Look!' I said. 'You just have to let me check that everything is safe.' I was worried that Lucy might be trapped beneath our carriage.

'Lucy!' wailed the woman.

'Let me check if it's safe!' I said. 'And we'll find Lucy and we'll get out!'

The shuddering and moaning of the carriage suddenly stopped and the baby paused in its crying and the woman looked at me as though having just woken.

'You must stay here,' I said, more calmly. 'Just for a moment. I have to check if it's safe. Do you understand? And then we'll get out together.'

She looked at me, terrified.

'Don't leave us here!' she said.

'I'm not leaving you here. I'm just going to check that there's a way out through the window and underneath the carriage and then—'

'Take my baby!' she said.

'What?'

'Take my baby with you and make sure he's safe. I'll wait here for Lucy.'

'Look, if you just wait here for a moment—' I began.

'You're not leaving us here!' said the woman. 'You take my baby and you look for Lucy and I'll wait for her.'

'But—'

'You! Take the baby!' she cried. 'And you make sure he's safe. And then you come back for me and Lucy.'

She was confused. She thrust the sobbing child towards me. I had no choice but to tuck him under one arm and crawl down with him through the window into the darkness underneath the train. If I got the baby out I could get the mother out. And then I could find Lucy.

Everything was wrong. It was dark, chthonic. There was a smell – a horrible sort of combination of hot metal and coal and oil and damp earth. I was breathing fast. It was as though we were being born. I made my way carefully with the baby underneath the carriage and across the tracks – I remember the rails somehow being greasy, with oil? – and then up into the light.

It was the most incredible sight: coaches were slewed across the tracks, rails were bent and twisted into terrible shapes, giant sleepers uprooted, the ballast ploughed through and scattered, and thick black smoke was everywhere. Passengers were emerging from their carriages and there were men running down the line towards us from up ahead. But what do I remember the most and the most clearly? It was the sound: the sound of birds singing. It seemed impossible, impossible that they could be heard above the din of breaking glass, and of grinding mechanical noises, and the rushing of flames, and the terrible cries of injured people, but there they were: birds, singing. It was like Spain, again. I deliberately took deep, deep breaths, trying to steady my nerves – and was struck suddenly by another smell, some sickening, thick, horrible smell that somehow I didn't recognise.

I ran a few yards with the baby heavy in my arms. Now I could see the full length of the train: it looked like a buckled toy, as though having been tossed up and destroyed by some malevolent child. Up ahead was Appleby Station, with its proud sign and its fine passenger footbridge and over to my left were the station's stables and cattle pens, the sound of the innocent animals joining the cacophony. And fire – fire was quickly spreading through the carriages, some of which had shattered entirely, stripped back to their thin pale wooden frames. It was a graveyard scene. It was pandaemonium.

Everything was wrong

One of the train guards was wandering up and down politely calling out, 'Are there any doctors on the train? Any doctors on the train at all? Any nurses? Nurses? Any nurses?' He might almost have been asking for passengers to present their tickets. A dining car steward was sitting down at the side of the tracks, stiff, stunned, blood on his starched white jacket, and – the most extraordinary thing – a refreshment trolley perfectly upright beside him, the Nestlé chocolate bars scattered around his feet, still glistening in their bright wrappers, broken cups and saucers like fragments of some vast whole. I ran over towards him and placed the crying baby in his arms.

'Sir!' I said. 'I need your help. Sir?'

He looked at me blankly.

'You must go up to the station and look after the baby,' I said. 'Yes? Until the mother comes.'

He continued to look at me blankly.

I repeated myself: 'You must take this baby and go up to the station. Do you understand? I need you to get up and take the baby with you up to the station, yes?'

He looked at me for what seemed like a long time but then nodded and I helped him up and he began walking slowly along the line towards the safety of the station.

'Go to the station with the baby!' I yelled at him again – he glanced back and nodded – and then I ran and plunged back down under the carriage to help the mother. Soon the flames from the other carriages would reach us.

She remained exactly where I had told her, in the corner of the carriage, entirely still now, and white, panic-stricken.

'Your baby is OK,' I said. 'A steward has the baby up at the station. We're going to get you up to the station.'

'Where's Lucy?' she said.

'I didn't—'

'I'm going to wait here for Lucy,' she said.

'You can't wait here,' I said. 'We have to go.'

'But Lucy will come and try to find me here!' She pressed herself into the corner of the carriage.

'No. Lucy's a sensible girl, she'll know what to do. She'll know where to find you. Come with me. Come on.'

She shook her head.

'Now!' I shouted, and I grabbed first one arm and then the other. 'Now!' I repeated, and she hit out at me and screamed but I wrestled with her and dragged her down and down through the window and under the train and up into the infernal daylight. As we emerged, a guard came staggering towards us, a terrible cut across his skull, his face sheeted with blood.

'Where's my daughter?' the woman yelled at him, as if he were personally responsible. 'Where's Lucy? And my baby? Where's my baby?' She grabbed at the poor man, but he was in no state to respond and he simply pushed her away and staggered on past, entirely lost and silent.

I held the woman's arms firmly. 'Look at me!' I said. 'Look at me!' And I looked deeply into her eyes, willing her to be calm and to understand and I explained that her baby was with the dining car steward up at the station and I told her to go on ahead, and that I would find Lucy and bring her to her.

'You promise that you'll bring her to me?' she said, heaving with tears.

I promised. I promised I would find Lucy.

I can remember to this day the look she gave me –

trusting, fierce, her eyes wide – and I can remember that she then gave a little jolt of resignation or offence, I don't know which, as if she had been pierced or branded. Then she turned and walked on, joining what was now a long stream of men, women and children passing alongside the burning train, many of them dragging their suitcases and belongings with them, some of them silent, others calling out for loved ones, or weeping and wailing, dishevelled and distraught. This is the end of the world, I thought: this is what it looks like.

A man somewhere close by was frantically yelling for help. I turned towards the sound and ran over to the noise. Our carriage was now in flames and the fire was encroaching on the next carriage: the man was yelling from inside. I clambered and pulled myself up and onto the carriage, using all my strength, and made my way across to the window, which was filthy – and shut. I could see terrified faces inside: the man with his wife and children were trapped beneath me. The maroon skin of the carriage was warped and already beginning to warm with flames. It was like looking down into a nightmare from a nightmare. I tried to open the window, pulling and tugging, but it was jammed where the walls of the carriage had buckled.

'Stand back!' I yelled. 'Stand back.'

The family disappeared from the window and I stood and attacked it with my heel, stamping and stamping with all my weight until the glass had shattered, until all that was left was a jagged gap in the glass and I could kneel down and one by one managed to help pull them free. They scurried up and out and over the ruined train and hurried up the line towards the station.

I jumped down and away from the train, exhausted. I tried to take my bearings.

There to my left was the station sign, 'APPLEBY STATION', and there was the station, with its big tall cast-iron water column, and the signal box on up ahead, and the signals, and to the right there was another large building, emblazoned with the words 'EXPRESS DAIRY COMPANY CREAMERY', the letters bold in red, with a fading image of a milk bottle substituting for the 'I' in DAIRY. And there, incredibly, was the engine, which had somehow parted company from the train and become embedded in this vast building, in the Express Dairy Company Creamery, milk flooding everywhere, soaking into the ground, lying in pools – black milk – and the crimson engine sunk and drowning, choking and gurgling like some dying animal, hot steaming coals sizzling in the darkening liquid. The engine's chimney had gone, and lying by the footplate I could make out the figure of a man – the fireman? The driver? – lying in a pool of liquid, his clothes smoking, his shovel next to him. Metal. Flames. Machinery disassembled. Like the devil's foundry. It seemed incomprehensible. Surreal. The stuff of nightmares and dreams – hashish dreams and opium nightmares.

And then I remembered: where was Lucy?

'Lucy! Lucy!'

I began searching. I yelled and yelled and yelled.

The first thing that Miriam and Morley heard, apparently, was my voice. They were nearly at the station themselves when the train crashed and Miriam had immediately pulled the Lagonda over and run down to the line, Morley close behind her, already making guesses and calculations as to the cause. By the time I saw them there were men everywhere with shovels and pickaxes and rope, clearing the carriages, and Morley was taking notes, Miriam assisting with the injured.

The hours that followed seem now like a blur. Men rushing with buckets to douse the flames, and then the fire engine arriving, and the ambulance, and finally the police. 'Ah, *potius mori quam foedari*,' muttered Morley, or something. We were herded together in the tiny waiting rooms at Appleby Station, rumours and theories beginning to spread as quickly as the flames from the engine: the train had run into a stationary goods vehicle; hundreds were dead; no one was dead; we had collided with an oncoming train. It was the driver's fault; the fireman; the signalman; it was a natural disaster; an act of God; a robbery gone wrong. There were terrible injuries, and great shock and tears, but there was also laughter and jokes – the appalling, disgusting, incomprehensible contradictions of humans thrown together in a crowd, first class, third class, and everything in between. I remember the young nurse who dressed my wounds assuming that Miriam and I were married – 'Your husband's very brave, madam, people say he saved a lot of lives. He's a good man' – and Miriam shooting back, as sharp as you like, 'First, he's not my husband. Second, as for him being good or not – in any sense – I couldn't possibly comment.' I think that's what she said. I think I remember the nurse saying that I had lost a lot of blood and that she wanted to take me to the hospital for treatment, and my refusing, and Miriam arguing with me, and . . . but, as I say, everything was a blur.

The only thing that remains clear is the moment I found Lucy.

She had been flung through the window of our carriage at the moment of impact.

If I hadn't lifted her to look at the River Eden she would have been with her mother and baby brother, safely recovering in Appleby Station.

But she wasn't. She was lying in a field, twenty yards or more away from the crash, entirely peaceful, her pinafore dress spotless and clean. Dead.

CHAPTER 5

WILD WEST APPLEBY

I THINK I'D KNOWN IT from the moment of the crash, but it was too difficult to comprehend. She looked so perfect. She looked unharmed. She lay on her back, looking up at the grey-blue sky. She could have been cloudwatching.

I don't talk about it unless I've drunk a bit – a lot – and even then I don't tell the full story. I never mention Lucy. I find ways to avoid it, to circumvent it, as I have always found ways to circumvent everything in my life. Finally writing it all down, I suppose, writing all this down, however feeble and forgettable it may seem, however anodyne and *nostalgisome* – one of Morley's favourite words, one he'd invented, I assume – is just a way of reassuring myself that it all really happened, and that it really meant something, that everything was linked together, that it wasn't nothing, and that it wasn't waste, that *she* mattered, that we all mattered. Morley's *County Guides* were designed as a bold celebration of England and Englishness: my recollections, I suppose, are some kind of minor, lower-case companion. If the *County*

Guides are a scenic railway ride then my own work is the scene of the crash.

So, first we were gathered in Appleby Station, us survivors, our wounds tended in the waiting rooms, and a cup of tea for our troubles, and then we were escorted to various hotels in and around the town to give our statements and to be offered shelter for the night. We were billeted at the Tufton Arms Hotel, right in the centre of the town, down past some railwaymen's cottages and across the River Eden. It was a short walk but it seemed like a long way, a desperate journey: some people in a hurry, some people going slowly; and many come to gawk at us; all of Appleby, it seemed, had come to find out about the crash. The police did their best to keep them away, but it was impossible to separate bystanders from survivors: we were all jammed together, shuffling forward as one. The only way you could tell the passengers from the locals was that the passengers all looked strangely alike, with that expression of surprise and horror from the moment when the crash had occurred.

'I've not seen it like this since t'fair,' said one woman, as I jostled my way past.

'Folk turning out to gawk,' said another. 'T' should be ashamed.'

People were not ashamed, but they were baffled, just as we were baffled. 'What happened?' came the endless murmur. 'What happened?'

Lucy's mother with her baby walked on up ahead of me, weeping. I made no attempt to go to her, to comfort her or to apologise: I simply lowered my head and walked on.

In Spain I had often suffered exactly the feeling of that afternoon in Appleby: of arriving in a strange town, and not quite knowing or understanding what was happening, and with the knowledge and feeling of already having done something terribly wrong, so that the whole place seemed alien and unkind, a foreign land inhabited by foreign people suffering their uniquely foreign woes in their uniquely foreign ways. According to Morley in the *County Guides*, Appleby is renowned for its beautiful main street, 'more Parisian boulevard than English High Street' but I must admit that on that first day I did not much notice its beauty, and which particular Parisian boulevard Morley had in mind is not entirely clear, since there are none, to my knowledge, that are furnished with butchers, bakers, chandlers, haberdashers, gentlemen's outfitters, greengrocers and pubs; Paris, for all its allurements, is no real comparison for a prim and proper English county town. A finer and – as it turns out – more fitting comparison for Appleby might be with a Wild West frontier town, in florid English red stone.

The Tufton Arms Hotel had seen better days, though it was difficult to say exactly when those days had been. It was a sad sort of place: scuffed, worn moquette carpets, cheap and pointless marquetry, cracked clerestory lights, plush, dusty furniture; like a vast dull first-class carriage. The hotel bar was the centre of operations. Tea urns had been set out on some of the tables, and plates of bakery buns. There was much bustling and much organising being done: volunteers from the local Band of Hope had somehow appeared, with their own banner, and had positioned themselves in the hotel lobby, arranging places for people to stay, and drawing up lists and matching locals with passengers; the Women's Institute were doling out the tea and buns; and the police had settled themselves in to conduct interviews. Morley later wrote in praise of the scene as a 'model of modest English efficiency'. It may have been. It may have been a demonstration of all that is best in the human spirit, a triumph of calm over distress and of civilisation over human wretchedness. All I know is that it was thoroughly depressing and that I was desperate to get away. I needed a drink.

'Yes, sir?' asked the barman – one of those old-style hotel barmen, a professional barman, a middle-aged gent, spruce and natty, in a tight little tie and a bottle-green waistcoat. He might just as easily be a town councillor or a greengrocer.

'Whisky, please.'

'So, were you in the crash?' he asked. My torn jacket and bloodied shirt, the bump on my head, and the ragged trousers must have been a give-away. I didn't answer. 'Very good, sir. Drinks are on the house for anyone who was in the crash.'

'In that case make it a double,' I said.

'There'll be no trains in or out for a week, I reckon,' continued the barman, as he was examining the bottles behind the bar. 'So I reckon we'll be getting through a lot of port and lemon.' He nodded towards the crowd around the bar, mostly women. 'So, Scotch: we've got Haig, Black and White, or Macnish's Doctor's Special. Irish, I'm afraid we've only Bushmills or . . .' He held up a full bottle of Irish whiskey. 'Bushmills.'

'I'll take a Bushmills then.' I had converted to Bushmills at one of Delaney's places: he served only Irish whiskey, his famous gin fizz, and other drinks even more distinctly suspect and of no discernible provenance.

'There was a little girl killed,' he said. 'Is that right?'

I said nothing. I drank the whiskey and ordered another. And then another.

I could see her face in the mirror behind the bar. I could see her smile. I could feel her hand holding mine. I could hear her asking questions. She seemed to be everywhere. But the more I drank the quieter she became. I also took a pinch or two of Delaney's powders – and eventually she was silent.

Morley, hectic and inquisitive as ever, had conveniently situated himself at the far end of the table at which the police had made their makeshift headquarters – the perfect location for a quiet spot of eavesdropping. He was armed with a cup of black tea, and was busy with his pen writing in one of his tiny German waistcoat-pocket-sized notebooks. He had about him his usual glow. Miriam was smoking and surveying the room with a look of pity and disgust. I sat down with them. I felt sick.

'Ah, Sefton,' said Morley. 'The hero of the hour.'

'Hardly,' I said.

'Come, come, we've heard all about your exploits, dragging people from their carriages and what have you, saving lives—'

I got up to leave, but Miriam gripped my arm and forced me to sit back down.

'He's had a shock, Father. Best to leave it.'

'Of course!' said Morley. 'Yes, of course, quite upsetting.'

'I wonder actually if, in the circumstances, we should perhaps call a halt to the book, Father,' said Miriam.

'Agreed,' I said.

'Yes,' said Morley, to my surprise. 'Perhaps we should.'

'Really?' said Miriam.

'Till tomorrow morning, perhaps?'

'What?' I said.

'Otherwise we would slip very far behind in our schedule, Miriam.'

'Our schedule,' I said, with contempt.

'Is something wrong, Sefton?' asked Morley.

'Father,' said Miriam, coming to my rescue. 'I was thinking we should perhaps take a longer break?'

'Agreed. Again,' I said.

'A longer break?' In all my years with Morley I rarely saw him riled or succumbing to petty rages, but this suggestion made him spiteful. 'Do you both want us to give up then?' said Morley. 'Just because there's been a train crash?'

'No,' said Miriam slowly, as if speaking to an ignorant child. 'But you're right: there has been a train crash.'

'And what on earth do you propose doing when real disaster occurs?' asked Morley. 'As it surely will.'

'Real disaster?' I said.

'A war, or a famine? Another Spanish flu? A crash is an accident. It may be a tragedy. But it is not, strictly speaking, a disaster. Do you know what a disaster is?'

'I think I do,' I said.

'Has there been great loss of life?'

'A little girl died, Father!' said Miriam.

'Which is tragic, but as I say, it is not—'

I moved to get up again and again Miriam held me back.

'I'm sorry but I have no intention of continuing to work with you on this book at this time, Mr Morley,' I said.

'And I have no intention of allowing you to give up our enterprise at this time, Sefton, simply because of misfortune. Would any great art ever have been created if we had given up because of some setback? Did any of us give up what we were doing during the Great War? Did I give up when my son and my wife—'

'And did I give up when in Spain—'

'Boys! Please!' said Miriam, slapping the table with both hands. '*I* have no intention of allowing you two to bicker like children. Of course Sefton won't be giving up on the project, will you, Sefton?' She glared fiercely at me.

'Well, it rather sounds like it to me,' said Morley. '*Tu ne cèdes.*'

'We are *not* talking about giving up, Father. But I do think we might at least pause in our endeavours until the tragic matters here are in some way resolved.'

Morley huffed. I gazed distractedly around the room.

'You know you can be terribly insensitive sometimes,' said Miriam.

'Insensitive?' cried Morley. 'Me? Insensitive?'

Fortunately – before I walked off, or struck Morley for his self-righteous stupidity – our conversation was interrupted by a young man who had sidled over, obviously intent on talking to us. He looked as though he might be a butcher's boy: his face was flushed, and he had that soft, odd, awkward manner of someone more at home with animals than with humans. He was not in fact though a butcher's boy: he was a reporter from the *Westmorland Gazette*. (Morley, who had of course started out as a muck-raking journalist, had little time for practitioners of his previous profession. In private he referred to them unflatteringly as 'Gobbos', after Shakespeare's word-mangling idiot in *The Merchant of Venice*. In *Morley's Defence of the Realm* (1939) he describes journalists as 'allowed fools, paid to express contempt for people, politics, religion and society as a whole'. Over the years he described journalists variously to me as 'vampires', 'grave-robbers', 'cutpurses', but also as 'the just', as 'valiant heroes', and as 'seekers after the truth'. His feelings and ideas were often inconsistent and contradictory.)

'*The Westmorland Gazette*!' cried Morley. 'Of course! Thomas De Quincey's old paper, is it not?'

'I believe so, sir, yes.'

'Founded when?'

'I'm not entirely sure, sir.' The young chap's red-flushed cheeks flushed all the redder.

'Don't know when? You write for the newspaper and you don't know when it was founded?'

'No, sir.' The poor fellow had round, pleading eyes.

'Do you know the date of your mother's birthday?'

'Yes, sir.'

'And your father's?'

'Yes, sir.'

'I rest my case,' said Morley, though exactly which case he was resting I was not entirely sure. His metaphors and analogies were not always entirely clear or helpful. ' I think you'll find it was established in 1818.'

'Sorry, sir.'

'"Sorry, sir"?' cried Morley, almost knocking over his cup of tea. '"Sorry, sir"? A little more gumption wouldn't go amiss, young man. I'm not at all sure you're cut out for this business. Well, do you have any questions for us?'

The young man began frantically flicking through his notebook.

'Wordsworth one of the original backers, I think?' said Morley. 'Was he not?'

'Of?'

'The paper, man!'

'I'm not sure, sir—'

'Everybody knows it was Wordsworth! Late Wordsworth. Reactionary Wordsworth. Prefer the young Wordsworth myself, but never mind. And De Quincey was the first editor, I believe – or the second? – though he was so drugged with his laudanum that he refused to go to the office. Still the case with your current editor?'

'Not as far as I'm aware, sir, no.'

'And does the paper still take the Tory line?'

'I'm not sure, sir.'

'You're not sure?'

'I've only just started work at the paper, sir.'

'Well, you'll not be working there long at this rate, will you, man? Original motto of the paper?'

'Erm . . .'

'"Truth we pursue, and court Decorum: What more would readers have before 'em?" Rather good, isn't it?'

'Yes, sir.'

'And do you pursue Truth and court Decorum, young man?'

'I suppose I do, sir.'

'Well, that's a start, I suppose,' said Morley. 'Offices where, in Kendal?'

'Yes, sir. On Stricklandgate.'

'You are a lucky young fellow. Probably the finest patch for a newspaper man in the whole of England, the *Westmorland Gazette*. From the hill farms of the Yorkshire Dales in the east to Furness in the west, and Helvellyn in the north to Morecambe Bay in the south . . .'

'I suppose so, sir, yes.'

'You suppose? You suppose? Well then, ask another question, man!' Morley produced a pocket egg-timer and placed it on the table. 'You've got three minutes.'

'I just wondered if you'd give me a quote, sir, about the rail crash, and your role in—'

'Give you a quote? One doesn't *give* quotes, young man. People speak, and one shapes their words, like a mother bear licking a cub into shape.'

'Well, if you wouldn't mind—'

'I am reminded of the words of the great Dean Swift, sir: "For life is a tragedy, wherein we sit as spectators awhile, and then act our part in it."'

'Is that a quote?'

'It's a quote of a quote.'

'Ah.'

'Just write it down,' said Miriam. 'It'll do.'

'I'm afraid I cannot comment on the accident until the police have conducted their investigation and compiled their accident report,' added Morley. 'Next question?'

'Is it true that the train was speeding, and that—'

'I refer you to my previous answer. Next question!'

'Is it true that you rescued a number of people from the carriages?'

'I can make no such claim. The person who did so is my assistant, Stephen Sefton, who is— Sefton?'

I had made myself scarce, slipping away from the table and behind Morley to the bar. I had absolutely no desire to hear him engage in Socratic dialogue with some poor young reporter from the *Westmorland Gazette*, and even less desire to appear in the *Westmorland Gazette*.

'Sefton?' called Morley across the packed room. I was only a few yards away, but the crowd was dense. 'Sefton?' I made no response. 'He's probably gone to get another drink. Do you indulge?' he asked the boy reporter.

'Indulge?'

'In drink?' said Morley.

'Well, I have occasionally—'

'Don't,' said Morley. 'The best advice I can give anyone is the same advice my father gave me as a young man: don't smoke, drink or fornicate, and never bring the police to the door.'

Such advice was too late for me, alas: I was already busy with another Bushmills and was immersing myself in the day's *Times*, looking for news of the police searching for a man following an assault outside Marlborough Street Magistrates' Court. There was nothing that I could find. I sank the whiskey.

'Three minutes!' I heard Morley announce, snatching up his egg-timer. 'That's your lot, boy. You're really going to have to work on that interview technique.'

The poor boy reporter got up and left, and I returned safely to the table.

While all this was going on the policemen at the other end of our table were conducting interviews with passengers: I knew that sooner or later they were going to want to interview me. I was dreading the moment. I had too much to say to them without making any admissions or speaking any untruths. They were a typically unlikely and unprepossessing bunch of country coppers: one of them had big ears like wingnuts, almost like a character in a children's comic; another was broad and squat, almost square, and was busy writing everything down, though it looked rather as though he was unaccustomed to handling a pen; and the third, clearly the most senior officer, had a bald head and a bottle-brush moustache, and he kept scratching at his rather scraggy neck and rubbing a hand across his brow, as though trying to soothe his troubled mind. Passengers were ushered before this trio by a formidable woman in a shop coat called Mrs Sweeton who seemed to have appointed herself as official usher. 'Thank you, Mrs Sweeton,' the senior policeman would regularly pronounce. 'Next, Mrs Sweeton.' I rather fancied that they knew each other very well. The passengers gave their statements and then were ushered away again. 'Thank you, Mrs Sweeton. Thank you, Mrs Sweeton.'

Morley was clearly keeping a keen and close eye on all this, and as I sat back down at the table he shushed me and indicated to me with his hand that I should sit and be quiet, attend to the conversations, and take notes. Another man was being ushered before the police – but this was no passenger.

The crowd in the bar parted as he was escorted to the table by two gentlemen dressed in LMS uniforms, like captains of the guard – thick black blazers, emblazoned caps and shiny brass buttons. I had seen the man they were escorting at the scene of the crash, frantically rushing first to the front of the train and then back to the rear. He was tall and good-looking, with high cheekbones, and though smartly turned out in his own LMS uniform he looked terribly afraid and uncertain.

'*He's* dishy,' said Miriam to me, as he sat down at the table: he was the sort of young man, I thought, who might easily attract the wrong sort of woman.

A total hush fell over the thronging crowd.

It was George Wilson, the Appleby signalman.

CHAPTER 6

THE LOCOMOTIVE ACCIDENT EXAMINATION GUIDE

THOUGH WE WERE SITTING NEARBY, close enough to hear, it wasn't possible to pick up every word of the police interview over the hubbub of the bar – after a few preliminary questions the crowd had returned to their own rumours and conversations – and it wasn't until the senior policeman raised his voice that the conversation with the signalman became entirely clear.

'So, can you think of any reason for the engine derailment?'

'Axle defect, bearing failure, boiler defect, bolt failure, brake failure, broken rail, debris, defective this or that, drive shaft failure, driver error, fireman error, excessive loading, excessive speed, lack of signal detection, landslip, signal layout defect. *Series implexa causaram.*' This was not, suffice it to say, the signalman's answer. It was Morley, interrupting.

'I beg your pardon?' said the policeman, looking across

for the first time at the three of us perched at the end of the table. 'I don't think you're a part of this conversation, sir, are you?'

'And signalman error,' said Morley, to the signalman. 'If you don't mind my saying so. Let's not assume. It's a checklist, from *The Locomotive Accident Examination Guide*, I think, first published by Hoyten and Cole in—'

The policeman looked despairingly at his two companions.

'I do mind you saying so, sir, actually. And I'd be grateful if you'd keep your thoughts to yourself for the moment. If you were involved in the crash you'll have an opportunity to give a statement, along with everyone else.'

'Father,' said Miriam, with a voice of restraint. '*Irritabis crabrones.*'

'It's only what the company's accident expert will say, when he arrives,' said Morley. 'I thought it might save you some time.'

'He's only trying to help,' said Miriam. 'Sorry, Officer.'

'*Si cum hac exceptione detur sapientia, ut illam inclusam teneam nec enuntiem, reiciam.*'

'What's he saying?' asked the policeman.

'If wisdom were offered me on condition that I should keep it bottled up, I would not accept it,' said Miriam. 'Roughly.'

'Well, he's going to need to bottle it up for the moment, if you don't mind. We're more than qualified to be able to get to the bottom of things, thank you. We're just trying to establish what might have happened—'

'I know what happened,' said the signalman.

'What?' asked Morley.

'Please!' said the policeman. 'I'm conducting an interview here.'

'Apologies, Officer,' said Morley.

'What happened, then?' the policeman asked the signalman.

'I was about to say,' said the signalman. 'I've already explained to Eric—'

'The stationmaster?'

Eric, standing smartly by the table, quietly nodded, his LMS cap lending the nod an air of locomotive authority.

'Well?' said the policeman.

'It was children on the line. I didn't have any choice.'

'Children?' said the policeman.

'Gypsy children. It's those ones that come for the fair, and then never went away,' said the signalman.

'The Appleby Fair,' said Morley to me.

I wrote it down.

'The Appleby Fair,' said the policeman.

'That's right,' said the signalman. 'They come up here and then they hang around and you can't get rid of the buggers and they let their bloody children run wild, and if it wasn't for them—'

'You know, I have always wanted to visit the Appleby Fair,' said Morley to me.

'You're not missing anything,' said the signalman to Morley. 'And if it wasn't for those bloody kids none of this would have happened. I didn't have any choice. I had to divert the train into the dairy siding.'

'The dairy siding?' asked Morley.

'The Express Dairy Creamery. The milk goes down to London.'

'I see,' said the policeman. He sat back in his chair and sighed.

There was an awkward silence. The police looked relieved. The stationmaster, his companion and the signalman looked devastated: this was their crash, after all. Morley, unfortunately, was determined to make it his.

'An interesting case, is it not?' said Morley.

'If you wouldn't mind leaving the police work to us, sir,' said the policeman.

'Philosophically interesting, I mean, Officer.'

'Sorry, sir, you are?' asked the policeman.

'Swanton Morley,' announced Morley, in his brisk, no-nonsense fashion.

'The People's Professor?' said the policeman.

'I am sometimes referred to as such, yes,' said Morley.

The policeman's manner changed entirely. 'Very nice to meet you, Mr Morley.' He leaned across the table and vigorously shook Morley's hand. 'My father was a great one for your books, sir.'

'I'm delighted to hear it.'

'He loved your books on wildlife,' continued the policeman.

'Very good,' said Morley.

'And the ones on hobbies and home improvements.'

'Excellent.'

'He was less keen on the philosophical ones.'

'Ah, well—'

'And I've never read any myself. We gave them all away when my father passed on.'

'Well, never mind,' said Morley. 'What we have here, funnily enough, is a classic philosophical problem.'

'Is it indeed?'

'It is. A classic moral dilemma.'

'You'd better write that down,' the senior policeman instructed his burly colleague.

'Really, Sergeant?' asked the burly one.

'Write it down,' repeated the policeman. 'It might be significant.' He stared at Morley as if beholding a work of art. 'The People's Professor, well, well. Lads, you've read the People's Professor?' The two other policemen shook their heads.

'Ah well,' said Morley to me. '*Non quivis suavia comedit edulia.*'

'What did he say?' the policeman asked Miriam.

'Not sure,' she said.

'Marvellous,' said the policeman.

'Notebook to hand?' Morley asked me. This usually meant that he had seen some opportunity and was about to deliver an impromptu lecture, which he wished to be recorded for posterity. An opportunity this clearly was. I did not alas have a notebook to hand. These are merely my recollections.

'Might I elaborate?' he asked the policeman.

'By all means, Mr Morley.'

Morley turned to address the signalman, who was looking defeated and ashamed. 'I'm so sorry you should have been faced with such a dilemma, young man. Mr Wilson, is it not, if I heard correctly?'

'That's right, sir. George Wilson.'

'Well, Mr Wilson, I'm afraid you have been confronted with one of the fundamental questions in ethics.'

'Has he?' said the policeman.

'Indeed he has. We might call it the "Changing the Points Problem".' (For a full elaboration of the problem, see Morley's article, 'The "Changing the Points Problem"' in the *Journal of Philosophy*, vol.113, summer 1938: another article that caused more trouble than it was worth.) 'Faced with the likelihood of causing harm to an individual or individuals, should one or should one not change the points?'

'Course you should,' said the wingnut-eared policeman.

'Indeed. It seems like the obvious answer. Though alas in this case, as so often, there are complicating factors.'

'Which are?' asked the senior policeman.

'Well, in this instance of course there is the complicating factor of causing harm to another individual or group of individuals.'

'The people on the train,' explained Miriam, who always liked to get in a word or two during Morley's musings. She was not someone, under any circumstances, ever to be out-done or outshone. Her father in full flow was always a challenge to her.

'Precisely,' said Morley. 'In which case, in the case of competing wrongs, as it were, our friend here can *only* have done wrong. The real question is therefore how wrong was the wrong?'

'What?' said George Wilson, the signalman, raising his voice. 'What are you saying? I didn't do wrong. I did what any signalman would have done. Eric, you tell him.'

Eric the stationmaster remained silent; he might just as well have been blacking the grate in the waiting room.

The crowd in the bar began to quieten.

'Yes, yes of course you did,' said Morley calmly. 'You did what any of us might have done. If you had chosen not to change the points, all the children on the line might well have died. How many were there?'

'Four or five.'

'Which would have been a terrible tragedy. But how many people were on the train?'

'We're waiting for the full head count,' said the senior policeman. He looked towards Eric the stationmaster.

'We think it'll probably be about five hundred,' he said, from under his LMS cap.

'So five hundred lives might possibly have been lost because of our friend's decision,' continued Morley.

'But they weren't!' protested the signalman.

'Thank goodness, no, though as it is . . .' Morley looked sympathetically at me. 'The loss of one child is of course a terrible tragedy.'

'And many more injured,' said the senior policeman. 'The fireman seriously.'

'Yes. But you can perhaps see that *theoretically* at least, from the purely utilitarian point of view, it might have been better for our friend here to have chosen *not* to change the points, possibly killing only four or five children rather than five hundred men, women *and* children.'

'Father!' said Miriam. 'That is really a quite monstrous suggestion.'

'But logically sound,' said Morley.

'You're saying it was a lose-lose situation?' asked the senior policeman.

'Precisely so,' said Morley. 'Which is what makes it truly a dilemma: if it weren't a dilemma it wouldn't be such a—'

'Dilemma,' said Miriam.

'Yes. Arguably, to participate at all in such an enterprise is

[65]

wrong, because the moral wrongs are already in place, established and unavoidable, meaning that you, sir' – he turned again to the signalman and spoke to him directly – 'had no meaningful choice at all, but were, rather, condemned to doing ill, whatever your decision and whatever the circumstances.'

In Morley's reckoning these were doubtless intended as words of comfort, but to any normal human being of course they were a terrible insult.

George Wilson the signalman was furious. 'It wasn't my fault!' he said, getting up from the table.

'No one is suggesting it is, sir!' said Morley. 'Please, sit down.' George glanced around him at the silent crowd now gathered around us in the bar. 'I'm simply drawing attention to the fact that in such circumstances it is impossible for someone to emerge blameless.'

'It was the bloody gypsy children!' said George. 'It was nothing to do with me! Did you hear me?' He had gone a deep shade of LMS red. 'Did you hear me?' He looked as though he were about to reach for Morley. Silence descended upon the bar.

Thankfully, Miriam intervened.

'I think it might be time to go to bed, Father, don't you? It's been a terribly long day.'

Morley seemed to be genuinely surprised at all the fuss he'd caused. 'I do hope I haven't upset you, sir,' he said to the signalman. 'I was simply trying to tease out some of the—'

'I think it might be best if you could go and tease them out elsewhere,' said the senior policeman. 'Just for now. We'll take a full statement from you tomorrow. Very interesting though, Mr Morley, thank you.'

'Come on, Father,' said Miriam.

George Wilson did not look or speak to Morley as he rose from the table and allowed himself to be led away. I got up to follow.

'Not so fast, you,' said the senior policeman, holding up a commanding finger. 'We'll also need a word with you, sir,' he said. 'You're Stephen Sefton, is that right?'

'That's right,' I said.

'Lot of people have been talking about you, sir.'

'Have they?'

'We have a few questions for you.'

'Of course,' I said.

The crowd of onlookers looked on expectantly. Miriam and Morley had disappeared. I was entirely alone.

'But it can wait till tomorrow,' said the policeman. 'Why don't you get some rest now.'

I got some rest by drinking quietly by myself in a corner of the bar until all the passengers had been found beds for the night and the Band of Hope had packed up and gone and the Women's Institute and the police, and the room was clear and all I could see was my reflection in the bar-room mirror.

'I think you've had enough, sir,' said the barman, some time after midnight.

He was right.

CHAPTER 7

PENCILARIUMS AND PHARMACOPOEIAS

I WAS PLAGUED BY TERRIBLE NIGHTMARES. I was being chased through a vast crowd of people who were moving around in a purposeless, random way – terrifying. Everywhere around me trees and houses had been levelled and there were rotting corpses. Delaney was there. He was in a white tuxedo, baring his teeth: white, perfect teeth. MacDonald and Mickey Gleason, my old International Brigade chums, were there, dressed as guards, cracking their knuckles, and the varsity boys from Marlborough Street Magistrates' Court, caked in blood. The little girl was there too, Lucy, taking photographs. And then I became lost in a dark tunnel, running along the tracks, and suddenly a train was coming towards me, lights glaring, horn blowing. 'Life is very like a train journey,' writes Morley in *Ringing Grooves of Change*, using a metaphor that will perhaps be lost on the younger generations and those without memories of steam. 'One sometimes enters long dark tunnels and the only thing to do is to shut up the window and wait for things to clear again.'

I was horribly hung over and the room was full of the sour smell of whiskey and cigarettes. I knew a man once, a Brigader, who decided to drink himself to death: people said it took him almost a week. I began to wonder whether I should try to find the time. I thought I might spend the day in bed and then make myself scarce. But when I opened my door to go and use the bathroom at the end of the corridor I found that Morley had left a pile of clothes for me outside the room, with a note that read simply: '*Nil desperandum*! Took the liberty to kit you out afresh. Breakfast promptly. Estimated time of departure 9 a.m.' I almost smiled. As so often, Morley was ahead of me. He had read my mood, or rather – more likely – he was proceeding simply and strictly by logic. He had worked out that the prospect of departure, any kind of departure, was going to be appealing to me. And also that I was going to need some new clothes, since my own had been ruined during the crash. Thinking ahead, he had successfully called my bluff, pulled me up short, taken me by the scruff of the neck, and set me back down again on the straight and narrow.

'Ah, Sefton,' he said, when I eventually presented myself at breakfast. 'All ready for departure? You're looking very smart.'

'Off to do a spot of grouse shooting, are we?' said Miriam, stubbing out a cigarette in a saucer.

'I do wish you wouldn't, Miriam,' said Morley. 'It's a filthy habit.'

'Oh shush, Father. Has the season begun, Sefton? I do

hope you'll allow me to join you – I love a weekend hunting party.'

The clothes were indeed of a kind that might have suited a country gent or a laird on his estate in Scotland – a particularly jolly laird with a taste for the more extravagant sort of hunting wear, for these were no rough tweeds and flannels. I was outfitted in plus-fours, enormous fat yellow socks, unyielding sunshine-orange brogues and a jacket that flared at the waist in a fashion that suggested the wearer might at any moment perform a pas de deux.

'Where on earth did you get those ridiculous fancy dress clothes, Father?'

'The night porter's brother works at a rather fine gentleman's outfitters in town. I'm afraid that at short notice this was the closest thing I could find to proper hiking gear.'

'We're not going hiking?' I said.

Miriam certainly didn't look as though she were going hiking. She was dressed, as always, with her usual verve – one might indeed say *panache*, if it weren't so early in the morning – in an outfit whose abundance of black ruffles and ruches suggested that even walking might prove a problem. Her make-up was perfect and her hair precisely and elaborately smoothed around her magnificent head, giving her the look of a very fine lacquerware painting. Morley of course was dressed in his customary outfit: bow tie, suit and brogues, 'suitable for any occasion', he would often claim, which indeed I can confirm, having seen him fell trees and chop logs, address meetings, read scripts on the BBC, go fishing, climb mountains, and entertain bishops, duchesses and lords, all in the self-same gear. 'Ladies and gentlemen might be able to afford the privilege of dressing appropriately,' he liked to say. 'The rest of us must make do with the merely practical.'

'I don't think I'm up to hiking,' I said.

'No, no,' said Morley. 'No time for hiking. I have taken into account your and Miriam's concerns about us proceeding with the book as planned – and we shall indeed be pausing in our enterprise—'

'Out of respect,' said Miriam.

'And also out of necessity,' said Morley. 'I feel the police might require our assistance.'

Miriam looked at me and raised her eyebrows. After last night's performance I think we both rather doubted whether Morley's assistance would be welcome.

'They're very keen to talk to you this afternoon, Sefton,' continued Morley. 'So I said I'd have you back after lunch.'

'I'm not sure,' I said.

'Not sure about what?' asked Miriam, extravagantly rearranging herself at the table, causing something of a commotion. She was the sort of woman who couldn't move without attracting attention.

'Not sure that I can help them with very much,' I said.

'I think you'll find you don't have much choice in the matter, Sefton,' said Morley. 'Eye-witness and what have you. And anyway we have a pre-existing arrangement this morning to visit an archaeological dig near Shap – part of our original itinerary – and Miriam and I both agree that we should probably fulfil that obligation.'

'It would be terribly bad manners to cancel at such short notice, Sefton,' said Miriam. 'Don't you think?'

'Bad manners?'

'Anyway,' said Morley. 'The main thing is we're off again!'

'That's the departure?' I said. 'That's where we're going? To an archaeological dig at a place called Shap?'

'That's right,' said Morley. 'Not far. And then we'll have you back this afternoon for your little chat with the police. I hope that suits?'

'Do I have a choice?' I said, feeling rather cheated.

'There's always a choice,' said Miriam. 'You could always stay here.'

I looked around at the glacial breakfast room of the Tufton Arms – full to capacity with guests, police and survivors of the crash, picking over their cold damp toast and their tepid tea and eggs – and shivered.

'I suppose I'll come, then.'

'Excellent!' said Morley, clapping his hands. 'Excellent!'

'It'll do you good,' said Miriam, patting my arm.

And so, after a hurried breakfast of coffee and cigarettes, and all done up in my ludicrous hunting outfit, I joined my companions in the Lagonda.

Miriam, as always, was driving, and I was stuck in the back with Morley, who was doing his best to educate me in the local lore and legends of Westmorland, from tales of dobbies and hobthrusts and other little people, to ruminations on the etymology of Old Norse place names, to the nature of the allurements of Ambleside, 'the hub of Wordsworth's wheel of Lakeland beauty'.

'And home to Harriet Martineau,' added Miriam. 'We mustn't forget Harriet.'

'*Dear* Harriet,' said Morley absentmindedly, proceeding

to praise the fascinations of Kendal, 'the cloistered auld grey town' and 'possessor of perhaps the country's most pleasingly punning motto, *pannus mihi panus*', the majesty of Patterdale, 'home to the mighty Helvellyn', and the 'soothing calm' of Windermere and Witherslack.

I did my best to stay awake.

'Can you name how many lakes there are in the so-called Lake District, Sefton?'

'Erm. No idea. Sorry, Mr Morley.'

'Guess.'

'Ten?'

'No.'

'Twenty?'

'No.'

'Thirty?'

'Wrong, wrong, and wrong again. There is in fact only one lake in the Lake District.'

'Really?'

'Correct. Bassenthwaite. The rest are properly tarns, waters or meres.'

'Ah.'

'That'll go in the book, of course.'

'Jolly good,' I said.

'Make a note,' said Morley, thrusting some notecards at me. 'We don't want to waste a minute, eh? Do you have a pencil?'

He handed me a pencil – his favourite, a Ticonderoga No.2, imported specially from America – sharp and ready to go.

'We should probably be using a Lakeland, of course,' he said. 'Or a Derwent. Excellent pencils. If we get up into

Cumberland we really must visit Keswick. Home of the English pencil – did you know?'

'Yes, Mr Morley,' I said. I had no idea that Keswick was the home of the English pencil and was less than interested, but was rather hoping that by pretending to knowledge I might avoid any kind of lecture – but no luck. With Morley, there was always a lecture.

'Cumberland plumbago,' he said. 'Absolutely unbeatable. And the availability of cheap timber, of course. The extraordinary history of pencil production in this part of the world is surely something that should be more widely celebrated. Don't you think?'

'Indeed.'

'One might perhaps consider constructing a shrine to the pencil, on the shores of Derwentwater.'

'One might,' I agreed.

'A pencilarium!'

'Uh-huh.'

'There's no such thing,' said Miriam.

'A Museum of Pencils then!' cried Morley. 'A temple to human ingenuity and humble engineering.'

'I don't think so, Father,' said Miriam. 'Who on earth would visit a museum of pencils?'

'I would,' said Morley. 'A room devoted solely to the Koh-i-nor. And the Everlast mechanical pencil. Perhaps a working exhibition—'

'Anyway!' cried Miriam. 'Let's assemble, Father, not disperse' – this being one of the phrases Miriam liked to use to refocus Morley's attention. (Other phrases included 'Interventions, not interjections', 'March, don't waltz' and 'Reality, not illusions'.)

'Yes,' said Morley. 'Quite right. Assemble, not disperse. Where were we, Sefton?'

'I'm not sure, Mr Morley.'

'Ah, yes! You were making a list. The tarns, waters and meres in Westmorland and Cumbria.'

'That's right.'

'They are?'

'Erm . . .'

'In order of size?'

'Erm . . .'

'Descending order of size?'

'Erm . . .'

'Windermere; Ullswater; Derwentwater; Coniston Water; Haweswater; Thirlmere; Ennerdale Water; Wastwater; Crummock Water; Esthwaite Water; Buttermere; Grasmere; Loweswater; Rydal Water; Brotherswater.'

'That's just what I was going to say.'

'Good,' said Morley. 'Do you know the entire population of the world could be stored in Lake Windermere, if you stacked them correctly?'

'Really?' said Miriam. 'How fascinating.'

'Or packed shoulder-to-shoulder on the Isle of Wight.'

'Well, that's good to know, Father.'

'Isn't it? Write it all down then, Sefton. Write it all down.' If there is only one thing I learned from my time with Morley it was probably that: the secret of successful authorship, summed up in just four words. *Write it all down.* Assemble, not disperse. Interventions, not interjections. March, don't waltz. Reality, not illusions. And always keep a pencil handy.

On our rather circuitous drive – 'We must stop here!' Morley would announce, every ten minutes, and 'No, Father,'

Miriam would invariably retort, before we did often end up stopping, for no good reason other than to admire a view. 'Aren't we just the William Gilpins!' Morley would exult – we passed a couple of gypsy caravans, tucked down narrow lanes away from the main road.

'Miriam!' cried Morley. 'Didn't our friend the signalman mention gypsy children on the line? I wonder if perhaps we should—'

'No, Father!' said Miriam. 'Sorry! No time. We're due at the dig.'

'But—'

'No ifs, no buts, no nothing. I have the wheel, in case you didn't notice. If you want to speak to the gypsies you'll have to do it later.'

'Do you know the gypsiologist John Sampson?' Morley asked me.

'I can't say I do, Mr Morley, no.'

'Terribly interesting. Bit of an oddball. Founding member of the Gypsy Lore Society. Rather romantic view of things – the gypsy as a kind of ur-ancestor of mankind. Interesting notion of course, and a long line of such thinking in the literary imagination: Arnold associating gypsies with resistance to the "strange disease" of modern life. Other examples?'

'Erm.'

'Miriam: other examples of representations of the gypsy in English literature?'

'Heathcliff?' called Miriam.

'He'll do, I suppose,' said Morley.

'He'll more than do,' said Miriam.

'Never seen the appeal myself,' said Morley.

'He's not *for* you, Father.'

'Well, who is he for? Dreadful man. Tortured romantic soul, prone to violence, troubled past. Can't see the appeal.'

'That's precisely the appeal,' said Miriam. 'Isn't it, Sefton?'

I forbore to answer.

'I rather prefer Arnold's scholar gypsy,' said Morley.

'You would,' said Miriam.

'Rather fascinating topic, though, eh?' said Morley. 'The English gypsy. Fascinating . . .'

(A complete history of Morley's fascinations would be very long indeed. There is, I believe, a doctoral student in the United States of America, a Mr Balokowsky, who is currently compiling an index of Morley's topics and themes, culled from the thousands of publications. It seems to me like an utterly pointless and very probably endless enterprise. I have made my views known to the young man and declined to become in any way involved. The task is simply too great, like compiling a list of *everything*. I doubt that there was *any* subject, place, person, entity, animal, vegetable or mineral that during our time together I did not hear Morley describe as 'fascinating'. The rules of etiquette: fascinating. Electroplating: fascinating. Falconry, fingerprinting, flower lore: fascinating. But as for the English gypsy, 'the Romanichal', this was more than fascinating: the Romanichal were an obsession.)

'Maggie Tulliver's defection to the gypsy camp,' he continued, 'and Jane Austen's Harriet Smith accosted by begging gypsy children on the outskirts of Highbury in *Emma*. The gypsy perhaps as the Englishman's surrogate self' – and certainly as Morley's surrogate self. He was in many ways a romantic wanderer, strange and set apart, just like the scholar gypsy in Arnold's poem. 'O like unlike to ours! / Who fluctuate idly without term or scope, / Of whom each strives, nor knows for what he strives, / And each half lives a hundred different lives; / Who wait like thee, but not, like thee, in hope.'

Anyway, Miriam, I am delighted to say, accelerated quickly past the gypsy caravans.

'Miriam!' cried Morley. 'Couldn't we stop just for a moment?'

'No time!' cried Miriam. '*Fugit irreparabile tempus.*'

'But they look like very fine wagons! You can't beat a gypsy vardo. I remember I was in the Carpathians once—'

'It's not happening, Father.'

'Have you ever been inside a gypsy vardo, Sefton?' asked Morley.

'I can't say I have, Mr Morley, no.'

'And he's not going to be today, Father,' said Miriam. 'Come on. No slacking, no shilly-shallying. No funking.'

'Very well,' said Morley. 'Very well.'

He returned to his typing, while Miriam let out a triumphant laugh, tossed back her head with typical dash, and floored the accelerator. I, as always, felt rather sick and wondered what on earth I was doing with these lunatics.

My leg, which had been expertly dressed by the nurse the day before, was now throbbing rather. And my head: the bump from the luggage rack had swollen into a lump the size and colour of one half of a bad potato. I did perhaps mention my pains once or twice, and perhaps more than once or twice, and certainly so much that as we were driving through Kirkby Stephen – 'Just a little detour?' Morley had petitioned Miriam. 'To see the parish church, the Cathedral

Kirkby Stephen: The High Street

of the Dales?' – Miriam pulled over the Lagonda and we parked outside a pharmacy in the centre of the town.

'Come on, you big baby,' she said, getting out and slamming the door.

'What?'

'Let's get you something for those bangs and bruises.'

Morley was about to leap out of the car and follow.

'We're not stopping here, Father,' said Miriam, pushing him back in.

'Well, we are, actually,' said Morley. 'Strictly speaking, we have stopped. We are no longer—'

'I mean we're not stopping here for long,' said Miriam. 'We'll only be a minute. You just stay in the car.'

'Fine!' said Morley, who was already hammering away at his typewriter again, his attention having been caught by some pillared shelter. 'Hmm. What do you think, early nineteenth century, Sefton?'

'Back in a moment, Father! Come on, Sefton. Chop, chop.'

Taylor's Pharmacy – 'ALL PATENT MEDICINES AND PROPRIETARY ARTICLES KEPT IN STOCK' – was a jigsaw-puzzle neat storehouse of brown and white bottles and pots in glass cabinets, decorated with gilt and mirrors and dark mahogany drawers. Mr Taylor, the pharmacist – for it was he – stood in his pharmacist's white coat, perfectly framed before this vast pharmacopoeia and behind a tiny set of shiny brass scales, like a god preparing to weigh mercy and justice, *sub specie aeternitatis*. He was younger than one might have expected for a pharmacist and might perhaps generously have been described as 'robust', sturdy around the chest and waist, though with a generous, soft clerical sort of face. He looked indeed like the perfect pharmacist: one could imagine him both dispensing and refusing to dispense you with absolutely anything. The drawers and bottles and cabinets behind him suggested a world of wonders and he the guardian to another realm. The whole atmosphere of the place, I have to say, made me rather excited. I felt like a cook, or a gourmand, surveying a well-stocked kitchen, come to petition the larder keeper.

Miriam explained that we were just passing through and were on our way to Shap, and that we required a little something for bumps, bruises and a headache.

'You're not locals then?' said Mr Taylor, gathering whatever it was he saw fit to dispense.

'No, sir, from Norfolk. We're here on a trip.'

'You heard about the crash yesterday, at Appleby?'

'Not only did we hear about the crash,' said Miriam. 'I'm afraid my companion here sustained his injuries in the course of it.'

'You're not the fellow from London who everyone's talking about?'

'Almost certainly!' said Miriam.

'The chap who saved the family from the burning carriage?'

'The man himself.'

I winced.

'Well done, sir,' said Mr Taylor. 'Congratulations.'

I had nothing to be congratulated on.

'I'm sure you must have been busy here yesterday with the crash?' asked Miriam.

'We sent over some supplies, yes,' said Mr Taylor. 'Terrible business.'

'Yes,' agreed Miriam.

'There was a little girl who died, from London, is that right?'

Miriam, kindly, did not answer, and Mr Taylor carried on with his tasks.

'They don't know yet what caused it then?' he asked.

'Not as far as I'm aware,' said Miriam.

At which point a bell rang in the shop, announcing another customer – and Morley wandered in.

'Father!' said Miriam. 'I told you to wait in the car!'

'I know, my dear. I know, I know. I just thought you were taking so long that there might be some sort of problem.'

'There's no problem, Father. Everything's in hand, thank you. You can go and wait in the car. Otherwise we'll fall behind schedule. Far far behind schedule. You know how far behind schedule we are already.' She looked at me imploringly.

'Mr Morley,' I said. 'We really must hurry along. This is not a part of the itinerary.'

'Oh, but I do love a pharmacy,' said Morley, beginning to fossick around, running a hand along a super-shiny wooden counter. 'I'm always reminded of Blake in a pharmacy, aren't you, Sefton? "If the doors of perception were cleansed every thing would appear to man as it is, Infinite. For man has closed himself up, till he sees all things thro' narrow chinks of his cavern." You have the keys to unlock the doors of perception, sir,' he said to Mr Taylor, who was concentrating on weighing and packing our prescription.

'Don't mind my father,' said Miriam. 'We'll be gone in a moment.'

'You certainly keep this place spick and span,' said Morley.

'I do my best, sir.'

'And are we to assume that you are *the* Mr Taylor of Taylor's Pharmacy?'

'That I am, sir. Gerald Taylor. Third generation of Taylors to be running this shop. Pleased to make your acquaintance.'

'Likewise,' said Morley. 'Likewise.' He was staring up at the many awards and certificates that were framed, high up on the walls.

'You appear to be supremely well qualified, Mr Taylor,' said Morley, gesturing towards the certificates. 'Inspires confidence, eh?'

'Them?' said Mr Taylor. 'Oh, no, they're not for the pharmacy. They're for the wrestling.'

'The wrestling?'

'Westmorland wrestling. Bit of a hobby. Goes back generations in our family. You've mebbe not heard of it, sir? It's local.'

'Westmorland wrestling!' cried Morley, becoming dangerously but predictably excited. 'Westmorland wrestling! Not only have I heard of it, Mr Taylor!' he exclaimed, standing up tall on tiptoes in his brogues. 'I am a great fan of wrestling of all kinds.' (This I can confirm. He was also an enthusiastic practitioner.)

'Father,' said Miriam. 'It's probably time we went. Mr Taylor, if I could pay you perhaps, for the—'

'Greco-Roman. Freestyle. Lancashire wrestling. Do you know William Litt's *Wrestliana*, perhaps, Mr Taylor, in which he claims that wrestling is of divine origin? Wonderful book. Jacob wrestling with the angel at the River Jabbok?'

'I can't say I do, sir. I just likes the wrestling.'

'You know, the most extraordinary bout I think I've ever seen was when I was in Turkey once,' said Morley, warming to another theme. (Note, Mr Balokowsky – *another* theme. There is no shortage. There can be no definitive list.) 'They have this most peculiar sport of oil wrestling. Have you come across it at all at all at all?'

'I can't say I have, sir, no.'

'The competitors oil themselves up until they're positively glistening – almost like they've been dipped in honey—'

'Mmm,' said Miriam involuntarily.

'And then the aim is not to throw the opponent but rather to hold on to them.'

'More like pig wrasslin,' said Mr Taylor.

'Precisely like pig wrestling,' said Morley. 'Rather spectacular, actually. Reminds one of Marcus Aurelius.'

'Father!' said Miriam. 'There's no time to be reminded of Marcus Aurelius! We really must press on.'

'"The art of living is more like wrestling than dancing."'

'Father!?'

'But do you know I have never once seen Westmorland wrestling,' continued Morley. 'Never had the opportunity.'

'Well, I'm going to be across in Egremont later, sir, at the fair. If you're interested.'

'Well, we really should, Miriam, shouldn't we?'

'You'd be very welcome, sir.'

'Thank you, Mr Taylor. Very best of luck to you today.'

'Thank you, sir.'

We took the medicines and left.

'What an absolutely charming fellow,' said Morley. 'And

he must be quite a wrestler, judging by all the awards and certificates.'

'Mmm,' said Miriam. 'Big hog of a man.'

'Break your neck quite easily, I would have thought,' said Morley.

'Oh, don't be morbid, Father. Now, Shap here we come!'

CHAPTER 8

ENGLISH ARCHAEOLOGICAL RECORDS

FOR INFORMATION ABOUT THE DIG at Shap I can only suggest that readers refer to Professor Alan Jenkins's standard work, *English Archaeological Records*, published by Oxford University Press in 1939 – though for reasons that will become clear it is not a book I can enthusiastically or wholeheartedly recommend.

Shap itself is a perfectly pleasant little Westmorland village, the sort of place where one can imagine living a perfectly pleasant life along the perfectly pleasant one-and-only street, going about one's perfectly pleasant business during the week and then on Sundays saying one's perfectly pleasant prayers to one's perfectly pleasant God in one's perfectly pleasant little church, and enjoying a perfectly pleasant pint of Westmorland ale in one of the perfectly pleasant country inns. Shap, like so much of England – and indeed like so many of the English, as they once were, until very recently – is perfectly pleasant. It is charming and inoffensive, and completely clogged on the day we arrived with car and lorry traffic escaping to Scotland and, presumably, with many Scots cars and lorries escaping to England in the opposite direction. Shap is not a destination: it is a place entirely en route, a perfect nowhere.

But the surrounding area! The surrounding area is something else entirely. The surrounding area – the wider parish of Shap, Shap Rural, as it is known, to distinguish it from the village – is simply astonishing. It is England at the extreme. It is ultimate England. Of all the places we visited during our time writing the *County Guides* it is probably Shap that remains in my mind as the most extraordinary. The vast plateau of fells and dales, the sudden peaks and valleys, the perfect dry-stone walls, the ravines and the waterfalls: it is a place entirely self-invented and self-contained, a place perfectly poised between the Lakeland mountains proper and the big bluff sweep of the Pennines, the remote kind of place where a man might wish to go late in life and wait happily to die. Sometimes, when I imagine for myself another life, a good life, a life of ease and peace, I don't think of the Caribbean or the Côte d'Azur, I think of Shap, maybe somewhere up above the village, or in the lonely valley of Swindale, with nothing to do but to admire the fells, the sheep and the heather, to think and to remember and to write. Our business in Shap that morning turned out to be a grim matter indeed, but the view was nothing short of magnificent.

Morley was already excited by the sight of the area's granite works and its limestone quarries, and by the beauty of the tiny little chapel in the hamlet of Keld – another 'essential' detour – but when he spied the standing stones of Shap he was, frankly, in ecstasy. He gave a deep sigh of satisfaction, took a deep breath in through his nose – one nostril, then the other, in his usual pranic fashion – and smoothed out the corners of his moustache. A pleasant smile spread across his face and he relaxed. This is what Morley lived for: England and its history. (Indeed, in *What I Live For* (1930), an anthology in which he asks various writers, politicians and all the other usual suspects what they live for he answers his own question, indirectly, by quoting Shakespeare from *Henry V*: 'Follow your spirit, and upon this charge cry "God for Harry, England, and Saint George!"')

Shap's stone circle stands at the south end of the village and consists of a collection of boulders of varying sizes which once formed part of a much larger collection of standing stones, what Morley in the *County Guides* calls 'one of England's many ancient reckoning places'. Over the centuries the stones have been gradually moved and manhandled and hauled away to be used for other purposes – for hardcore and foundation stones, and doubtless for decorative garden features – and yet for all the destruction wrought upon the site what remains is still rather impressive, like a small ruined Stonehenge. It was all the more impressive the morning we arrived for being the scene of a busy archaeological dig, with all the associated tents and equipment and tools. That day it undoubtedly felt like an important place, a place where something might happen. Shap, according to Morley, is 'the Avebury that nobody knows': it is, moreover, 'a sacred space'. I am not entirely convinced. But it is certainly a site of great drama.

'Look! Look!' cried Morley, like a boy coming across a travelling circus or a country fair. 'We're here!'

The first thing I noticed on our arrival at the dig was not

the stones but an old motorbike and sidecar parked at the entrance to the field leading to the stones. It was no ordinary motorbike and sidecar. The sidecar had been converted into the most peculiar contraption: where the passenger might usually sit, a large black metal box had been installed, connected by a series of coiling pipes and wires to the motorbike's upswept exhaust. Miriam parked the Lagonda and Morley of course leapt out and became instantly and utterly intrigued by the thing, and stood examining it in some detail, warming his hands on the sides of the box and then carefully sketching the design on one of his waistcoat-pocket notecards.

'Remarkable,' he kept saying. 'Remarkable. Look at this, Sefton. English ingenuity, eh?'

The sidecar itself was painted in the most ornate fashion, with the words DORA'S STATION CAFE AND OUTSIDE CATERING – CATERING FOR ALL TASTES picked out in bold – if rather unskilled – gold calligraphic lettering.

As we stood admiring this peculiar machine a buxom woman came hurrying across the field towards us, becoming all the more buxom as she approached. She would have made an excellent Carmen, Morley later remarked. ('With that accent?' said Miriam. 'The perfect accent,' said Morley, who claimed that the accents of the north of the country came closest to the sound of the ancient settlers of Europe, and thus brought us closer to our common ancestors and our true selves. At least, he sometimes claimed that it was the accents of the north of the country that brought us closer us to our common ancestors and our true selves. At other times he suggested it was the accents of the south of the country. And the west. And the east. His ideas were not always entirely consistent. For a snapshot of his view at a single point in time – during a particularly 'northern' phase – see his paper 'In Search of the English Ur-Accent', in *Pictorial Geographic* magazine, vol.26, no.2, 1934.)

'Aye, aye,' she said. 'Can I help you?'

'Aye, aye,' said Morley in return, in what I assumed was supposed to be an approximation of the local accent. 'Excelsior Triumph and a Steib sidecar. If I am not mistaken.'

'And surely you are not mistaken, sir,' said the woman. 'My pride and joy.'

'That's quite a little stove you have there,' said Morley, who had thankfully returned to his normal speaking voice. 'I was just warming my hands.'

'On my hotbox?' said the woman.

'Quite magnificent,' said Morley. 'I was just saying to my colleagues here.'

'Well, thank you.'

'A beautiful machine. The motorcycle and the stove.'

'Do you know anything about motorcycles?' she asked. It was a silly question; Morley knew a thing or two about everything.

'Only a little,' said Morley.

'Well, I'm sure I could take you for a ride some time,' said the woman. 'If you were interested?'

'Do you know,' said Morley. 'I might just take you up on that. Dora, is it?'

'It is indeed,' she said. The pair of them shook hands.

'And you cater for all tastes, I see?' said Morley, indicating the lettering on the sidecar.

'I certainly do my best,' said Dora.

'I'm sure you do,' said Morley. 'I'm sure you do.'

Miriam coughed loudly several times during the course of this carry-on and frowned noisily and disapprovingly towards Morley. He took no notice, of course. No slouch herself in the art of English flirting, Miriam knew exactly when her father was getting out of his depth, which was often. Morley was endlessly flirting with women without apparently realising that he was doing so – and this sometimes got him into serious trouble. (The episode with the Texan oil millionaire's widow certainly springs to mind: that was a narrow escape. And all the trouble with the German countess. And the wife of the Scottish laird. The mixed-up divorcee who bought him a pet leopard. The poetess. The actress. The other actress. The list is surprisingly long.)

'I'm afraid we really don't have time to talk about motor-cycles at the moment, Father, do we,' said Miriam, making a statement rather than asking a question. 'Remember, we're here for the dig.'

'Don't let me hold you back then, my dear,' said Dora, who was busy getting busy about her business. 'They're over there. You can't miss them.' She hauled a couple of trays out of the sidecar hotbox, using a pair of old leather motorcycle gloves, and stacked them one on top of the other. The trays were full of golden steaming pies in white enamel pie plates.

'Of course, of course,' said Morley. 'Don't let us hold you up.' He took a long, lingering theatrical sniff, which sounded rather like the reverse of a trumpet fanfare: this was yet another of his less than pleasant habits. 'But may I say, whatever those pies are, Dora, they smell absolutely delicious!'

'Well, thank you, sir. Herdwick lamb and juniper pies,' she said. 'A local speciality.'

'I wouldn't mind a little nibble on that myself,' said Morley.

'I might be able to treat you to some leftovers,' said Dora.

'Oh, for goodness sake!' said Miriam.

'Here, let me help you, Dora,' said Morley, entirely unconcerned. And he moved to take a tray from her.

'That's very kind of you, sir,' she said, giving him one of her motorcycle gloves. 'You don't want to burn your fingers now.'

'Quite,' said Morley.

'Father!' said Miriam.

'Where do you want these then, my dear?' Morley asked Dora, holding the tray aloft in a gloved hand, for all the world as though he were a waiter serving drinks at the Criterion.

'I'm just taking the last few bits over for the professor and his students,' she said.

'Jolly good,' said Morley.

'Father!' said Miriam again.

'What?' he said. 'Come on, lend a hand. Sefton? Chop chop.'

Miriam tutted and folded her arms in disgust – she was hardly going to act as a waitress – but I dutifully took another tray from the hotbox, this one full of boiled potatoes and enamel pots of mushy peas, and all four of us strode across the field towards a big white bell tent. Or rather, three of us strode, and Miriam sulkily followed, picking her way between cow pats in her unsuitable heels.

'This is where they eat,' whispered Dora, before we entered the tent. 'And don't mind him.'

'Who?' said Morley.

'The professor. He's full of babblement, but his bark's worse than his—'

'Bite?' said Morley.

'Exactly,' said Dora, winking at Morley. 'Don't let him badger you.'

We entered the tent to find perhaps a dozen people seated around a long trestle table which was set out with simple picnic food: oatcakes and oat bread and pickles, modest Westmorland fare. At the head of the table was a man who held a glass of dark wine in one hand, his eyes screwed small against the smoke of the cigarette held in his other. He wore a white shirt and cravat, and his long greying hair was swept back from his forehead, giving him the appearance of a poet or perhaps a playboy film director, the kind of bohemian fool I sometimes came across in Soho. He was not in fact a poet or a playboy film director. He was Professor Alan Jenkins, of Oxford University no less, and the author of *English Archaeological Records*, published by Oxford University Press in 1939 (as previously mentioned, though again, might I emphasise, not wholeheartedly recommended). Professor Jenkins is, I understand, generally considered to be the world's leading expert on megalithic structures, and he may well be – it is a subject about which I am ill-equipped to comment. I can safely say however that Professor Jenkins is undoubtedly one of the world's leading experts in incivility. Of all the preening pompous twits we ever came across in our perambulations, Jenkins ranked among the very greatest.

'Herdwick lamb and juniper pie, Professor,' said Dora, serving him with a pie in its enamel plate.

'Not exactly high table, is it?' said the professor, snorting, to the attractive young woman seated on his right, who laughed uproariously at what was presumably intended to be a joke.

'More damson wine, Professor?' asked Dora.

The professor waved a hand and Dora indicated to Miriam with a nod of her head that she should fill up his glass from a bottle on the table, while she continued to dole out the pies. Miriam vigorously shook her head in response, indicating that she would be doing no such thing, and Dora shook her head back in disappointment, while Morley nodded to indicate to Miriam that she should bloody well do as she was told. It was quite the little dumb-show we were enacting, though the diners – young and earnest, mostly male and mostly dressed in expensive rough tweeds – were so absorbed in their meal and their apparently hilarious conversation that none of them seemed to have noticed us. But when Miriam sullenly reached across the table to take the bottle to pour the wine – she and Morley having been vigorously nodding and shaking heads at one another now for quite some time – Jenkins did take note. Miriam's, after all, was not a wrist to be ignored.

'Well well,' said Jenkins. 'And who is this?' He turned around to look at Miriam, apprising her instantly with a wolfish grin. But then he saw Morley and then he saw me and his smile and his tone immediately changed. 'And who on earth are you?'

Morley drew himself up to his full height and announced himself in his customary fashion – 'Swanton Morley, sir, at your service' – which I always thought marked him out as a provincial, suggesting someone who might have come to perform some lowly tradesman's task, unblocking a sink perhaps, or sweeping a chimney, hanging a door, or some wallpaper. ('For the working classes I am a builder of great palaces, Sefton,' he once told me, many years later, in his darkest hours, when he had rather come to doubt his achievements. 'But for the bourgeoisie I will never be anything more than a cheap paper hanger.')

To my great surprise, Jenkins greeted us warmly.

'Well, well, Mr Swanton Morley! We have been expecting you. Very good of you to join us.'

Little did we know we had walked into a trap.

Jenkins clapped his hands to silence the table.

'Ladies and gentlemen!' he announced. 'We are honoured to have with us at our humble dig today a very distinguished visitor. A very distinguished visitor indeed. You may be familiar with his work in the popular press. He is a journalist and the author of a number of books for children – isn't that right, Mr Morley? And it seems he also has an interest in archaeology—'

'A very amateur interest,' said Morley.

'Indeed,' said Jenkins. 'Indeed.'

Dora, having finished distributing the pies from her tray, took Morley's tray from him and went on around the table.

'It is extraordinarily kind of you to allow us to visit, Professor,' said Morley.

'Kind?' said Jenkins, taking a great swallow of his damson wine, and setting the glass down firmly on the table. 'Kind?' He made a sort of doleful face. 'Oh no, Mr Morley. I don't think it was my intention to be *kind*, sir. One is *kind* towards children and animals, isn't one?' He appealed here with a smirk to his gathered students, who smirked readily in response. 'No, you seem to have misunderstood, Mr Morley. I wasn't being kind. I was simply curious to meet the man who had the audacity to suggest in some inferior daily rag that I am the poor man's Howard Carter!'

Some of Jenkins's students, to their credit, winced at this rather sudden and direct attack and even Morley himself – accustomed as he was to being patronised by the rich, the superior, the university educated, and the upper middle classes – was clearly rather taken aback. He coughed apologetically.

'I think I know the article to which you are referring, Professor, and I can assure you I was merely suggesting—'

'"Merely suggesting!"' Jenkins interrupted. '"Merely suggesting?" And who are you, sir, to "merely suggest" anything to me? You who base your superior knowledge on . . . sorry, *what* exactly? The fact that you have written *The Children's Guide to Archaeology*?'

Jenkins was playing to the gallery here – and they were enjoying the show. Several of the male students guffawed, others tittered. Everyone was grinning: everyone except for me, Miriam, Morley and Dora.

'I have certainly spent much of my working life doing my best to offer some schooling to those who have no access to a formal education—' began Morley.

'Well, bully for you,' said Jenkins, taking up his glass of damson wine again and knocking back a final mouthful. 'Bully for you. Well done.' He held out his glass towards Miriam, indicating that she might refill it for him. She did no such thing.

I was beginning to feel extremely uncomfortable, and fearing the worst. It wouldn't take much more provocation for either Miriam or Morley to explode.

'Just tell me this, Mr Morley,' continued Jenkins. 'Have

you suffered for knowledge at all, as I have? And as my students have? Living outside' – he waved his hands around him – 'in this sort of squalor.' The site was not in fact in the least squalid. On the contrary. It was rather better appointed, and certainly less damp and draughty than my old digs back in Camden. 'Have you made sacrifices for knowledge, sir?'

'I believe I have, Professor, yes,' said Morley modestly. His life in many ways was a living sacrifice to the cause of knowledge.

'And do you have the degrees and professional qualifications to prove it? The *credentials*?' – which are of course the only things that count to men of Jenkins's stature. *Credentials*. Awards. Certificates. Citations. Chaff.

Morley remained silent.

'No? Really?' Jenkins made another sad, clownish face. 'I thought not. In which case might I suggest, sir, that in future you leave serious scholarship to *serious* scholars and stick to scribbling about whatever pathetic subjects you actually know something about?'

This caused another ripple of laughter among the students.

Miriam had had enough.

'How dare you, sir!' she said, hands firmly on her hips. It is a terrible cliché of course to describe someone's eyes as 'blazing' but Miriam's eyes were indeed in that moment alight with indignation. I had seen them before. And I can see them still.

'Pardon?' spluttered Jenkins, who was clearly not accustomed to being challenged.

'I said, how dare you! Do you talk to every stranger you meet like that?'

'I talk however I damn well please to whoever I damn well please, miss,' said Jenkins, pushing back in his chair.

'Whomsoever,' Miriam corrected him.

'And who are you exactly?' said Jenkins.

'Never mind who I am, sir. Whoever I am I would expect a show of better manners from a gentleman of your so-called education and standing.'

'Would you now?' said Jenkins, twitching rather like a horse dug by a sharp spur. 'Would you now, girl?'

'Yes I would. And I am a woman, sir, not a girl, thank you. I'm assuming you can tell the difference?'

The young woman sitting on Jenkins's right gave a tiny clap of her hands at this.

'Have you quite finished?' said Jenkins, glancing from the young woman and back to Miriam.

'No, I have not,' said Miriam.

'Well, might I point out, young lady, that we are engaged in serious scholarly research here and that you would be—'

'And might I point out, *sir*, that any man of any education would rather be called a rascal than—'

'– be accused of a deficiency in graces,' said Morley, finishing what was presumably a quotation.

'Thank you, Father,' said Miriam.

'Finished, the pair of you?' said Jenkins.

'No,' said Miriam. 'I have not. I'll tell you when I've finished. To paraphrase Dr Johnson, sir, I find you utterly deficient in graces. You invited us here to join your dig, we came in good faith, and you have proceeded to insult us. Is this how you teach your students to behave?' That seemed to hit the mark. Jenkins shifted uncomfortably on his seat and set his jaw in defiance. 'Is it? I think you'll find you owe us an apology, sir. At the very least.'

'Young lady,' said Jenkins through gritted teeth and lowering his voice. I wasn't quite sure whether he was going to get up and strangle Miriam or whether he was going to knock Morley down. Either way, I feared for our safety. In fact, he stood up and made an elaborate bow. 'Please forgive me. I seem momentarily to have forgotten myself. Please: I insist that you join our luncheon.' He clicked his fingers and beckoned Dora over with a finger. 'Set some more places for our guests, woman.'

'Certainly,' said Dora.

'And I'd expect you to show rather more manners to those serving you, sir,' said Miriam.

Jenkins laughed. 'Do you know, I think you may be one of the most impertinent creatures I have ever met.' He paused here for effect. 'I rather like it.'

'Whether you like it or not is of little interest to me,' said Miriam, seating herself at the table, while tossing back her head in a way that suggested that it was actually of great interest to her. 'And I am not a creature.'

'Oh, I think you are,' said Jenkins. 'But do forgive me for any offence caused. It was perhaps the wine talking.' He waved towards the bottles of damson wine. 'Local plonk. One perhaps underestimates its effect. Stronger than one thinks.'

'Really?' said Miriam. With which, she poured herself a glass, I took a seat beside her, and Morley beside me.

'Go easy on him,' said Morley, leaning over to Miriam. '*Mortuum flagellas.*'

And so – eventually – we all settled down to a lunch of

Herdwick lamb and juniper pies in a tent at the archaeological dig at Shap.

After the lunch, and before getting back to work, the students stood around chatting and smoking, invigorated, excited, full of vim and vigour, clearly having enjoyed the little spat between Miriam and Jenkins. It probably wasn't every day that an archaeological dig saw such a spectacle: Miriam had become quite the centre of attention, as no doubt she had fully intended. ('There is more than one way to prove the existence of God,' as Morley liked sometimes to remark. 'All of them inconclusive. Most of them incomprehensible. And none of them particularly interesting.' And there is more than one way to become the star of the show: most of them mysterious, some of them nefarious, and Miriam expert in them all.) Morley was still eating slowly at the table, but then he did insist on chewing every mouthful of food thirty-six times or more ('If it was good enough for Gladstone, Sefton, then it's good enough for me'). Jenkins wisely kept a safe distance from both Morley and Miriam, briefing students and quaffing yet more of the admittedly delicious damson wine, while Dora bustled around, tidying up. It was a scene of peculiar domestic contentment, in the middle of a field, in the middle of nowhere in Westmorland, though my thoughts, as usual, were bellowing in my mind. I calmed myself with cigarettes, the wine and pinch or two of Delaney's powders.

Miriam had struck up a conversation with the young woman who had been at Jenkins's side during the lunch.

She was tall and thin and strikingly good-looking – almost another version of Miriam, indeed – and she was laughing at Miriam's jokes as enthusiastically as she had earlier been laughing at Jenkins's. Her name, I gathered, was Nancy. I stood by, listening to the conversation. She was explaining something about the dig to Miriam.

'. . . but I don't think he'll be allowing you to get too close to his trench!' she said.

'Well, I wouldn't touch his trench if you paid me, Nancy,' said Miriam.

Nancy stifled a laugh as Jenkins approached.

'Something funny?' he asked.

'Oh, you know, just *girl* talk,' said Miriam, flashing him a sarcastic smile.

'Well, sorry to break up your party, ladies, but it is probably time to get back to work,' said Jenkins, looking at Nancy with, I thought, a rather proprietorial air. 'If you wouldn't mind, Nancy?'

'Do you not want me to show them round, Professor?' she asked.

'I'm not sure there's anything much to show,' said Jenkins, 'that would be of interest to the . . . amateur.' He smiled unpleasantly at Miriam. 'Did you say it's some sort of guidebook your father is writing?'

'That's correct, Professor,' said Miriam, taking a deliberately long time to light a cigarette. 'But not an archaeological guidebook. That would be rather *de trop*, don't you think?' (Again, as mentioned, for an entirely *de trop* archaeological guidebook, see Jenkins's own *English Archaeological Records*.) 'No,' continued Miriam. 'Father's guide is to the whole county of Westmorland. Part of a series of guides to all the counties of England, covering history and geography, and topography, and . . . well, all the -ologies and -ographies and -onomies.' She took a long draw on her cigarette. '*Including* archaeology, of course. Of little or no interest to a specialist like you, naturally. But I know Father is interested in including some information about your little dig here. I'd certainly *very* much appreciate it, if you might allow us to have a peek at what you're up to.' She moved a little closer to him as she spoke. 'In fact, I wouldn't mind if I could spend a little time in your trench with you.'

Nancy did her best to keep a straight face.

'Well,' said Jenkins, clearly not quite knowing what to say and doubtless both offended and flattered by Miriam's extraordinary attentions – as men were often both offended and flattered by Miriam's extraordinary attentions. She really had the most peculiar effect on people. He adjusted his cravat. 'I'm sure you couldn't do any harm. Nancy, you stay with them and make sure they don't get up to any nonsense.' He smiled – uncertainly this time – at Miriam and with that strode off, his students following him, trowels in hand, back to dig in the trenches.

I allowed Miriam to finish her cigarette with Nancy and went to fetch Morley from the tent. He was still at the table, all alone, but had finally finished eating. He looked lost in thought. He looked pale. He sometimes had these moments – where he seemed to be thrown out of gear, and out of time. He wiped his mouth distractedly with a napkin as Dora came to clear his plate.

'Now pay you no mind to the professor, Mr Morley,' she said. 'Billy the Bully I calls him.' She leaned over him and Morley smiled up at her.

'You know, Dora, if you don't mind my saying so, you remind me of someone. Something about you . . .'

His eyes, I thought, looked a little watery; indeed, he seemed overcome with emotion. He sighed deeply and then, to my great astonishment, he half closed his eyes and moved to lay his head against Dora's not inconsiderable breast.

'Mr Morley?' said Dora, more in pity than in shock. She looked at me, concerned. 'He's come a bit all-owerish,' she said quietly.

Morley was suddenly very embarrassed.

'Is everything all right, Mr Morley?' I asked.

'No, yes, I mean . . . please forgive me.'

'That's all right,' said Dora patiently. 'What is it, love? What's the matter?'

'My wife . . .' Morley began. 'She . . . Only recently . . . I'm so terribly sorry. It's just I sometimes get these . . . It's . . .'

Dora touched his arm gently. 'You're all right,' she said. 'I understand. Grief has its own timetable, Mr Morley. Nothing you can do about it. You just have to find a way to carry on, don't you?'

Morley looked up, clearly consoled by this, while Dora, entirely unfussed and calm and practical, began to wipe down the table beside him.

'There's my husband today, up there in his signal box. I said, "George, there's no trains running, stay at home, love." But he feels like it's his duty, you know.'

'Your husband's a signalman?' asked Morley. 'In Appleby? George Wilson? Was it him who . . .'

Dora nodded and continued with her work.

'I'm so sorry,' said Morley. He reached out and touched

her arm. 'I had no idea, my dear. It must be a terrible time for you.'

Dora nodded again. The two of them seemed to have understood one another: an understanding had passed between them. Morley suddenly seemed rejuvenated.

'Right. Come on then, Sefton. We should leave this good woman to her work. Let's have a little look around, shall we? Thank you so much, Dora.'

'No, thank you, for all your help,' she said. 'I appreciate it. Man like you, sir. Thank you.'

I was glad to get back outside the tent and Morley seemed to be restored to his usual self. We joined Miriam and Nancy by a vast stone, several hundred yards from the centre of the dig where Jenkins was busy working. He could be heard clearly in the distance, barking out orders to his students.

'Some sort of Oedipus complex, I shouldn't wonder,' said Miriam. 'Are you familiar with the work of Sigmund Freud?'

'I'm afraid not,' said Nancy. 'I'm studying archaeology.'

'Archaeologist of the mind, Freud,' said Miriam. 'You simply must read him.' She was forever recommending Freud to people. 'You'd very much enjoy it.'

'I'm sure I would,' said Nancy, gazing at Miriam in admiration.

'Now, young lady, tell us about this stone,' said Morley.

'Well,' said Nancy. 'This is what is known as the Googleby Stone. Though the locals sometimes call it the Goggleby Stone. Something like that. Shap, as you probably know, Mr Morley, is an area famous for its standing stones and this one seems to have been part of what may once have been a whole series of avenues and circles stretching right across the landscape.' She spread her arms to include the vast space around us.

'Mmm,' said Morley. 'It must really have been quite spectacular.'

'Oh, absolutely,' said Nancy. 'Particularly when you think that when they were first quarried you'd have been able to really see the pink crystals in the granite here.'

Morley peered closely at the stone and stroked it affectionately, as if it were one of his dogs at home and he were looking for ticks.

'Indeed,' he said. 'Quite quite remarkable. The achievements of our ancestors. Astonishing, really.'

As Nancy continued to explain the history of the area to us, Morley walked all around the stone, once, twice, three times, stroking it and humming to himself as he did so. The thing towered above us. It looked rather like a huge fat triangle poking upside down out of the earth, or like an arrowhead piercing the ground. Having walked slowly all around it, having seemingly absorbed every aspect of it, Morley then paced back several steps, in the direction of a dry-stone wall, in order to get a distant look. He squinted his eyes and stretched out his arms and made little box shapes with his fingers, framing the stone against the backdrop of the landscape.

'Might be worth a photograph or two, eh, Sefton?' He took out his notebook. 'What do you think?'

'Indeed, Mr Morley.'

'Just trying to work out the geography of the place. Just trying to understand the pathways and the shape of things. The elevations and depressions and the . . .' He took another step back again and stamped on the ground to establish his place and then looked down, having clearly noticed something underfoot.

'Has Jenkins been digging here?' he asked Nancy.

'No, not as far as I know,' she said.

'Well, someone has.' He knelt down and examined the earth beneath him, and then peered through a hole in the base of the dry-stone wall. 'Hmm. What do you think of this, Sefton?'

'Erm.'

'I think this is what the locals might call a hogg-hole,' he said, 'to allow sheep to pass from one pasture to another. Isn't that right?'

'I'm sure it is, Mr Morley.'

'But no sign of sheep here, are there?'

I looked around. There was indeed no sign of sheep.

'And what about this?' said Morley. Next to the hogg-hole was a patch of bracken and heather that looked to have been recently piled up. 'A site of some interest, for someone.'

'Well,' said Nancy. 'It's all very interesting around here, I suppose.'

'With the standing stone just there,' said Morley. He turned his back to us. 'And the river there.' And then he turned again. 'The wall following the lie of the land. The perfect spot, I would have thought.'

'Perfect for what, Father?' asked Miriam.

'Some structure of some sort?'

'Like?'

'I don't know,' said Morley. 'But someone's clearly found something here. Or made something here . . .'

'Locals, probably,' said Nancy. 'You occasionally see a

few of them up here, looking around, hunting for treasure, I expect.'

'Hmm.' Morley's moustache began twitching: I knew all the signs. 'Well,' he continued, 'I wonder if we should just have a little explore ourselves.'

'Oh but I really don't think you should,' said Nancy, becoming flustered. 'No. I don't think that would be a good idea at all. Jenkins'll absolutely blow his wig if he sees you.'

Morley peeked round the Googleby Stone towards Jenkins and his students in the distance. There was absolutely no way he could have seen us behind the stone.

'I don't think that's very likely to happen,' he said. 'Do you?'

Nonetheless, Nancy looked worried. 'He did say for you not to get up to any nonsense,' she said.

'But we're not getting up to nonsense, are we, Sefton?' I thought it best not to answer. 'On the contrary. It would be such a shame to have come all the way here to a dig and not actually to have dug, wouldn't it? *That* would be the nonsense. Don't you think?'

'I'm really not sure it's a good idea,' said Nancy.

'Just a little dig around here,' said Morley, pointing to where the earth had been disturbed around the bracken and heather.

'We'd need a spade, Mr Morley,' I said, hoping that this might put him off.

'Well, I just happen to have a little something with me,' he said, proudly producing a small trenching tool from his jacket pocket. 'Always carry one with me.' (Among the many other things he claimed always to carry with him, depending on our predicament, was a hunting knife, a penknife, string, a compass, a flint for making fires, a complete first aid kit, a good book, a pack of cards, a whistle, a harmonica and a change of underclothes.) 'It's a beautiful day, we have a spade and history all around us and beneath us. It would be remiss of us not to explore just a little, would it not?'

Miriam huffed and folded her arms. She'd seen it all before.

'I'll tell you what,' said Morley. 'You two ladies keep a look out for Professor Jenkins and Sefton and I will have just a quick poke around here. Give us some colour for the book, wouldn't it, Sefton? We can hardly say that we were at Professor Jenkins's famous dig at Shap but we didn't actually get to dig.'

Nancy looked at Miriam. Miriam rolled her eyes.

'Quick dig,' said Morley. 'Couple of photographs. One of me. One of Sefton. Then we're away, Nancy. I promise.'

Which is how I ended up down on my knees with the little spade, digging deep into the ground, Morley standing above me, Miriam and Nancy watching nervously from a distance. I cleared the bracken and heather and dug for a few minutes. There was nothing of course but earth. And more earth. Morley took a couple of pinches and examined it carefully. I kept digging. Yet more earth.

And then suddenly there wasn't earth any more. There wasn't anything any more. As I dug a shaft opened up below me and then the ground gave way and I found myself falling forward, swallowed up into some kind of pit.

I fell face forward several feet into total darkness, thudding down with incredible force. Winded and terrified, I quickly wrestled myself around and scrambled to my feet, thinking I might be buried alive. Gazing up I could see light above my head. The first thing I heard was Miriam. She didn't sound overly concerned.

'Oh Father. What on earth have you done with him?'

'I haven't done anything with him,' said Morley.

'Is he all right?'

'I don't know,' said Morley. 'Sefton?' he called rather sheepishly. 'Sefton? Can you hear me?'

'I told you we should have left it alone,' said Nancy.

'I'm fine,' I called up. 'Thank you.'

'There we are!' said Morley triumphantly. 'Can you see me, Sefton?' He was leaning out over the edge of the hole, his face just two or three feet above the top of my head.

'Yes,' I said.

'Are you hurt?' cried Miriam, who did not deign to lean over the edge.

'I don't think so,' I said.

'Thank goodness,' said Miriam, although in fact she sounded rather disappointed.

'Now, Nancy, are you thinking what I'm thinking?' said Morley.

'I don't know, Mr Morley,' said Nancy.

'What do you think it is?'

'It could be a souterrain,' said Nancy.

'Exactly what I was thinking!' said Morley.

'A what?' said Miriam.

'An Iron Age structure,' said Morley. 'Sort of an underground pit. Used for storage.'

'Well, if it is,' said Nancy, 'Jenkins is going to be absolutely furious!'

'Or delighted?' said Morley.

'Furious,' said Nancy. 'He was convinced there was a

souterrain around here, but it looks as though he's been digging in the wrong place!'

'But someone has been digging in the right place,' said Morley. 'They must have been down here recently for it to open up like that. Probably looted it already . . .'

'Shouldn't we get him out?' said Nancy.

'We probably should,' said Miriam.

'But you never know,' continued Morley, 'we might be lucky, might find an artefact, some coins, or some pottery or some such. No harm in looking, is there? Sefton, I don't know if you want to have a little look around while you're down there? Before we get you out?'

'I'd quite like to get out, actually,' I said.

'What can you see?'

'Nothing at the moment.' I was staring into darkness and at earth walls, but as my eyesight became accustomed to the dark, and with the little light filtering through from up above I thought I could make out a sort of primitive shelf built into the passage – and I gingerly put my hand out towards it.

Which is when I discovered the body of the woman.

CHAPTER 9

DEATH AND DECEIT
AND DESPAIR

MORLEY – OF COURSE – had jumped straight down into the souterrain, so now we were both staring at the woman's body. It was not the body of a woman who had been here since the Iron Age. It was the body of a woman who had not been here for very long at all. The sight of her made me feel quite sick: a corpse in pretty summer clothes, dumped in a pit underground. It was appalling, mind-boggling. I thought for a moment I might have been hallucinating. I strongly wished I hadn't drunk so much damson wine and smoked so many cigarettes, nor snorted so much powder, and I wished more than ever that I had never set off with Morley on another foolish adventure. Sometimes it seemed like all we ever encountered was death. Death and deceit and despair. (Morley of course saw it otherwise. Or at least he wrote *as though* it were otherwise, desperate to convince himself and others. To quote his preface to *The County Guides: West-morland*: 'Reports of the death of England have been greatly exaggerated. England is not dead and is not dying. It remains an enchanted realm, a world beyond time and place. This is England, our England, now and for ever.' It was hardly convincing in 1937. Now, frankly, it seems absurd.)

'What do you think, Sefton?' asked Morley. 'Rigor mortis?'

'I'm not sure, Mr Morley.' It was dark down in the pit and the only light was from above.

'She looks – what? – about the same age as Miriam, wouldn't you say?'

'I don't know, Mr Morley.' I was very keen to get out.

'In her early twenties, perhaps. Mid-twenties at most. And . . . light summer dress. High heels. The gay outfit makes it all the more poignant, does it not?'

'I suppose.'

'And it certainly suggests that she did not die here. In this pit. Or in this field. My guess is her body was moved here. But from where?' He looked around. As far as I could see the pit was no more than a few feet wide. He was fiddling around with something in his pocket. You never knew what he might produce. I wouldn't have been surprised if he had the original architectural plans for the place. Or a stepladder. 'Mmm.' He had in fact produced a pencil, which he used to lift what appeared to be some kind of thin gauze material covering the poor woman's face. I had no desire to see her face.

'Interesting,' he said. 'I wonder why her face has been covered.'

'You probably shouldn't touch it, Mr Morley,' I said.

'It?'

'Her, I mean. You'd be tampering with the evidence.'

'Indeed. I am taking precautions, Sefton.' He brandished

the pencil. 'Remains the most useful tool in any workman's toolbox. I've said it before. The 2B. Essential. But I am glad you're thinking like I am. This is clearly a crime scene, is it not?'

'I suppose.'

'Suppose? She didn't climb down here by herself now, did she? Someone brought her down here.'

'I think I need to get out, Mr Morley,' I said.

'Yes, yes, all in good time, Sefton. But first of all I need you to take some notes, if you wouldn't mind.'

'Down here?'

'Indeed. Do you have your notebook and pen?'

I began half-heartedly hunting in my pockets, but he quickly thrust a notebook and pen at me.

'You can use mine. But you really must get into the habit of keeping your notebook to hand, Sefton. I have mentioned this to you before, haven't I? Girdling, the ancient medieval practice of—'

'Yes, Mr Morley.'

'Right. Now . . .'

'I can hardly see here to make notes,' I said.

'Hardly is more than enough in such circumstances, wouldn't you say?'

I took the pen and paper and began to make cursory notes as Morley spoke.

'Cause of death – broken neck, it looks like. Some sign of rigor mortis, which suggests she has been dead for more than twenty-four hours. But not much more by the smell of her. Which . . .' He sniffed closely at the body. 'Isn't bad, actually, all things considered. What do you make of this sheet over her face, Sefton?'

I didn't make anything of it.

'Mmm. And look at this.' He indicated something on the shelf beside her. 'A candle, if I am not mistaken, in a rather fetching jam-jar holder. Quite ornate. Take a note. Very interesting. Whoever came down here lit their way perhaps with the candle, placed the gauze across her face, and then snuffed out the candle, just as the poor girl herself had been snuffed out. Or . . . Or! Ah! Perhaps they lit the candle in order to lead her into the other life. Which do you think, Sefton?'

'No idea,' I said.

'I'm sure I've read something about it somewhere. It's just remembering where . . . One has to learn to think like a murderer, you see, Sefton. Come on. You can do it.'

'I need to get out,' I repeated. I was in Spain. I was in the crash. I was outside Marlborough Street Magistrates' Court.

'What about her hands?' said Morley.

'I don't want to look at her hands.'

'Come on. Here. Look. What do you see, Sefton?'

I reluctantly looked at the woman's hands. Even in the shadows and darkness it was clear that her hands were blackened.

'So?'

'Black marks,' I said. 'Bruises.'

'Black marks. Yes. Bruises. No. And what stains the skin in this manner?'

'I really don't know, Mr Morley. I think I'm going to be sick actually.' Spain. London. Lucy. It was all too much.

'Nonsense! You're made of sterner stuff than that, man. And you're a photographer. Come on, think.' He clicked his fingers. 'Hands, black stains?'

'Silver nitrate?' It was something we'd started using in the makeshift darkroom back at St George's.

'Precisely!' said Morley. 'Now we're in business!'

'So?'

At which point, thank goodness, I could hear voices from up above. Miriam and Nancy, very wisely, had clearly gone to fetch help.

'Quick,' said Morley. 'Hold this.' He produced a specimen jar and a brush from one of his capacious pockets. 'Come on, before the police get here. You know what they're like. *Terram coelo miscent.*'

'What?'

'Hold it here, please.'

'What the hell is this for?'

'Here, please, Sefton.'

I held the specimen jar by the woman's shoes while Morley proceeded to brush dirt from her soles.

'What on earth are you doing? Where did you get that from?'

'Free with every *Children's Encyclopaedia of Archaeology*. They've been terribly popular actually. I knew it'd come in handy.'

∽ ∾

We were pulled up out of the pit by a couple of Jenkins's students. An ambulance had arrived, and the policemen who were investigating the train crash in Appleby, and there were more policemen down at the site of Jenkins's dig. Miriam stood over by the Googleby Stone, her arm around Nancy's shoulder – the poor thing seemed quite upset. Our police-men weren't exactly delighted to see us.

'Mr Morley,' said the policeman. 'We meet once again under difficult circumstances.'

'I'm afraid so, Officer.'

'Unfortunate.'

'Quite.'

He introduced a man in a thick black overcoat, an awkward-looking fellow, physically – was it a hunchback? A war wound? – with an unlit pipe clamped in his mouth.

'This is Chief Inspector Banks, from Penrith.'

'Pleased to meet you,' said Morley.

'It was you who found the body? Is that right?'

'In fact it was my assistant, actually, Mr Sefton,' said Morley.

'Ah, yes, the notorious Mr Sefton?'

I smiled nervously. 'Yes?' I said.

'I've heard a lot about you. I was looking forward to getting to talk to you this afternoon, sir. But I suppose events have rather overtaken us now, haven't they?'

'Yes, I suppose they have.'

'So. Now is probably as good a time as any then, isn't it? Do you want to tell me what happened?' Morley was about to speak. The chief inspector held up a finger to silence him. 'In your own words, please, Mr Sefton? You'll get a chance in a moment, Mr Morley.'

I did my best to explain to him what had happened. He did not look at all convinced by what I said, but then I suppose that was his job.

'Well. Yesterday's hero finds himself once again at the

very centre of an unfolding drama. Very interesting. We'll need to take a full statement at the station, obviously.'

'Of course,' I said.

'Speaking on behalf of myself and Mr Sefton,' said Morley, interrupting, 'if I may?'

'Yes, Mr Morley?' said the chief inspector wearily.

'Can I just say that as the first on the scene, as it were, we are of course more than willing to help the police in whatever way possible.'

'I'm not sure that you can help us very much at the moment, sir, except perhaps as potential suspects.'

'As suspects?' said Morley. 'Witnesses, do you mean?'

'Suspects, Mr Morley.'

'Really? I'm afraid I rather fail to see the logic, Officer.'

'Well, put yourself in my position, Mr Morley.' The chief inspector removed his pipe from his mouth and used it rather as a conductor might use a baton. 'You're two days in Westmorland and you and Mr Sefton here have already been involved in a train crash in which a young girl died and now you've gone and found yourselves a dead body. One might perhaps view that as rather suspicious, don't you think?'

'Or unlucky,' said Morley.

'I don't believe in luck, Mr Morley. I only believe in innocence or guilt.'

'Ah, well, that's where we differ then perhaps. I do believe in luck, Officer, you see, in the sense of meaningful coincidences, rather than prescriptive fate, of course.' The chief inspector looked nonplussed. 'And as for innocence and guilt, one might ask, which of us is not stained? "For though thou wash thee with nitre, and take thee much soap,

yet thine iniquity is marked before me, saith the Lord God."
Jeremiah 2, verse 22.'

'There's no need to bring the Scriptures into this, Mr Morley, thank you.'

'Oh, but there is, Officer, there is. I thought you might be interested to know that we detected traces of silver nitrate on the victim's hands.'

'You examined her hands?'

'Well, I wouldn't say we *examined* her hands exactly.'

'Did you touch her hands?'

'No, no, no.'

'Or any other part of her body?'

'Goodness me, no!' said Morley. 'But you see I wonder if the silver nitrate might suggest she was involved in the pharmaceutical industry in some way? If one needs to identify the body. Silver nitrate is used extensively in the preparation of wart creams, you see, as I know to my own cost—'

'Right, thank you,' said the chief inspector.

'I just thought it was important to present all the evidence before jumping to conclusions or determining innocence or guilt.'

'As I say, Mr Morley, we'll doubtless be talking to you and your colleague in much more detail later, bearing all the evidence in mind. We just need to establish the identity of the body first.'

Another man had arrived: burly, middle-aged, with a ginger beard. He reminded me rather of those rather forbidding portraits of Henry VIII, and looked equally unhappy.

'Dr Harris,' said the policeman. 'Thank you for coming at such short notice.'

'Hmm. Where's the body?'

The chief inspector pointed over towards the souterrain.

'Right. I'll have a quick look. I can probably perform the autopsy this afternoon.'

'Really?' said Morley. 'Might I attend? I am thinking of writing a guide to pathology, actually.'

The doctor looked at Morley, as people often looked at him, utterly appalled and perplexed. 'Who are you?'

'Swanton Morley, sir, at your service.'

'He's the writer,' said the chief inspector.

'He's a damned cheek,' said the doctor, ignoring Morley entirely and walking over towards the souterrain.

'He's got his hands full at the moment,' said the chief inspector.

'Of course,' said Morley. 'Though if I could attend the autopsy?'

'Absolutely out of the question,' said the chief inspector, exasperated. 'I'll need you and Mr Sefton just to sit tight in Appleby, if you wouldn't mind. You're staying at the Tufton Arms, aren't you?'

'That's right.'

'Well, we'll be along to take statements from you in due course. All you need to do is remain here in Westmorland for the moment. I hope that won't be an inconvenience. You've got your guidebook to be getting on with, I believe?'

'Yes,' said Morley. 'We have. Plenty to do. And we have made extensive notes, Officer, from when we discovered the body, which we can make available to you?'

'I think it'd be best for you to leave us to do our job, Mr Morley, and you can get on with yours, eh? You keep your note-making for your book, eh?'

The woman's body began to emerge from the souterrain,

hoisted up on a stretcher by the two ambulancemen and several of the students. Our little crowd by the Googleby Stone instinctively drew closer as the body emerged from out of the earth. The cloth that had covered her face had been removed.

'Oh my God,' said Nancy, turning quite pale. 'I know her. It's Maisie – Maisie Taylor. She works in the chemist.'

'Taylor's Pharmacy in Kirkby Stephen?' said Morley.

'That's right.'

'Daughter of the pharmacist?'

'Wife,' said Nancy. 'She's Gerald's wife.'

'Oh dear,' said Morley. 'That's a shame.'

Nancy began sobbing.

'Though it does explain the silver nitrate,' he said, in the general direction of the chief inspector.

Suddenly from behind, Jenkins appeared, trailed by his students, clearly having finished his own discussions with the police down at his dig.

'What on earth is going on here?' he thundered. 'Morley, I blame you for this! Turning my dig into a bloody fiasco! Nancy, why didn't you stop them? I told you they—'

And then he saw the body of Maisie Taylor and stopped in his tracks.

'Maisie?'

'Do you know who this is, Professor?' asked the chief inspector.

'Yes. I mean no. I mean, not really. I do know who she is. But I have no idea what she's doing here.'

'And where do you know her from exactly?'

'She works in the pharmacy in Kirkby Stephen, and I . . . We sometimes . . . That's where I met her anyway.'

Nancy suddenly flew at him and began beating him about the face, her fists flailing. Jenkins made no attempt to protect himself, but merely stood with his arms outstretched as she punched and pounded at him. It took two policemen to drag her off.

'You bastard!' she was screaming. 'You bastard! You filthy bastard!' She was like a thing possessed, writhing around in the arms of the police. 'Everyone knows he was at it with her! They know!' She was nodding furiously at the terrified students, who were cowering in the shade of the Googleby Stone. 'They all know! He'd bring her up here at night. To the tent. He tried it with all of them. All of us! He was . . . the filthy bastard! Look what you've done to her! You bastard!' It looked as though she might break free from the grip of the policemen at any moment.

'Right, that's enough,' said the chief inspector, raising his hands – and his pipe – to calm things down. 'Enough!' He pointed at Nancy. 'Enough!'

'You murdering bastard!' she screamed.

'All right, you don't say another word, miss. Understand? Not another word, or I'll have you arrested for a breach of the peace. You don't want that now, do you?' Nancy was still struggling in the arms of the policemen, but she remained silent. 'And you' – the chief inspector turned and pointed to Jenkins – 'you, sir, are accompanying me to the station.'

'But—'

'No ifs or buts. Now.'

'And we—' began Morley, picking – as usual – an inopportune moment.

'Get out of here,' said the chief inspector.

CHAPTER 10

MERRIE ENGLANDE

'MR TAYLOR'S WIFE,' said Morley. 'The pharmacist's wife.'

'Indeed,' said Miriam. 'Very sad.'

'Poor man,' said Morley.

'Poor woman,' said Miriam.

We were back in the Lagonda, ready to head to Appleby. Morley was rubbing his fingers and thumbs together, in a gesture he sometimes used when trying to work out something difficult, as if literally sifting ideas through his hands.

I was looking forward to a stiff drink back at the Tufton Arms.

'Where did he say he was going this morning, when we saw him?'

'Who?' said Miriam, reapplying her lipstick in the car's rear-view mirror: there were times when the Lagonda came to resemble a kind of mobile beauty parlour.

'Mr Taylor, the pharmacist. The poor widower.'

'Can't remember, Father,' said Miriam, checking her application of make-up. 'Sorry.'

'*In exornando se, multum temporis insumunt mulieres,*' muttered Morley.

'I heard you,' said Miriam.

'What did he say?' I asked.

'Just ignore him,' said Miriam.

'Where did Mr Taylor say he was going?' asked Morley again, trying to summon up the answer from between his fingers.

'It was the Egremont Fair, I think, Mr Morley,' I said.

'Whatever that is,' said Miriam, puckering her lips together and blowing herself a kiss.

'Ah, yes, the Egremont Fair, that's right!' said Morley. 'Or the Crab Fair, strictly speaking.'

'Something to do with crabs, presumably?' said Miriam, manipulating an eyebrow and glancing in my direction.

'Crabs?' said Morley. 'Crab apples, Miriam! The Lord of Egremont traditionally distributed crab apples to the people, I think. What's the date?'

'It's the eighteenth of September, Father. All day.'

'There we are then!' said Morley. 'Third Saturday of September. The Egremont Crab Fair! One of the great remaining English medieval fairs! Traditionally took place on the feast of the Nativity of St Mary, I believe, but was moved for practical reasons during the last century, probably to do with changing working patterns and—'

'Fascinating I'm sure,' said Miriam, starting up the car. 'Anyway.' We set off in the direction of Appleby.

'Yes, he said he was going for the wrestling, didn't he?'

'That's right, Mr Morley,' I said.

'I bet you'd like to see a bit of wrestling, Sefton, wouldn't you?'

'I bet he would,' said Miriam. 'But no chance.' She smiled sarcastically, her lipstick underlining the emphasis.

'Egremont,' said Morley. 'Strictly outside our boundaries, of course, over in west Cumberland—'

'Oh no,' said Miriam, clearly foreseeing where the conversation was going. 'No way.'

'No way where?' said Morley.

'We are not going to Egremont, Father. If that's what you're thinking.'

'How do you know what I'm thinking?'

'Because I always know what you're thinking.'

'Always?'

'Invariably.'

'Not always then,' said Morley. Another small linguistic victory. 'It's only a couple of hours' drive.'

'No.'

'What would it be . . . ?' Morley consulted the map of the British Isles that he seemed to have on permanent display in his mind's eye. 'Penrith. Keswick. Whitehaven even? Or up to Cockermouth and then the road south . . . Mmm. Beautiful scenery. While we're here, you know, it would be a terrible shame not to take the opportunity.'

'No!' said Miriam.

'It would add quite a lot to the book, my dear. We've hardly begun with Westmorland. Apart from the scenery there are all the monuments, and the castles, and the industry—'

'No, Father. I said no.'

'And of course there's the fair itself, for when we come to write up Cumberland. We'd be ahead of ourselves, actually. Two counties for the price of—'

'No. No. And double no,' said Miriam emphatically.

'And we'd be able to let poor Gerald know that the police need to speak to him back in Appleby. So it's win-win-win—'

'No it is not, Father. It is not win-win-win. It is no, no, no. Do you understand?'

'Miriam!'

'Father! We are not driving all the way to Egremont. We are here, in case you've forgotten, to write a guidebook to Westmorland, plain and simple, in which task we are already conspicuously failing, without wandering off into Cumberland and goodness knows where. And besides, the policeman asked us to remain in Appleby, if you recall?'

'He didn't really mean it,' said Morley.

'Yes, he did really really mean it! He's a policeman, for goodness sake!'

'My point entirely.'

'Someone has died, Father, and I think you need to take it rather more seriously.'

'I am taking it very seriously, my dear. Not only has someone died: a man's wife has died.' He paused, composing himself. 'And Sefton and I discovered her body – so I think perhaps we have a duty to poor Mr Taylor to let him know as quickly as possible that the police will be wanting to speak to him, don't you?'

'Well in that case we can just let the police know where Mr Taylor is and save ourselves the bother of the journey. Obviously.'

'But . . .' Morley was clearly looking for reasons to justify the journey. 'The journey is the journey!' he said, gazing around, in that annoyingly mystical way of his.

'The journey is the journey?' repeated Miriam. 'And what on earth is that supposed to mean, exactly?'

'This *is The County Guides*, Miriam. This is it, the very spirit of the thing. The three of us, en route, in transit. *In loco!*'

'Oh! Father!' cried Miriam. 'Sefton? Talk to him. We are not driving all the way to Egremont. And that's final.'

We arrived in Egremont in the late afternoon. The drive there was, of course, utterly spectacular, the automobile equivalent of a ride on the Settle–Carlisle line, Morley taking notes and typing as we travelled, as well as continually tossing out observations about the history and topography of Westmorland and Cumberland, and the history of English fairs, and the meaning of the sublime in English literature, and the nature of traditions and customs in rural English life pre-, post- and during industrialisation – the usual sort of conversation for a pleasant afternoon's outing. With Morley, every jaunt became a lecture, and every lecture a jaunt. The Egremont Fair, I discovered, dates back to the thirteenth century, and is to be clearly distinguished from the likes of the Appleby Fair, which is strictly a gypsy fair, dating back only to the reign of James II, and also from the Grasmere Sports, which is really a sporting occasion, though all three are apparently an integral part of the Lakeland social calendar and therefore play an important role in maintaining what Morley in *The County Guides* describes as the 'ancient and noble traditions of Merrie Englande'. It was perhaps therefore no surprise to be greeted on our arrival in Egremont by the sight of a gang of merrie Englishmen happily brawling outside a pub far advanced in its decrepitude and cheered on by a crowd who one might easily imagine having enjoyed bear-baiting during the late Middle Ages.

'Ah! The Englishman at play!' said Morley.

'Bloody gypsies!' cried one woman in the crowd to the brawling men. 'Go back to where you belong!'

'Oh, Father,' said Miriam. 'Look at this. Is it safe?'

'High spirits,' said Morley. 'Nothing to worry about. Rather quaint in many ways. Now, a quick tour of the fair, we'll find Gerald and then we'll be gone. We'll be back in Appleby by nightfall. Perfectly straightforward.'

In all my years with Morley nothing was ever straightforward – and so it proved at the Egremont Crab Fair.

Miriam parked the car on a residential street near the centre of the town. There were cars and vans and horses and carts everywhere you looked, men and women in their finery – and their not-so-finery.

'Probably best if we split up,' said Morley, 'and then whoever finds Gerald can say that we'd like a word and we can perhaps rendezvous back here in – what? – an hour or so?'

'Very well,' said Miriam.

'Mind your car, miss?' asked a young lad who had clearly seen an opportunity to make some money during the festivities.

'No, thank you,' said Miriam, shushing him away.

'Here you are, boy,' said Morley, giving him a handful of coins. 'Spend it wisely!'

'Father!' said Miriam.

'It's a fair, for goodness sake, Miriam!' said Morley. 'Go and enjoy yourselves!' And with that he promptly disappeared into the crowd.

I was about to do exactly that and head for the nearest pub when Miriam called me back.

'You're not going to leave me alone here, Sefton, are you?'

'But Mr Morley said we were to split up and meet back here in an hour or so.'

'I know perfectly well what he said, but I'm not at all sure I want to be on my own with all these . . . people.'

Miriam could be snooty and she could be snobbish, and there were times when she was just plain rude. The influence of her London set – the Mitfords and the Guinnesses and the actresses and the mannequins – could be quite unfortunate. But this was admittedly quite a crowd, and quite a mixed crowd, and quite an unruly crowd, and as we neared the centre of town more and more young men and women and families began pressing all around us from every direction, with hawkers and flower sellers and boys and girls begging for change, and women selling rag dolls and – could it have been? – puppies from baskets, and tea stalls and booths and tables piled high with tall pies and flat cakes. Someone had somehow attached a gramophone horn to the top of a tall pole and somewhere nearby – and very recently – a farmer had been spreading muck. The combination of the sound of Tommy Dorsey's 'The Dipsy Doodle' and the stench of manure, and the sweet smell of crab apples crushed underfoot was really quite intoxicating. Miriam was accustomed to the city, with its strict and peculiar rules governing crowd behaviour: this was classic country chaos.

She took my arm and we began walking together. 'Let me hold on to you, Sefton, just in case,' she said. And sure enough, we'd not gone more than a few steps when we were accosted.

'Hey, young lovers, do you want your fortune told?' asked a gypsy woman, who really would have made a Carmen; she was wearing the typical clothes of her tribe, a costume of such fine colours, and with loud clacking bangles and bracelets, that it almost eclipsed Miriam's own.

'We are not young . . . anything, thank you,' said Miriam, picking up her stride.

'Is that right? Are you sure?' said the woman, who had fallen into step alongside us. 'Good-looking young lady like yourself, with such a fine young gentleman.'

'We're not buying anything today, thank you,' said Miriam. 'Good day to you!'

'I'm not selling anything,' said the woman.

'Good,' said Miriam.

'You sure you two are not together?'

'Quite sure, thank you,' said Miriam. 'I am practically engaged to someone else, actually.'

'Ah! Ah, that'd be it,' said the gypsy. 'I could tell, you see. Dordi, dordi. It won't go well.'

'What won't go well?'

'Your engagement, my dear.'

'How dare you!' said Miriam.

'Oh, I thinks you know it, my dear,' said the gypsy. 'I thinks you know it. And I thinks you know that you two are destined to be together.'

'Pah!' cried Miriam. 'I'll tell you what I do know. I know we're destined to go and visit the fair, madam, and I'd be very grateful if you could let us get on and do so in peace, thank you.'

'You don't want to know your destiny then?'

'I make my own destiny, thank you,' said Miriam.

'Do you, now?'

'Yes, I do, thank you.'

'And what about you, boy?' the gypsy asked me.

'Me?'

'Shall I reveal your future to you?'

'It's not his future that's the mystery,' said Miriam.

'Oh, but I can tell you all about his past as well,' said the woman.

'Really?' said Miriam.

'I don't think so,' I said, and began to speed up even more. 'Come on, Miriam.'

But the gypsy grabbed my arm and brought her face close to mine. 'Oh, I know all about you,' she said.

'Go away!' I said.

'Oh yes. I know all about you. You know you're one of us, don't you?'

'What?'

'I can tell. You're one of those condemned to wander the world without ceasing, running and running, never finding peace.'

'Thank you,' I said, brushing her off and speeding away. 'Much appreciated. Goodbye!'

Giving up with us, the woman immediately caught on to another man and woman and tried the same patter with them. 'Hello, young lovers, do you want your fortune told?' The man was rather more brisk with the gypsy than even we had been, and she duly passed on again to the next couple.

'Bloody gypsies,' said the man to me, as he walked past. 'Gunnan folk. They've got their own fair, why can't they leave us to ours?'

'They say the crash down in Appleby is o' alanga them,'

said the woman. 'The children live on nobbut bread an' scrape.'

We wandered together round the fair, Miriam rather irritated and anxious, clearly annoyed with the gypsy woman, and with me, and with Appleby and Egremont, and with the whole of Cumberland and Westmorland, but gradually she calmed down and began to enjoy herself. We drank tea and ate cakes. We watched men playing quoits and children attempting to climb a greasy pole. It was another warm September afternoon and the tea and cakes and the general air of gaiety slowly began to work a subtle autumn magic: we laughed at the same things, and shared a few small confidences. It was probably the most time we had ever spent in one another's company alone, and certainly the most time we had ever spent together without arguing and without having to intervene to save Morley from some ridiculous predicament or other. I thought for a moment that life might actually be like this: some kind of surreal rural idyll. There was, in a field, a pipe-smoking competition; Miriam was sorely tempted to have a go, but participation seemed to be restricted to old men in flat caps and suits, all puffing up a storm. Elsewhere in the field we witnessed what a local informed us was something called 'Gurning Through a Braffin' – a sort of face-contorting contest that I wisely declined to enter. And a sign outside a tent advertised something called 'Biskeys and Treacle'.

'Biscuits, do you think they meant?' asked Miriam.

'No, I think they mean "Biskeys", whatever they are,' I said. (See the entry under 'Biskeys and Treacle' in *The County Guides: Westmorland*.)

It was as though we were discovering a foreign country

together, Egremont Fair being about as exotic as England gets, a spectacle of the utterly odd and the perfectly everyday. But there was no sign of Mr Gerald Taylor, and soon it was time for us to return.

As we began wandering back towards the Lagonda, away from the centre of the town, my eye was caught by what was effectively a mini-bazaar set up on a patch of scrubland by the side of the road, tended by an ancient being wrapped in layer upon layer of clothes as though for a Russian winter. The thick grey braided hair and the large hooped earrings through large low-hanging earlobes suggested a woman of advanced years, but it was difficult to tell: if it was a woman it was a woman with a man's face; the defiant face of a Geronimo. She had a variety of items set out on a blanket before her: wooden spoons, lucky horseshoes, candles and jars of cloudy liquids.

Miriam sensed me pausing.

'Thinking of buying me a present?' she asked.

'Why, what would you like?'

'Not sure. Not exactly Selfridges, is it?'

'Perfumes, miss?' asked the old woman. 'Ointments? Creams? Something for your fiancé?'

'He's not my fiancé,' said Miriam.

'Something for your pretty lady?' the old woman asked me.

'Let me buy you something,' I said. I had started to feel rather comfortable with Miriam, perhaps for the first time. 'I'd like to.'

'Seriously?' she asked.

'Absolutely. As a memento of our day together.'

'Well, Sefton, you do know how to treat a woman.'

The defiant face of a Geronimo

She picked up a jar of cloudy liquid.

'What's this?' she asked the old woman.

'Oh no, no, you'll not be wanting that, my dear,' the woman replied, in her thin, strangulated voice.

'I just wondered what it was,' said Miriam.

'No, I can't let you have that,' said the woman.

'What do you mean, you can't let me have it? Isn't everything for sale?'

'It's not for you, my dear.'

'I'll be the judge of that, shall I? I was simply enquiring what it was.'

The old woman fixed Miriam with a defiant stare. 'It's hotchiwitchi oil,' she said.

'It's whatty withchy?'

'Hotchiwitchi.'

'Hotty witchy?'

'*Hotchiwitchi*. You'd call it a hedgehog.'

'It's hedgehog oil?'

'That's right.'

'How do you get hedgehog oil? Is it some sort of secretion?'

'It's from the fat, from the cooking,' said the woman. 'From when we bake the hotchiwitchi.'

'Ugh,' said Miriam, placing the jar quickly back down on the blanket. 'And what on earth's it for?'

'Hotchiwitchi oil? It does for everything, my dear. Cure for baldness. Cure for heartache. Cure for chilblains. Cure for your diarrhoea. Cure for your constipation.'

'A cure for constipation *and* for diarrhoea?' said Miriam.

The woman laughed one short barking laugh so loud and so violent it sounded like someone coming up for air, and then she held up another jar that looked exactly the same as the hedgehog oil.

'You don't need that one. You want to try this one, miss. This one's for you.'

'And what is that?'

'Comfrey ointment.'

'It looks exactly the same as the—'

'Comfrey ointment,' insisted the woman.

'And what's that for?'

'What d'you want it to be for, my dear?'

'What is it *actually* for though?' asked Miriam.

'Comfrey ointment does for everything.'

'Like hotchiwitchi oil?'

'Totally different. Boiled up with a bit of lard, it does you for burns and cuts. Lubricates your engine. And it's good in a nice stew.'

'Are you mocking me?' asked Miriam.

And the old woman laughed again. 'Where's your gorgio sense of humour then?'

'I have a perfectly good sense of humour, thank you,' said Miriam.

This made the old woman laugh even more.

'Come on, Sefton. This woman is clearly not interested in our business.'

'No, no, no,' said the old woman. 'Seriously, my dear. Seriously. This is for you,' she said, scooping up a handful from a pile of what looked like small dirty pieces of diced ginger. 'This is what you need.'

'Really? And what is this? Dried starling oil? Purified pansy ointment?'

'This?' said the woman. 'It's mandrake, my dear.'

'Is it?' said Miriam. 'I've never seen mandrake.'

'Good for the blood, mandrake,' said the woman. 'You takes your little nutmeg grater, puts it in a pot, boils it up and then you takes it like tea, with sugar.'

'And what does it do?'

'It eases you proper,' said the woman. 'In every way.'

'Well, perhaps I will take some of that then,' said Miriam.

'Told you,' said the woman. 'I know what you need, miss. And he knows, eh?'

Miriam clearly bridled and became tense at this suggestion: no one should ever know what Miriam needed, apart from Miriam. She produced her purse, as I reached for my wallet.

'Let me,' I said.

'I pay my own way, thank you, Sefton,' said Miriam, her tone hardening. The warmth of the afternoon seemed suddenly to have vanished.

'Did you find the mandrake yourself, madam?' I asked the old woman.

'No, no. That's the girl, Naughty, who finds the mandrake.' She pointed to a little girl behind her who was bathing a baby in a handsome washtub made from what looked like half of an old beer barrel.

'Naughty?'

'That's right.'

'Is that her name?'

'That's right. And her little sister's Nice.'

'Right,' I said.

'Naughty finds mandrake. She's a gift.'

'I see.' Naughty did not look as though she had a gift – she looked like a dirty ragamuffin – though of course it's difficult to tell. (I have certainly met enough poets and artists in my time who have blurred the distinction between dirt and art, and who were neither naughty nor nice.)

'I'm afraid I don't have anything smaller,' said Miriam, producing a crisp brown ten bob note.

I reached again for my wallet.

'Here,' I said, 'let me, please.'

'No, no,' said the old woman. 'That should suffice.' And she snatched the note.

'Hey!' said Miriam. 'I'm not paying that much for a handful of dried roots!'

'Very rare, mandrake,' said the woman. 'Very rare.'

'That's outrageous!' said Miriam.

'Hey!' I said. 'Give the lady her money back.'

Suddenly a man came, as if from nowhere, from behind the old woman and stood protectively beside her. He was wearing a white vest and a leather apron and had a wild head of dark hair shaved high and tight on the sides. With wide-set eyes and a long profile he looked remarkably like a horse preparing to charge; indeed, he had a horseshoe tattoo on one arm, and was carrying an actual horseshoe in his other hand. In the near distance behind the woman I noticed that he had a makeshift workshop set up: a forge by a fire in a clearing by some trees, beside a vivid gypsy caravan.

'Problem, Mother?' said the man.

'No!' she said. 'These good people were just buying some of our mandrake.'

'Good.' He stared at me. 'That's all good then?'

'I'm afraid there's been something of a misunderstanding,' I said.

'Is that right?'

At that moment Morley appeared beside us.

'Ah!' he cried. 'Found you! Have you had a good afternoon?'

'Very good, thank you, Mr Morley,' I said.

'Did you try your hand at quoits?'

'No,' I said.

'What about the greasy pole?'

'No.'

'Oh you should have, Sefton! Reminds of the time I was in Lucknow, fabulous place, and they had a not dissimilar—'

'Did you find Mr Taylor, Father?' asked Miriam.

'No,' he said. 'I'm afraid not, but there's some wrestling about to start. I think we might just find him there, if we're quick.'

The horseshoe man had wandered back over to his anvil and was settling down to his bellows when Morley caught sight of it.

'Well, well,' he said. 'Well, well, well, well, well. What is this? Tinsmith? Blacksmith? Silversmith? Worth an investigation perhaps, Sefton? A quick photograph, at least? "Cumbrian Country Crafts"? I can see the caption now. Come on.'

'We just need to sort something out here, Mr Morley, actually,' I said.

'Miriam can sort it out, can't she?' said Morley. 'She's a big girl. Come on, quick. We need to get back for the wrestling.'

And so, reluctantly, I left Miriam arguing with the old woman over the price of the mandrake and made my way with Morley over to the man, fearing – in all honesty – for both Morley's safety and my own.

'What do you want?' the horse-faced man asked, without looking up.

But Morley's attention had already wandered.

'I was just admiring your wagon here, sir, actually,' said Morley. 'It really is a thing of tremendous beauty, if you don't mind my saying so.'

'It is, and you may.' The man stood up and looked proudly towards his caravan.

'Did you build it yourself, may I ask?'

'I did not, sir, no.'

'Would you mind awfully if I asked who made it then? It's just, I have always had rather a hankering after a vardo myself.'

'You know the proper name?'

'Oh yes,' said Morley. 'I am something of an enthusiast for the gypsy way of life.'

'Is that right?'

'Oh, very much so. *Very* much so.'

'Well it's a shame others don't share your enthusiasm,' said the gypsy, fixing his eyes suspiciously on me. 'Lot of "misunderstandings" between us and the gorgio. No offence.'

'None taken, sir,' said Morley. 'I understand completely. We are all, alas, as strangers to others, and sometimes even unto ourselves.'

Morley was by now in reverie, up close to the caravan, examining the big bright yellow wooden wheels and the carriage's incredibly ornate carvings.

'Look at this, Sefton! I mean, just look at it!'

'Made by Tom Tongs of Manchester, sir,' said the man. 'Finest vardo maker in the land – in my and many another's opinion.'

'Yes. Yes. It really is quite magnificent,' said Morley. 'Like a cathedral, almost. Have you ever been to Notre Dame?'

'Can't say I have, sir, no. Palace on wheels, I calls it,' said the man.

'Exactly,' said Morley. 'Couldn't have put it better myself. A palace on wheels! A portable Versailles!' Morley slapped the vehicle as if slapping the hindquarters of a prize-winning heifer. 'And it weighs it, I'm sure. It must be, what?'

'Fifty hundredweight, I would guess.'

'My goodness,' said Morley.

'She's a two-horse carriage, really,' said the man.

There was a horse tethered by the wagon, and a lazy-looking dog lounging on the steps that led up inside. Morley glanced across at the animals.

'That's why we're here,' said the man. 'Our other horse died that we bought at Appleby. Blue roan mare. We used her as a sider.'

'A sider?'

'To go alongside,' said the man.

'Ah, of course,' said Morley. 'Well, sorry to hear that.'

'I knew we shouldn't have bought her. Something wrong with her. But you know what the fair's like. Allowed my heart to rule my head.'

'Yes, I think we've all experienced that,' said Morley, stroking the caravan's woodwork. 'The Appleby Horse Fair, you mean?'

'That's right,' said the man.

'I've never been, alas.'

'You want to come next year, sir. It's not like this. Proper gypsy fair, so it is. You get wagons all the way from Borough-bridge to Catterick Green; you could plot your way home by the fires at night. And horses everywhere. Piebalds, skew-balds, roans. Quite a sight.'

Horse grazing in a field

'Well, one year I would very much like to see that,' said Morley. 'Very much indeed. One of the great festivals and customs of the English year.'

'That it is, sir.'

'The Nottingham Goose Fair, the Durham Miners' Gala, May morning at Magdalen College, Lewes Bonfire Night—'

I coughed very loudly, sensing one of Morley's long lists in the making.

'Are you all right, Sefton?'

'Yes, fine, thank you,' I said.

'Well, you should look in on us, if you do ever make it to Appleby for the fair,' said the man.

'I will,' said Morley, 'thank you.'

'You know Appleby?'

'Just a little.'

'It's up by Gallows Hill but you get the vardos everywhere, all up Boroughgate. We usually try to set up down there. Naughty and my mother like selling the potatoes and pig's trotters. They do a roast potato with a trotter for a farthing, plus your salt and vinegar.'

'That sounds delicious,' said Morley. 'And very good value.'

'Aye, better value than the horse,' said the man, sighing, glancing at his weary-looking animals.

I'll be honest: I rather doubted the man's hard-luck story. I assumed that he had simply spotted Morley as an easy target – a soft touch. During our years together I saw Morley swindled out of hundreds if not thousands of pounds by men and women of all kinds and classes – businessmen, 'artists' and ne'er-do-wells – who clearly spied the same vulnerability in him. For someone so smart he could be incredibly stupid: I wondered sometimes if he made himself stupid for the benefit of others. I saw him give money to ex-servicemen who were clearly not ex-servicemen, to women pretending not to be prostitutes who clearly were prostitutes, and to children whose only appeal was the fact that they were indeed children. He was generous to the point of utter foolishness, if not complete idiocy. If I was right, and judging by the usual shape and structure of these scams, the man would avoid any direct appeal for cash, but would instead slowly reel Morley in with ever more pathetic tales of hardship: first, a dead horse; then, a dead child; a dead wife; a fatal illness. So far, the conversation was going exactly as I might have predicted.

'I should never have bought that horse. Should have stuck with a piebald. You can rely on a piebald.'

'Yes, a good reliable horse, a piebald,' agreed Morley. 'I think I'm right in saying that George Washington preferred a piebald.'

'So we're stuck here for the moment. We just need to make enough money to buy a good horse – a mare, so we can breed a foal – and then we're gone. Not asking for much, is it?'

'No, no, not at all,' said Morley.

'Trouble is, people are always trying to move us on.' He looked menacingly at me again.

I looked menacingly back. I knew his game.

'Yes,' said Morley. 'It's the old story, isn't it, I'm afraid. You are fugitives and vagabonds.'

'I don't know about that, sir.'

'In the biblical sense, I mean,' said Morley. '"When thou tillest the ground, it shall not henceforth yield unto thee her strength; a fugitive and a vagabond shalt thou be in the earth." Genesis, chapter 4, verse 12. The fate of many of us, I'm afraid, whether we know it or not.' Morley looked at me and I looked down at the ground. 'Anyway.' He was now at the foot of the steps of the caravan, stroking the dog.

'You're good with the dogs,' said the man, buttering Morley up even further.

'I am an animal lover,' said Morley. 'Yes, certainly. Lurcher, is she?'

'That's right. A good dog, a good horse, and maybe a game cock, for fighting – that's all a man needs, isn't it, sir?'

'Quite,' said Morley. 'Though I'm afraid I can't share your enthusiasm for the fighting cock.'

'Well, you're not one of us, sir, are you? You wouldn't understand. You can't stop a cock from fighting. It's not natural.'

'"Don't be natural, be spiritual," says St Paul.'

'Does he?'

'He does indeed.'

'Well, I'm sure I don't know much about the Bible, sir, but I can tell you what I do know: St Paul bain't keep cocks, that's for sure.'

'Ha,' said Morley. 'Very good. I like that. "St Paul bain't keep cocks." I might use that, if I may.'

'Free to you, sir,' said the man. 'Free, gratis and without charge.' He was totally transparent: get Morley into his debt, and then Morley would feel obliged to help him out.

I thought it was probably time to go. 'Mr Morley, we should probably head on here, if we're to make the wrestling.'

Morley ignored me and stepped back to gain a better view of the vardo.

[144]

'You know, your paintwork reminds me of something,' he said. 'I just can't think what.'

The man looked up. 'The purple and gold?'

'Yes. Rather like Cleopatra's barge, isn't it?'

'The barge she sat in, like a burnish'd throne?' asked the man.

'Indeed,' said Morley. 'That burned on the water.'

'And the poop was beaten gold?'

'That's right!' said Morley. '"Purple the sails, and so perfumed that / The winds were love-sick with them; the oars were silver, / Which to the tune of flutes kept stroke, and made / The water which they beat to follow faster, / As amorous of their strokes."'

'You know your Shakespeare then,' said the man.

'And so do you!' said Morley. 'So do you! Very impressive, sir. You are truly the scholar gypsy!'

'I wouldn't say that, sir. Learned it from a book, just, a long time ago.'

'Well, you learned it well,' said Morley.

'It was a good book. You should read it. You might learn something,' said the man.

'I'm sure I might,' said Morley.

'*Morley's Book for Boys*. One and only book I ever read.'

'I don't believe you!' said Morley.

Neither did I. I assumed the man had saved this up as his *coup de grâce*: this was guaranteed to squeeze money out of Morley. He must have recognised Morley from somewhere.

'Really?' said Morley.

'I can swear on the Bible I can read, sir. You ask me to read anything and I can read it.'

'No, no, I believe you can read, my good man. But *Morley's Book for Boys*? Really?'

'I've got it in my vardo still. Taught myself to read with it.'

'Well.' Morley puffed out his chest a little, I thought; perhaps the only time I ever saw him do so during our years together. 'That really touches me, sir, more than you will ever know.'

'Does it?'

'It does, yes.'

'Have you read it then?'

'Not only have I read the book, sir. I wrote it.'

The man looked at Morley for a long time, and then broke into a smile. If he was acting – and I was certain that he was – it was certainly a good act.

'It's you, isn't it? I recognise your photograph from the book. You're older.'

'Aren't we all.'

'But you're still Swanton Morley.'

'For better and for worse,' said Morley. 'At your service. And you are?' He reached to shake the man's hand.

'Noname,' said the man, wiping his hand on his apron before shaking. 'Pleased to meet you.'

'Noname?' I said, in a tone that I hoped clearly suggested that he was called no such thing, and that this entire episode was a ridiculous sham.

'That's right, sir.'

'That's your name?'

'It is, so it is.'

'I don't think I've ever—'

'You wouldn't have done, sir. My mother, God rest her soul, took me to church to get me christened.' He began climbing up the steps into his wagon. 'And when the vicar asked what name she'd chosen she told him Jehovah.'

'Jehovah?' said Morley.

'It's a good old biblical name, sir,' he said.

'It certainly is,' said Morley. 'It is in fact arguably *the* good old biblical name.'

'Anyway, t' vicar kicked up a fuss and said she bain't have that and so she said that was the name she'd chosen and if I wasn't to be called Jehovah then I'd have no name. And so he christened me Noname, out of spite. But it's served me well enough.'

He wiped his hands again on his apron. 'Swanton Morley. Well, well. Swanton Morley.' He stood now at the top of the steps, looking down on us, for all the world as if he had indeed been picked out as a Jehovah but was equally proud to be Noname. 'Do you want to come and look inside?'

'I would be honoured, sir,' said Morley.

'The wrestling, Mr Morley?' I said.

'Yes, yes,' said Morley. 'Plenty of time. Come on, quick look inside won't take long.'

Reluctantly I made to follow Morley up the steps into the gypsy wagon. Noname glowered at me.

'Sorry,' said Morley. 'I forgot to introduce you. This is my companion, Stephen Sefton.'

'Funny name,' said Noname. 'Never heard the like of that before. But I suppose if he's a friend of yours, Mr Morley . . .'

The inside of the wagon was all dark varnished wood but it was spick and span, with not a thing out of place. It reminded me of a little theatre, or an old London gin palace. There was a squawking parakeet in a cage in the corner, and a huge old oil lamp swinging from a chain, and piles of neatly stacked and brightly coloured Scotch blankets, and a little stove on the left, and a built-in bed at the back, half hidden by paisley curtains, and a woven basket full of cups and crockery by the stove.

'Well, this *is* cosy,' said Morley.

'We like to keep the wagon nice and clean, sir,' said Noname. 'People say we're dirty, but you can see for yourself.'

'I've been in mansion houses that your wagon would put to shame, Noname,' said Morley.

'I'm sure you have, Mr Morley. I've met rich folk myself, and half of them live like dirty grunts, if you don't mind my saying so. There's not a lot you couldn't learn from us gypsies.'

Certainly not a lot about sweet-talking and thievery, I thought – and then tripped over a bucket by the door, which rattled loudly, setting off the dog barking outside.

'Quiet, Rusty,' shouted Noname, and the dog immediately became quiet.

'You have him well trained,' said Morley.

'You have to have a dog well trained,' said Noname. 'You teach him who's boss, or he'll think he's the boss of you.' He straightened up the bucket I'd kicked over.

'Sorry,' I said.

'S'all right,' said Noname. 'It's just the jar pot.'

'The jar pot?' asked Morley.

'The children collect jam jars, so we can reuse what the gorgio throw away,' said Noname. 'They make candleholders, little bit of solder with a metal handle. Beautiful.'

'Very good,' said Morley. 'If only we were all as conscientious and industrious.'

'Conscientious and industrious is right,' said Noname. 'That is exactly right. People forget that about us.'

The hypocrisy of the man!

Morley looked the caravan up and down, peering into every nook and cranny, asking questions about this or that aspect of construction, and about gypsy life generally, which Noname eagerly answered, while carefully looking Morley up and down in return, carefully examining his every feature and every move. I found it rather creepy.

'You know, it's funny, Mr Morley,' said Noname. 'I always thought one day I might meet you.'

'Really?'

'Yes. I just . . . had a feeling, I suppose. An intuition. My father wasn't around for most of my childhood, but it was him who gave me your book and I learned so much from it, I sort of felt like . . . I don't know.' He couldn't take his eyes off Morley. 'I almost felt like I knew you, Mr Morley. That's stupid, isn't it?'

'It's not stupid at all, sir. Far from it. I think that's why we all read books, is it not, Sefton?' Morley asked me.

'Yes,' I readily agreed. I wasn't listening to a word he said. I was planning an exit strategy. The gypsy had clearly set his sights on Morley and was planning some sort of elaborate con, while Morley, like a fool, had clearly warmed to the gypsy, as he seemed to warm to everyone: it was one of his great failings. The best I could hope for was to get us out of there without him losing the entire contents of his wallet.

'In order to get to know others,' said Morley. 'That's partly what books are for.'

'I haven't read enough books to know, sir. I've only read yours.'

'Well, I am honoured.'

'I always felt I could trust you, Mr Morley.'

'You certainly can, sir,' said Morley. 'You certainly can.'

I coughed loudly. 'Gentlemen,' I said. This seemed like the right moment to leave. 'I hate to interrupt, but—'

'You know what?' said Noname, ignoring me. 'Let me show you something, Mr Morley.' And he reached up above his bed to retrieve something from a high shelf. 'Here we are then. I don't show this to many people.' He paused. This would be the con, I thought. 'My library.' And he brought down a book. Or rather, *the* book. *Morley's Book for Boys*.

'There it is,' he said, looking triumphantly at me. If this was a set-up then it had been elaborately planned. 'What do you think of that?'

'Well, well,' said Morley. 'It's a while since I've seen this.'

'I could recite you from every page, sir. "It is my hope and expectation that this book contains everything that a young boy needs to know and is likely to be interested in." That's how you start, isn't it?'

'I think it is,' said Morley. 'Yes.'

'Can I just check?' I said. 'You don't mind?' I thought that Morley was now so entranced with the thought that a gypsy had learned to read using his book and his book alone that he would have believed it if the man had started reciting the opening pages of the Koran. I opened the book to the first page. Noname had it exactly right.

'"But to be clear,"' Noname went on, '"this is not a book of facts. It is possible for a boy to know many facts and yet still be ignorant." Which is quite right, Mr Morley. "The truly educated boy knows how to find things out for himself." Quite right again, Mr Morley.'

'Yes!' said Morley, absolutely delighted. 'Yes! That's absolutely correct. And then I go on about having to learn all the most important things in life for oneself, is that right?'

'Quite right once again, Mr Morley; though I have to say that all the information things about camping and setting fires and tracking animals I certainly found them very useful, as you can imagine.'

'Me teaching you of all people about outdoor crafts!' said Morley. 'My goodness me. Would you like me to sign it?'

'Sign what?' asked Noname.

'The book?'

'Sign what in it?'

'My name. Write my name in the book?'

'Certainly not!' said Noname, snatching the book from me. 'I've got my name written in the book.'

'Of course,' said Morley. 'My apologies.'

'How exactly did you come across this book?' I asked.

'Like I say, my father bought it for me,' said Noname, holding the book close to his chest. 'He used it to teach me to read and write.'

'Unbelievable,' said Morley.

'Yes,' I agreed.

'Which was a rare thing among us, Mr Morley, I can tell you.'

'I can believe it,' said Morley. I couldn't.

Noname held the book up in front of him, as if having unearthed some precious artefact. 'I was about thirteen or so, I suppose. I knew how to shoe a horse, and how to cut willows and peel 'em and dye 'em and make bread baskets, and all the other things we learn. But I didn't know how to read and I don't know why but I got this hankering for it, this hunger to be able to put things properly in sentences and paragraphs, and so my father he got me this book and we worked our way through it together, him teaching me all the rudiments like as we went.'

'That really is a remarkable story,' said Morley. 'Isn't it, Sefton?'

'Remarkable,' I said.

'I don't know about remarkable, Mr Morley, but it is a true story, that's all,' said Noname, looking at me.

'But surely all true stories are remarkable stories,' said Morley.

'Ah! And that's how I knows you are truly Swanton Morley, sir, and not some impostor, saying things like that! That is the true sign of you being yourself.'

Miriam was calling from outside.

'Father! Father!'

All three of us shuffled out and down the steps.

'Ah, Miriam!' said Morley.

'Father, I'm afraid I am really having terrible trouble explaining something to this woman and I wondered if you could . . .' The old woman was standing by her, leaning on a stick, looking entirely pathetic. 'You see she has taken some money of mine for—'

'That is a mistake,' said Noname. 'A misunderstanding.' He looked at me. 'Mother'll not be charging today, will you, Mother?'

'I won't?'

'No, she won't.'

And then he said something in Romani and the old woman handed back Miriam's ten bob note, glaring at her, before shuffling back off towards her makeshift stall, muttering.

'What did he say?' Miriam asked.

'No idea,' said Morley. 'My Romani's a bit patchy, to be honest. Best leave her be.'

'As I say, Mr Morley,' said Noname, 'if you're ever in Appleby, you must come and we'll sit by the yog.'

'The fire?'

'That's right, sir. You're a true scholar!'

'I wish,' said Morley.

The little girl who had been bathing the baby came running over, carrying her little sister.

'These are my little girls, Mr Morley, Naughty and Nice.'

'You certainly have a fine line in names,' said Morley.

'I like to think so,' said Noname. 'Naughty,' he instructed the little girl, 'say hello to Mr Swanton Morley.'

'Goodbye!' said Naughty, sticking out her tongue and running off.

'And goodbye to you,' said Morley, laughing. 'Actually . . .' He consulted his wristwatch. And his other wristwatch. And his pocket-watch.

'The wrestling!' he said. 'Sefton, why didn't you say? You've made us late! Come on! Miriam! Quick! Goodbye, Noname! Pleasure to meet you, sir!'

'Likewise, sir,' cried Noname. 'And you, Mr Sefton.'

I wouldn't trust him as far as I could throw him.

CHAPTER 11

STEPHEN 'JAWBONE'
SEFTON

In *Morley's Book of Sporting Heroes* (1938) Morley devotes several chapters, as one might perhaps expect, to the great cricketers, including W.G. Grace and K.S. Ranjitsinhji, whom he describes as 'the supreme batsman of all time', though his own personal all-time cricketing favourite, who doesn't get a mention, was his good friend the fearless wicket-keeper Les Ames; Morley was scrupulous about being even-handed and avoiding even the slightest hint of favouritism. (In Morley's personal opinion, however, which he was often keen to express, Ames's achievements were nothing short of astonishing: the only Englishman ever to score more than a hundred runs before lunch in a Test; the most stumpings and the most dismissals in an English county cricket season; and one of the few people to emerge from the famous Bodyline tour of Australia with his dignity intact.) Morley also devotes chapters, perhaps rather more surprisingly, to Jack Johnson, John L. Sullivan, Jesse Owens – a 'man of unimpeachable integrity' – and an entire chapter to the 'big five' English billiards players of the 1920s and 1930s: Walter Lindrum, Clark McConachy, Willie Smith, Joe Davis and Tom Newman, 'the baronetcy of the baize'. Miss D.D. Steel, 'the incomparable Miss Steel', the lady croquet player, enjoys a chapter to herself in the book and, more eccentrically, so does Mick the Miller, 'England's first great racing greyhound'. But perhaps the most surprising entries in Morley's sporting hall of fame are for those he describes as 'God's wrestlers', a group of Cumberland and Westmorland clergymen who 'wrestled not only with God but with human souls – and with human bodies', including the Reverend Abraham Brown, one-time rector of Egremont and one of the great wrestlers of the nineteenth century. Morley loved nothing more than a good old-fashioned Lakeland wrestling clergyman.

There were, alas, as far as I could tell, no clergymen wrestling on the afternoon we attended the Egremont Fair, but then there are presumably no requirements for them to wrestle in clerical collar and robes. Everyone was in fact wearing the traditional Westmorland wrestling garb of white vest, long johns, dark embroidered trunks and dark socks, a get-up that made them appear like nothing so much as giant babies rolling around on the greensward under Dent Fell. It really was the most extraordinary sight. There were multiple bouts taking place at once. The wrestlers stood facing one another, legs apart, bent over, chins resting on each other's shoulders, hands clasped behind their opponents' backs, and then the referees – dressed in flat caps and suits – would cry 'Hods' and the bouts would begin, with the men attempting to slide their arms up to somehow up-end their adversary. I had no idea about the rules and regulations of the sport, but

The great combat sport of the English countryside

I had to admit it was rather fascinating – a bit like high-speed human chess.

'How does this work exactly?' asked Miriam.

'The person to touch the ground with any part of their body rather than their feet is the loser,' said Morley.

'Right. Is that it?'

'Best of three decides the bout.'

'Hmm. Not exactly a game of skill, then, Father, is it?'

'On the contrary,' said Morley. '*Au contraire!* It is not only a game of skill, Miriam, it is a game of strength and speed and – as you can see – an extraordinary spectacle.' At least in this last regard Morley was indubitably correct: as well as the dozens of contestants there were, to my astonishment, hundreds and hundreds of spectators, all of us crowded round in a vast circle, with many children on their father's shoulders and others perched atop cars and lorries, creating a kind of impromptu tiered amphitheatre. 'The great combat sport of the English countryside,' continued Morley, 'hunting, shooting and fishing notwithstanding. A sort of combination of street theatre and the enactment of ritual violence. Might be worth an essay, actually, Sefton. "Fighting on the Fair Field Full of Folk: Ritual Violence in the World of Rural Wrestling". What do you think?'

'Very good, Mr Morley.'

'Yes, it is, isn't it? Good. Make a note.'

There was, thank goodness, no time to make a note.

'Oohh,' the whole crowd gasped as one, witnessing a particularly tough fall.

'Ouch,' said Morley. 'Don't fancy that, eh, Sefton?'

It was Miriam who spotted Gerald Taylor first: he towered above his opponent and easily toppled him. We shuffled our way around the edge of the crowd to get a closer view and had almost reached him by the time the bout was over and he was shaking hands with the referee. As he modestly raised his arms in triumph and the crowd applauded, I spotted our old friend the chief inspector making his way through the crowd.

'Oh no,' I said. 'I think it might be time for us to get back to Appleby, Mr Morley. We're not actually meant to be here, you know.'

'Nonsense,' said Morley, who had been deep in conversation with a local about the current state of Cumberland and Westmorland wrestling. 'You don't want to see the final?'

'I have a feeling Gerald Taylor might not make it to the final, Mr Morley,' I said, pulling at Morley's arm and pointing out the chief inspector, and the other policemen. The crowd fell silent as the chief inspector at first approached the referee and then Gerald and spoke quietly to him. It was impossible to hear what was said but we knew, as no one else at that moment knew, that Gerald Taylor's world was about to change for ever.

At first, he simply shook his head, disbelievingly. The chief inspector then said something else quietly in his ear and Gerald pushed him away from him.

'I don't think he's taking it very well,' whispered Miriam.

'No,' said Morley. 'But what did you expect?'

I for one did not expect what happened next.

Gerald let out a roar of pain that echoed around the field and beyond Egremont and which could probably have been heard as far away as the Isle of Man. It was a pitiful sound and a terrible sight – this giant of a man, all done up in his bright white wrestling finery, brought suddenly and publicly so low.

'The Philistines are upon you, Samson,' sighed Morley quietly; this was one biblical allusion that even I could follow.

The chief inspector put a hand out to try to calm Gerald, but it was no good.

'She's not dead!' he shouted. 'Do you hear me? She's not dead!'

'I'm sorry, Mr Taylor,' said the chief inspector.

'Do you think we should do something?' said Morley.

'Definitely not,' said Miriam, too late. We certainly should have done something, before something happened to us.

'Mr Taylor. Gerald, please,' protested the chief inspector.

'How?' roared Gerald. 'How did she die?' This was the pharmacist in him speaking, obviously. The whole crowd was silent, but was also asking the same question.

'You need to come with us, Gerald,' said the chief inspector.

'She is not dead till I say she's dead!' yelled Gerald, placing a heavy hand on the chief inspector's shoulder. He was still in wrestling mode and the chief inspector had become his opponent.

'Gerald – I'm sorry.' The chief inspector caught my eye. He was clearly desperate, looking to deflect Gerald's rage – and he found in me a way of doing so. I didn't really blame him. I'd have done the same. He pointed at me. 'In fact it was this gentleman here who found her. Mr Sefton, do you want to explain to Gerald . . .'

Gerald took one look at me standing at the front of the

crowd and before I could even shake my head he came charging at me, demented – like a bull at the Plaza de Toros de Las Ventas in Madrid, according to Morley. ('You were magnificent, Sefton,' he congratulated me later. 'Oe! Oe! Oe!') All I recall is that Gerald had me by the neck and was doing his best to throttle me, yelling, 'She's not dead!' again and again. This was most definitely not a bull-and-matador move: it was not an elegant move; and it was not a wrestling move. It was an act of rage and grief – which is probably what saved me. Of all the moves I learned to defend myself against over the years the attempted choke is perhaps the easiest to counter, and a man lashing out in sorrow is always easier to defeat than a man acting in anger or in fear. In the face of such a reckless attack, survival is an instinct rather than a skill, and all my instincts came into play. As his grasp tightened around my throat, I stamped on Gerald's feet, raised my fists to strike him directly under the chin, flipped his arms over, got him in a quick armlock and eventually managed to wrestle him to the ground. There were oohs and ahhs from the crowd as the chief inspector rushed forward to pull me away.

'Enough!' shouted the chief inspector. 'My God, man! What do you think you're doing?' He was talking to me.

'I'm trying to protect myself from him!' I said.

'You might have broken his jaw!'

'I haven't broken his jaw,' I said. I might have broken his jaw. He was certainly holding his jaw as if it were broken.

'We'll take it from here, thank you.'

'Be my guest,' I said, stepping back and holding up my hands in the traditional sign of surrender. 'Look! He came at me. I made no attempt—'

'Shut up!' said the chief inspector, helping Gerald to his feet.

Members of the crowd also came forward to assist; people were patting Gerald on the back, offering their sympathies. His white vest was stained with blood. He looked punch-drunk and bewildered. 'Come on, Gerald,' people were saying. 'It's all right, Mr Taylor.' But no one spoke to me: I had instantly become the scapegoat.

'I'll be talking to you later, Mr Sefton,' said the chief inspector, jabbing a finger at me. 'And I can tell you now, you'll be lucky if I don't charge you with assault.'

'What?' I said.

'No, no, no, Officer,' said Morley, shaking his head and wagging a finger, speaking loudly above the hubbub. 'I don't think so, do you? Self-defence, plain and simple, sir. In front of – what?' He looked around at the stunned crowd. 'A thousand witnesses?'

'He's right,' said Miriam, defiantly crossing her arms.

I wasn't so sure we could rely on the goodwill of the crowd: it seemed to me that everyone was looking towards us with more than a little hostility. We had effectively spoiled the Egremont Fair. We had ruined the spectacle: we had brought real violence to a scene of holiday theatre.

'Well,' said the chief inspector, who was rather struggling to keep on top of events, and who clearly sensed the crowd's hostility also. The last thing he wanted was a riot on his hands. 'I think we'll all just have to . . . sort this out back in Appleby.'

'Exactly,' said Morley.

'Absolutely,' said Miriam. 'Good idea.'

'I'll see you back in Appleby then,' said the chief inspector.

'Of course,' said Morley.

'That's all, folks!' the inspector called out to the crowd. 'Get about your business. Move along now. Plenty more to see and do at the fair.'

We made a very hasty exit through the crowds, leaving Gerald in the hands of the police, and it wasn't until we were safely back in the Lagonda and on the road that any of us spoke.

'Wow,' said Miriam. 'That was really very impressive, Sefton.'

'Wasn't it!' said Morley. 'You know you are really quite . . . unexpected sometimes. That's what I like about you. You know Gerald was the winner of the wrestling this year at Grasmere?'

'Mmm,' I grunted. I felt a headache coming on.

'I wonder perhaps if I should consider giving up on the *County Guides* and becoming your manager? I've always rather fancied myself as a boxing or a wrestling promoter. We could tour the fairs. "Swanton Morley Presents Stephen 'Jawbone' Sefton, in the Fight of the—"'

'Maybe once we're finished with Westmorland, Father?' said Miriam.

'Yes,' said Morley. 'Yes. We should finish with Westmorland first.'

As far as I was concerned we couldn't be finished soon enough.

CHAPTER 12

THE STENCH OF
CABBAGE AND ONIONS

'OH, DO STOP WRIGGLING, Sefton and take it like a man!'

Miriam's comments, as always, were attracting attention.

We were safely back in Appleby, in the bar at the Tufton Arms, which was still full of survivors of the train crash, and still hanging on for dear life to its faded glory. In the dim yellowy light no one and nothing was looking particularly well. Dinner had consisted of something called 'tattie pots' – a local dish, apparently, consisting of mutton and black pudding, topped with potatoes, a meal that looked like a sorry pint of porter, and which was served with an inexplicable side dish of gigantic pickled onions. Only the onions were lively and enthusiastic: the tattie pots themselves had long since given up all hope and might easily have been sucked through a straw or supped with a spoon. I rather suspected that the ingredients had been assembled some time ago, and that this was merely the latest iteration of an endless combination of pre-cooked parts: mutton-and-potatoes-turning-into-stew-becoming-tattie-pots-soon-to-be-bubble-and-squeak, the English restaurant food chain. The odour of cabbage and onions was all-pervasive. It was one of the great culinary curiosities of our travels the length and breadth of England that almost all local dishes tasted and smelled of cabbage and onions, whether or not actual cabbages and onions were involved. ('The cabbage is a superlative vegetable,' according to Morley in *Morley's Essential English Food and Drink* (1930), 'with an unforgettable aroma,' and the onion is 'the ever-fragrant foundation stone of old-fashioned English home-cooking'.) There was – one can only conclude – something horribly sulphurous about England during the late 1930s. The exact source of the smell was difficult to put one's finger on, until of course it was too late.

We had established ourselves by the fire, where Miriam was angrily applying iodine to my various cuts and bruises, Morley was drinking barley water, I was drinking whiskey, and everyone else in the bar was looking at us in amazement. Just as we had caused absolute chaos in Egremont earlier in the afternoon the three of us were now providing free entertainment for the patrons of the Tufton Arms on a Saturday night.

'Where on earth did you learn to fight like that, Sefton?' asked Miriam. 'I thought for a moment you might have killed the poor chap.'

'Yes, interesting moves,' said Morley. 'The combination of the upper cut and the elbow jerk. Very inventive.'

'And very effective,' said Miriam. 'Almost knocked the poor bloke's head off.'

'Well, you just . . . sort of pick these things up as you go along, don't you?' I said.

'I certainly don't,' said Miriam.

'Maybe you should though, my dear,' said Morley. 'Come in handy, wouldn't it?' He raised his right index finger and stroked his moustache with his left hand, in that way he had of suggesting that he were receiving an idea through the ether, his body serving as an antenna on a wireless set. 'Yes. Yes. Some sort of – what would we call it? – "self-defence" training for women? That wouldn't be a bad idea, would it?'

'That would never catch on, Father,' said Miriam.

Undaunted and caught up mid-transmission, Morley began describing a programme of boxing and wrestling training for women. '"Wroxling" we could call it,' he said, 'or "Brestling"?'

'Father!' said Miriam – and then attempted to garner opinion about his proposed programme from the poor defenceless women in the bar. 'Would you like to learn how to throw a man on his back, madam?'

There were concerned glances over the assembled port-and-lemons. At which juncture, thankfully, Nancy – the young woman from the dig at Shap – walked in.

She had changed from the outfit she had worn at the dig – an entirely inoffensive sort of get-up, suitable for any all-weather archaeological adventure – and was now wearing a rather more startling red velvet trouser suit, belted high at the waist, with a black tie, and with her blonde hair Brylcreemed back, a high bohemian-Sapphic sort of look that would certainly not have suited outdoor pursuits, and which I suspected was not seen every day in Appleby.

'Oh, Nancy!' cried Miriam, delighted to find some respite from Morley's latest madcap scheme, and her iodine application (she was not a natural nurse), and thrilled no doubt to find another dedicated follower of fashion. 'You must join us!'

'You're sure you don't mind?'

'Please do, my dear,' said Morley.

Nancy pulled up a chair and sat, I thought, uncomfortably close to Miriam.

'You look absolutely wonderful,' said Miriam.

'Thank you,' said Nancy. 'You too.'

'Would you like to know how to wrestle a chap to the ground?' asked Morley.

'Ignore him,' said Miriam.

'I'm afraid I'm really not that bothered when it comes to wrestling chaps to the ground,' said Nancy.

'There we are, Father, you see,' said Miriam. 'It would never catch on. We can perfectly well take care of ourselves, Nancy, can't we? Ladies?' Miriam appealed to the middle-aged and elderly women in the bar who were continuing to enjoy our entertainment.

'Of course we can,' said Nancy, touching Miriam's arm in approval.

'Pity,' said Morley. 'I thought it was rather a splendid idea.'

'Anyway, I was rather hoping to find you here, I must admit,' said Nancy. 'I have some news. Have you heard?'

'Heard what?' asked Miriam.

'The results of the autopsy?'

'On poor Mr Taylor's wife?' said Morley.

'Mrs Taylor,' said Miriam, 'as we call her. Maisie. She does have a name, Father.'

'Well?' said Morley.

'Apparently, she died of a broken neck,' said Nancy.

'Aha!' said Morley loudly, clapping his hands – entirely inappropriately. 'As I thought. What did I say, Miriam? What did I tell the police? Broken neck, I said! Broken neck!'

'Yes, you did say you thought it was a broken neck, Father. Well done. Congratulations. You correctly identified the cause of death of an innocent woman who was unceremoniously dumped in a hole in the ground.'

'Corkscrew neck-breaker maybe?' said Morley.

'A what?' said Miriam.

'Wrestling move,' said Morley. 'We should ask our wrestling correspondent here. Isn't it, Sefton?'

'I have absolutely no idea, Mr Morley,' I said.

'Hmm,' said Morley. 'Puts a rather different complexion on things, though, doesn't it?'

'How so, Father?'

'Well, I'm just thinking out loud,' began Morley.

'Probably best if you didn't, actually,' said Miriam, nodding at the people at the other tables, who had now fallen entirely silent and who were staring at us agog.

'Ah, yes. Quite.' Morley lowered his voice and we all leaned in to hear him. 'It's more than possible that Gerald could have broken his wife's neck, is it not?'

'Father!' said Miriam.

'Well, he could, couldn't he?' said Morley. 'With a single stroke.' He made a chopping move with his hand. 'You saw him this afternoon, Miriam. Quite some force behind him, eh, Sefton? Not a man unable or unwilling to throw his weight around.'

'Yes,' I agreed. I had the cuts and bruises to prove it.

'But what about Professor Jenkins?' asked Miriam.

'Hadn't the police hauled him away as the most likely suspect? You'd identified him and Maisie as lovers, Nancy?'

'Yes,' said Nancy. 'And so they were. Everyone knew – apart from Maisie's husband, perhaps. But apparently Jenkins is claiming that he and Maisie had broken up ages ago!'

'Well, they've certainly broken up now,' said Morley.

'Father!' said Miriam.

'How well did you know Maisie Taylor?' asked Morley.

'Oh, everybody on the dig got to know Maisie,' said Nancy. 'She was very popular.'

'Good-looking sort of girl?'

'Gorgeous!' said Nancy, and then, calming herself slightly, added, 'I mean, she was very pretty.'

'And what was she like?'

'She was great fun! She just loved life. She was one of those people – you know, always out, keen to have a good time. You know the sort of person.'

'Yes, I'm afraid I do,' said Morley, looking at Miriam. 'And Mr Taylor?'

'I don't really know Gerald, I'm afraid.'

'But similar to Maisie, would you say?'

'No. He's more . . . Well, he's got all his responsibilities at the pharmacy, obviously.'

'Yes,' said Morley. 'Struck me as a very diligent hardworking sort of fellow.'

'By all accounts,' said Nancy.

'Yes. And when exactly did she die, did the autopsy say? You don't happen to know?'

'Well, the funny thing is, the chap who told me about it—'

'Who is?'

'He's a reporter on the *Westmorland Gazette*.'

'Young chap with a face like a butcher's boy?' This was the poor fellow Morley had encountered last night.

'That's right.'

'Well, at least he's good for something,' said Morley.

'He shouldn't really have been letting on, I don't think, but . . . well, I used my feminine wiles, shall we say?' She touched Miriam's arm again, confidentially.

'Really?' I said.

'Yes, and he says the doctor believes that Maisie died on the same day and around the same time as the train crash!'

'My goodness!' said Morley.

'Yes. I know. Odd, isn't it?'

'She couldn't have died in the crash, could she?' I asked. 'And then her body was transferred for some reason to Shap?'

'Of course not, man!' said Morley. 'Died *in* the crash? Sometimes I do wonder about you, Sefton. Why would any-one want to move the poor woman's body from the crash and hide it? It doesn't make any sense.'

'None of it makes any sense, Father,' said Miriam.

'True,' said Morley, half closing his eyes in concentration.

'It was probably just a coincidence then?' said Nancy.

'The trouble is—' began Morley.

'Father doesn't believe in coincidences,' said Miriam.

'A coincidence,' said Morley, in confirmation, 'is only ever an unexplained part of a puzzle.'

'Anyhow,' said Nancy. 'Didn't want to put a dampener on your evening. I just wanted to let you know, seeing as you found her and everything. Seemed only right. And also a few of us from the dig are going over to Penrith later. There's a band on.'

'Oh, really?' said Miriam.

'Only local. Not exactly Nat Gonella! But you'd be very welcome to come along. All of you, I mean.' She didn't mean.

'I don't think so,' said Morley. 'Thank you anyway.'

'Father's not a fan,' said Miriam.

'How about you?' Nancy asked me. 'You look rather as though you could do with cheering up.'

'I'm fine, thank you,' I said. 'I think I might skip an evening out. It's been rather an eventful day.'

'No stamina, you chaps!' said Miriam. 'That's your trouble!'

'No match for you young ladies, certainly,' said Morley, getting up. 'Way of the future, I fancy. Women on top, eh, Sefton?'

'Yes, Mr Morley,' I agreed reluctantly. 'Quite.'

'A cock may crow, but the hen lays the egg,' said Morley. 'Mmm.'

'Maybe not the worst thing that could happen, all things considered. Matriarchy. Interesting alternative to patriarchy. Might be a way ahead, given the direction things are heading?'

'Yes, Mr Morley.' He often had these ludicrous flights of fancy. I also got up to leave and was about to make my excuses and say goodnight to Miriam and Nancy, but they were already engrossed in one another's company – they might almost have been long-lost friends, or lovers – so I slipped away unnoticed and began trudging up the stairs behind Morley, the stench of cabbage and onions catching in my throat.

'I wonder,' said Morley, as he hurried along the corridor and began turning the key to his room.

'You wonder what, Mr Morley?' I asked.

But he didn't hear me and slipped into his room, to do his wondering alone.

And so I made my way back to my own room to do my own wondering: why bother? What's the point? And what did it any of it mean?

CHAPTER 13

THE JOY OF PICKLING

I MADE NO PROGRESS IN MY WONDERING, of course, but Morley wondered with purpose. He had clearly been working on something overnight. He had a plan. He always had a plan. (For a purview of his pondering on plans, see his popular pamphlet on project planning and preparation, 'The Five Ps', published in 1927, which outlines principles of modern project management which have now of course been widely adopted by businesses, in factories, government departments, by primary and preparatory school teachers, and in secretarial training colleges in England and throughout the world.) The police had left a message at the Tufton Arms, asking if we would be kind enough to speak to them later in the afternoon, which was perfect, according to Morley: 'That means we can put the morning to good use, eh, Sefton?' he declared enthusiastically over a breakfast of kippers in the hotel's dingy dining room.

He had, in fact, already put the morning to good use. The police may have had a murder to solve, the terrible death of young Lucy was of course still to be properly investigated, and there were still no trains running on the Settle–Carlisle line, which meant dozens of people remained stranded in Appleby, with no means of leaving; but none of this was going to put Morley off his stride or his schedule. He had been up from five, as usual, and had his typewriter and pads and pens arrayed before him on the table, much to the annoyance of the other guests, no doubt, whose boiled eggs, tea and toast were accompanied by the sound of hammering typewriter keys and the frantic scribbling of handwritten notes, noises unwelcome at any time of the day, frankly, but particularly so at breakfast. He was busy working on the page proofs for *Devon* by the time I arrived downstairs and had already knocked off an article or two for the newspapers: something or other on wicker work, apparently, and something else on the chemistry of home-fermentation, inspired no doubt by the inescapable smell of cabbages and onions in the hotel, which meant that even breakfast smelled like some hideous Bavarian workhouse supper. (For Morley's history of sauerkraut, incidentally – one of his more esoteric interests – and for his original sauerkraut recipe, reprinted in *Morley's Joy of Pickling* (1934), and which was said to be a great favourite of George V and Queen Mary, ironically, see his article 'Sauerkraut Connections' in *Human Nutrition*, vol.26, no.4.)

I enjoyed my customary breakfast of two cups of coffee and a cigarette, with a delicious side order of a lecture on the health benefits of fermented food and the role played by Captain Cook in developing methods for the storage of perishable food items on long journeys, and we were eventually joined by Miriam around nine. She arrived wearing a silk turban, a supercilious smile, and a grey silk dress that might have been nightwear and might have been evening wear but which was certainly not breakfast wear. She was whistling a dance tune.

'Good morning,' said Morley. 'Good evening?'

'Fabulous!' she said, over-emphasising the 'fab'. 'Fab-u-lous. Out of this world!'

'Out of this world? Literally?'

'Literally, Father. You really should have come.'

'I would only have cramped your style, my dear.'

'Do you think?' She struck a pose, like a mannequin in a shop window. 'I doubt it. Sefton, you should have come too. You might enjoy frisking your whiskers occasionally.'

'Yes,' I said, because it was easiest.

'Or on second thoughts, maybe not.' She lit herself a cigarette, poured a cup of coffee and proceeded to do her best to slouch languorously at the breakfast table.

'Now, children,' said Morley, 'you'll be delighted to hear that I do have a plan for today.'

'Good!' said Miriam. 'Can we go home?'

'Hardly, my dear. The police are still very interested in what we have to offer.'

I coughed. The police were about as interested in what we had to offer as a pig is interested in the people who throw out the swill: it is a purely functional relationship.

Morley continued. 'And there's still the rest of *Westmorland* to cover.' It was difficult sometimes when he was speaking about a county to know whether he was referring to the actual county or to his book on the county: for him, the two were synonymous. Norfolk was *Norfolk*. Devon was *Devon*. Westmorland was *Westmorland*, and etcetera.

'But is there really *much* more of Westmorland for us to

[174]

see, Father? I know we've only been here a few days, but I do feel we've seen enough now for the book.'

'Oh, plenty of things left to see,' said Morley. 'I mean, apart from Ambleside – and we must see Ambleside! – there's Barbon and Barton and Beetham and Bolton and Brough and Brougham and—'

'Yes, I don't need an alphabetical list, thank you, Father. I'm really just looking for the highlights.'

'The highlights?'

'Yes. Something uplifting and sublime.'

'We had Shap, Miriam.'

'I'm not sure I'd count that – lovely as it undoubtedly was. Little bit spoiled for me by the discovery of a dead body. I was thinking more of pretty mountains and lakes. Something with grandeur.'

'We might have to leave the pretty mountains until we get on to *Cumberland*,' said Morley. 'I'm afraid the highlight today is probably going to be a trip to Kirkby Stephen.'

'But we've already been to Kirkby Stephen, Father!' She lifted her coffee cup and sat up straight. 'Oh goodness! You're not losing your memory, are you?'

'No, I am not losing my memory, thank you, Miriam.' This was to become a familiar exchange in the years to come. 'But I do want to have another little look around Gerald Taylor's pharmacy.'

Miriam took a sip of coffee, realised it was cold and called over a waiter.

'This coffee is cold!' she said. 'Is it too much to ask for hot coffee in the morning?'

'No, miss, not at all,' said the waiter.

'Really,' she said, 'the service here is quite atrocious.'

'We have been waiting for you for quite some time,' I said.

'Beside the point, isn't it?' said Miriam. 'Anyway, why on earth do you want to go back to Gerald Taylor's pharmacy?'

'Just, because, Miriam,' said Morley.

'Because what?'

'Because . . . The poor man's lost his wife and I feel we have a responsibility, having found the poor woman.'

'Responsibility?!' said Miriam. 'To do what? Get ourselves in more trouble with the police?'

Our fellow breakfast guests seemed unusually subdued, I thought. Had they nothing themselves to talk about? All I could hear was the scraping of butter on toast.

'Probably not a good idea, Mr Morley,' I said quietly. 'Under the circumstances.'

'The thing is,' continued Morley regardless. 'I don't really want the police to know that I've been looking around.'

'Ah!' said Miriam, clapping her hands. The waiter arrived back with a fresh pot of coffee. 'Marvellous!' said Miriam. 'And perhaps some toast?'

'So we just need to be a little bit stealthy in our approach,' said Morley.

'Stealthy?' I said. Morley's idea of stealthy did not alas extend to his governing the volume, tone or manner of his table talk.

'It's a Sunday, for goodness sake,' said Miriam. 'Gerald's still helping the police, as far as we know, and his poor wife is dead. There won't be anybody at the pharmacy.'

'Which would be perfect,' said Morley. 'But just in case there is, I will need you two to come up with some good reason why you're there, and to provide a bit of a distraction. I hope you don't mind?'

'Well, I think I can safely say that I can always provide a distraction,' said Miriam, looking towards me, doing her best Jean Harlow impersonation.

'And I don't need long,' said Morley. 'I should be in and out in no time.'

'As the bishop said—'

'Enough of that sort of talk at breakfast – or any other time for that matter – thank you, Miriam,' said Morley.

'It was a joke, Father!'

'If that's the sort of thing you pick up at these dances I do rather despair, my dear.'

'That is the least of what one picks up at the dances, Father!'

'No doubt. Right.' Morley consulted his wristwatches and his pocket-watch, and began gathering up his papers. 'Estimated time of departure for Kirkby Stephen, 09.30. That's twenty-three minutes by my watches. No shirking!' With which he rose to leave, typewriter under one arm, reference books under the other.

'No funking,' said Miriam loudly, getting up and sweeping out, grabbing a couple of slices of toast on the way from the poor confused waiter, who had re-emerged from the kitchen with a tray laden with a toast-rack, butter and jams.

'Sefton?' cried Morley, halfway out the door of the dining room.

'And no shilly-shallying,' I muttered quietly, slinking out behind them.

'Sir!' called the waiter, as I was leaving. 'Sir!' I turned back, almost having escaped. The waiter handed me a brown paper bag full of a dozen hard-boiled eggs. 'Your father—'

'He's not my father,' I said.

'The gentleman asked the kitchen to prepare some eggs, for your outing.'

'Very good,' I said. 'Thank you.'

'And some flasks of black tea.' He handed me two flasks. 'Thank you,' I said.

'And I just need a signature, sir, for breakfast.'

'Yes, of course,' I said.

I duly signed and left the dining room as quickly as I could.

I had the strong feeling that the staff and our fellow breakfast guests were glad to see us gone.

The heavens opened as we drove to Kirkby Stephen, the mild September weather finally giving way to grey autumn rain and wind. This prompted Morley, alas, to start quoting Coleridge, from 'Dejection: An Ode', at great length. By the time we arrived in the town my head was throbbing and when Miriam and I presented ourselves half-bedraggled at the front door of Taylor's Pharmacy I was wondering whether they might be able to provide some cure for those suffering from Romantic poetry recited by middle-aged men in droning tones – some kind of poetry emetic. (I was so pleased with this notion that I made a note in my notebook to compose a long free verse epic against the recital of poetry, titled 'Poemetic'. The poem, alas, has never been undertaken: my years with Morley rather sapped my poetic strengths. My *Complete Poems, 1937–1940* consists of a single sonnet, a sestina, some limericks and a ballad. *The County Guides* became my *Poly-Oblion*.)

Morley made himself scarce, looking for an entrance round the back, while Miriam knocked loudly once, twice and three times on the pharmacy's big black double-width front door. On the third knock the door was opened by a woman who looked more than a little pained and discombobulated. She was carrying a coat, gloves, a hat and a Bible.

'Good morning,' said Miriam.

'Can I help you?' said the woman, distracted, fussing around with her coat, her gloves, her hat and her Bible.

'I do hope so,' said Miriam, clasping her hands together, in a wretched fashion.

'I'm just on my way to church, actually,' said the woman. 'Can it wait?'

'Unfortunately . . .' said Miriam, doing her best to look utterly pathetic. The rain certainly helped: pathetic was not her forte; triumphant was more her style.

'You know I can't dispense? It's a Sunday.'

'Oh no, we don't need you to dispense,' said Miriam.

'Good. Is there some sort of trouble then? Is it something to do with Gerald? With the police?'

'No, no, no. Nothing like that.'

'Well, as I say,' said the woman, peering outside the front door at the rain. 'I'm afraid—'

'It's rather awkward, actually,' said Miriam. What had been a drizzle had now become a shower and was threatening to become a downpour. 'I wonder if we could come inside, just for a moment . . .'

We were clearly one more trouble to add to the woman's long list of difficulties. This proved fortunate; after all, what's another trouble when you already have enough of your own? ('Suffering is never shared equally,' writes Morley in 'Man's

Lot in the World' (1931), one of his odd little syncretist pamphlets. 'The wounded can often bear wounds that would prove fatal to the faint of heart.' And, 'To be whole is to be broken.' And 'To know weakness is to be strong.' He was deeply susceptible to such proverbs and maxims. I did my best to deter him, but they were always creeping back into his prose. I blamed his interest in Buddhism, Daoism, Confucianism, and all his other favourite Eastern -isms, which tend to rely on wise sayings and stories. He admired Jesus and Moses and Mohammed, but he revered the Buddha.)

'All right,' she said. 'You can come in. But just for a moment. Until this shower's passed.'

'Thank you so much,' said Miriam. 'Thank you.' One might describe Miriam's tone as patronising – if her tone wasn't always patronising.

The pharmacy was deliciously dry and warm inside and my eye was caught again by the array of brown-bottled elixirs lined up on row upon row of dark mahogany shelves.

'What was it you wanted?' asked the woman, who was searching in a cane umbrella holder by the door for a suitable Sunday umbrella.

'We are terribly sorry to bother you,' said Miriam. 'It's just . . .'

I thought I heard a noise from the back of the pharmacy – a kind of thudding. Morley? Had he got in already? Miriam was going to need to think on her feet.

'. . . it's just, my fiancé and I are travelling up to our wedding.' Miriam smiled mischievously at me. This was fast becoming her favourite diversionary tactic.

I smiled sarcastically in response.

'Congratulations,' said the woman, having chosen an umbrella. She seemed not to have heard the noise. She unfastened the umbrella's straps and gave the thing a vigorous shake.

'Thank you!' said Miriam.

'Marriage is a blessing.'

'I certainly hope so,' said Miriam. 'All advice welcome.'

'I haven't myself been so blessed,' said the woman, shrugging on her coat.

'Well. I'm glad to say this is my first time as well!'

The woman made a sour face. 'And where are you getting married? Here? In Westmorland?'

'Gretna Green,' said Miriam.

'Really?' said the woman, pulling on her gloves.

'Yes, we're just travelling up,' said Miriam. 'My father doesn't approve, you see.' This was spoken with an attempted sob in the voice.

'Oh dear,' said the woman.

'I have no doubt he'll come round though,' said Miriam more brightly.

'I do hope so.' The woman looked at me, clearly attempting to assess my suitability as a husband.

Miriam was looking a little stuck. She raised her eyebrows at me, pleading for assistance.

'My fiancée was previously engaged,' I said. I was about to add 'several times'.

'Ah,' said the woman.

'And was horribly let down by her previous suitor.'

'Ah. Yes. I see,' said the woman. 'So your father is concerned for you, that you don't make the same mistake again?'

'Yes, that's right,' said Miriam.

The woman peered past Miriam to the open door to check the rain. I thought I heard more rumbling from out back. What on earth was Morley up to?

'Was that thunder?' asked the woman.

'I think it was,' I said. 'Yes.'

'Definitely,' said Miriam. 'It's just, the reason we're here . . . we . . . forgot one or two essential things for our honeymoon, and I wonder if you might be able to provide us with . . .'

'What sort of essential things?'

'The sort of essential things . . . that a young . . . innocent couple might need as they . . . set out on the path of married life together,' said Miriam.

'Ah,' said the woman. 'Those sorts of things.'

'Yes,' said Miriam. 'So I was hoping . . .'

'I'm not sure,' said the woman, sniffing in my general direction. 'Marriage is created for the procreation of children.'

'It is, it is,' said Miriam. 'Yes. It is, isn't it? I'm very much a Christian myself, actually, and a very devoted churchgoer. In fact we both are, aren't we, darling?'

'Yes,' I said, with as much Christian grace as I could muster.

'And we are very much hoping to start a family right away. But as you can imagine I really would like to gain the approval of my father before we do so.'

'Quite right,' said the woman.

'And so we just wanted a little time to . . . bed in, as it were.'

'Hmm,' said the woman.

She huffed and she puffed, weighing us in the moral balance, just as she would weigh out potions and lotions using the brass scales behind her on the counter.

'Well,' she said eventually, laying down her Bible by the scales. 'I know he keeps them here somewhere.' She went behind the counter and began opening drawers.

'My brother would know, of course, but he's otherwise indisposed. Or my sister-in-law, but she's . . .'

'Oh, yes, we heard,' said Miriam.

'You heard?' said the woman, looking up, confused.

'We were staying in Appleby last night, and someone mentioned there'd been a death. The pharmacist's wife, they said. Is it poor Maisie Taylor, your sister-in-law?'

'Yes,' said the woman. 'Unfortunately.'

'I'm so sorry for your loss.'

'Well, that's very kind of you, miss.' She continued rootling in drawers. I checked my watch. Morley had had five minutes. 'Aha!' cried the woman, having discovered what she was after. 'Were you looking for rubber? Or Gerald has these local ones, made from lambskin, I think? I don't know what they're all about.' She held up the range for me to see.

'Rubber or lambskin, darling?' said Miriam, trying to keep a straight face. 'What do you think?'

'Rubber is fine,' I said, unamused.

'You don't want to try the lambskin?'

'No, thank you,' I said.

'We'll take the rubber,' said Miriam.

'Good,' said the woman, utterly unfazed; she clearly felt she was acting in a righteous manner, assisting two young innocent Christians on their way to wedded bliss.

'And our deepest sympathies once again,' said Miriam.

'Thank you.' The woman was wrapping our honeymoon supplies in brown paper. 'Though I can't say I'm surprised, to be honest.'

'Surprised at what?' said Miriam.

'Well, you'd maybe understand, miss, as a . . . woman of the world. My sister-in-law was quite a . . .' She looked around, to ensure no one else might overhear. 'A gallivanter.'

'Maisie? A gallivanter?'

'Yes,' said the woman, 'ruined even before she met my brother.'

'Ruined?'

'I'm afraid so. She wasn't right for him. We all said so. Everybody said so. He's a good, decent person, my brother. A respectable person.'

'I'm sure he is.'

'And she is – was . . . Well, this shop's been in our family for a hundred years or more.'

'Lovely shop,' I said.

'Yes,' said the woman. 'I think she saw her opportunity and took it.'

'Ah,' said Miriam. 'I see. A social climber.'

It takes one to know one, I thought.

The woman sighed and gave no answer.

'But how is your poor brother?' continued Miriam.

'Gerald? I'm hoping to see him later. He was attacked by some madman at the Egremont Fair yesterday.'

'Oh dear!' said Miriam. 'There are some very strange people around, aren't there?'

'Lucky he didn't break his jaw, apparently. He's helping the police at the moment. Not that they think he's . . . I mean, they haven't charged him or anything. It's not like that.'

'Well, that's good.'

'He's not guilty of anything. The only thing he's guilty of is being gullible.'

'I'm sure no one's suggesting he is guilty.'

'Well, you know what people are like.'

'Yes, of course.'

'It's terrible to say it, I know,' said the woman. 'But I blame her.'

'Maisie?'

'One doesn't like to speak ill of the dead.'

'No, no, of course not.'

'But she was always . . . Turning people's heads. Even after they'd married. I told him I don't know how many times. But he's so soft, my brother.'

'Not that soft,' I muttered.

'Sorry, darling?' said Miriam. 'Did you say something?'

'No, no,' I said. 'Just talking to myself.'

'Men!' said Miriam to the woman. 'You have keep an eye on them all the time. He wasn't the jealous type then?'

'No, no. The opposite. I sometimes wondered if he was happy to turn a blind eye.'

'I see.'

'He was potty about her, the little . . .' She composed herself and picked up her Bible. 'Sorry. I shouldn't be talking like this. It's just . . . It's all happened so quickly.'

'Of course,' said Miriam understandingly. 'Of course. When was the last time you saw her?'

'Maisie? Friday morning.'

'The morning of the crash?'

'That's right. She always insisted on doing the rounds.'

'The rounds?'

'With the medicines. Prescriptions.'

'Ah.'

'She had the bike, you see, with the big wicker basket and

all. She fancied herself as a – goodness knows what . . . flying around, dispensing her . . . Anyway. I really should go. Sorry to trouble you with my woes.'

'Not at all,' said Miriam.

'These should do you for a little while.' She patted the brown paper parcel.

'Thank you so much,' said Miriam. She laughed, mock-innocently. 'You know, I've no idea how much these things cost. Darling?' She looked at me. I looked back at her. She produced her purse.

'No, no, I wouldn't take money for those,' said the woman.

'Really?'

'No. It doesn't seem right, on a Sunday.'

'Are you sure?'

'It's my good deed for the day.' How Miriam had persuaded the woman that she was doing us a favour I had no idea.

'Well, thank you. I'm so glad we stopped by.'

'You got here just in time, actually,' said the woman. 'I'm going to be shutting up the shop for a few days after I've been to church. We'll have the funeral to arrange. And Gerald with the police. I'm going to get him to come and stay with me.'

'Yes, that is a good idea,' said Miriam. 'After all your troubles.'

The woman walked over towards the door, weighed down with her troubles and her Bible, and ushered us back out into the drizzle. Church bells were ringing in the distance.

'Must hurry,' she said. 'Good luck with the wedding. Family has to stick together – you remember that.'

'Yes, of course,' said Miriam, waving the brown paper parcel in thanks. 'Thank you again.'

'I hope your father comes round.'

'Yes, I'm sure he will,' said Miriam. 'Thank you! Thank you! Goodbye!'

The woman strode away to church, umbrella aloft and we got back into the Lagonda, to find Morley already in there, hiding, lying down on the back seat.

'What was all that about?' he asked. 'I hope your father comes round to what?'

'Nothing,' said Miriam, shaking rain out of her hair, like a fancy dog. 'It was a distraction, that's all, as requested. And a very successful distraction it was too, was it not, Sefton? What did you think? Have I missed my vocation as an actress?' She ran her fingers through her hair, flicking rain everywhere – I'm sure I'd seen a film in which an actress did the same. Miriam often acted roles, even when behaving instinctively.

'Undoubtedly, Miriam,' I said. I was now wet not only with my own rain, but with hers.

'Sefton here picked himself up a couple of little treats, actually,' she said, tossing the paper parcel into my lap. 'Not that they'd be much use to you.' Her taunting and teasing could be very tiresome. She looked at herself in the car's rear-view mirror. 'Do I look absolutely dreadful?' She looked like a mannequin left out in the rain. 'I'm going to have to get back and fix myself up again. Oh well. Any joy round the back, Father?'

'All locked up,' said Morley, 'and I couldn't open the door. Locked.'

'I suppose with all those chemicals and medicines inside.'

'Yes,' said Morley. 'Exactly. Couldn't crack the blasted thing.'

'You shouldn't be picking locks anyway, Father.'

'No. Of course not.'

'Illegal.'

'Exactly. And the only other way in would have been to break a window, but I thought it would attract too much attention on a Sunday morning.'

'Yes,' said Miriam. 'Never mind. Not to worry.'

'Bit of a wasted trip,' said Morley. 'Sorry about that.'

'No, no,' said Miriam. 'We learned an awful lot from Gerald's sister.'

'It was his sister in the shop?'

'That's right. And I can tell you, there was no love lost between her and Maisie Taylor.'

'I see.'

'Maisie was a young woman of some renown, apparently,' said Miriam. 'Gerald's sister absolutely hated her. Loathed her.'

'Oh dear,' said Morley.

'I wouldn't be surprised if she had something to do with Maisie's murder. Didn't you think, Sefton?'

'No,' I said.

'Really? Unmarried sister resents her brother's attractive young wife, is determined not to let the shop fall into her hands, takes decisive action.' Miriam was clearly warming to her fantasy. She was, after all, her father's daughter, and I fancied she'd been reading too many of Morley's beloved pulp fiction magazines. 'In fact, maybe they did it together?'

'Who?' said Morley.

'Gerald and his sister! Gerald finds out that Maisie's been dispensing more than medicines on her rounds round the villages and confides in his sister, who encourages him to do the honourable thing and—'

'Get rid of her?' asked Morley. 'It's possible. It's not something I'd have thought of. What did you make of Mr Taylor's sister, Sefton?'

'She seemed perfectly pleasant and polite to me, actually,' I said. 'Under the circumstances. And without a trace of malice.'

'Oh come on, Sefton, she was a bitter, shrivelled-up old maid,' said Miriam.

'Well, let's not jump to conclusions, Miriam,' said Morley. 'You only just met the poor woman.'

'Well, she was, Father! Sefton, tell him!'

'I speak as I find,' I said. 'And as I say, I found her perfectly pleasant.'

'Really, Sefton? Well, you're not a very good judge of human character, then, are you?'

'Not if being a good judge of human character means going around accusing every unmarried woman of murder—'

'Oh really!'

'In which case,' I continued, for good measure, 'your new friend Nancy might have been locked up a long time ago.'

'Nancy?'

I was being spiteful. I suppose I didn't like the way Miriam had been carrying on with Nancy the night before – all that pawing and exchanging of intimacies. And it felt like time to counter Miriam's ludicrous suggestions with some ludicrous suggestions of my own.

'Yes,' I said. 'Why not? Nancy might have had just as much cause to resent Maisie as Gerald's sister. What if Nancy had a thing for Maisie—'

'A *thing*, Sefton?' said Morley. 'What on earth do you mean?'

'You know what he means, Father!'

'And Maisie spurned her?' I continued. 'She was very quick to accuse Professor Jenkins of being involved in a relationship with Maisie. What if she was merely using that as a smokescreen to hide her own guilt? She's clearly someone with her own agenda.'

'Her own "agenda"?' Miriam laughed. 'Nancy? What is that supposed to mean? I think it simply means you're jealous, Sefton, aren't you? That you can see that Nancy might possess charms that you don't?'

'Children!' said Morley. 'This is Kirkby Stephen, it's not . . . Los Angeles! I think we all need to get back to Appleby, and calm down, change out of our wet clothes, and then we can talk about this with some degree of common sense and rationality. We only came here to see if we could help poor Gerald Taylor, not to throw around baseless and vulgar accusations! We're trying to help solve a little Lakeland unpleasantness, not add to the weight of the world's woes!'

'Quite right,' said Miriam. 'And well said, Father. Sefton is being utterly ridiculous.'

We had got carried away, but before common sense and rationality could intervene we were presented with yet another unexpected example of Lakeland unpleasantness. Just as Miriam started the car, and as the rain began truly pouring from the heavens, a little girl came running down Kirkby Stephen's deserted Main Street towards us. She was being chased by a gang of boys: it was like watching a small wet fox being run to ground by hounds. The boys raced after her, chanting the old song, familiar to me from the school playground, and doubtless familiar to generations of English children: 'Ipsy Gypsy wed in a tent, / She couldn't afford to pay the rent / So when the rent man came next day / Ipsy Gypsy ran away!' They were yelling and running full pelt, but the little girl was outpacing them and heading straight for us. 'Come back, you dirty gypo!' they were calling.

'Look! It's Naughty!' cried Miriam.

'Naughty?' said Morley.

'The gypsy's little girl from the Egremont Fair!'

'Noname's girl? What on earth is she doing here?'

There was no time to find out.

As Naughty approached the car, sopping wet, I got out one side and Morley swung open his door and got out the other. He commanded the boys to stop. Which, in fairness, they did; they'd have caused a terrible dent in the Lagonda otherwise. Naughty ducked in behind Morley. The rain was now chiselling down from a thunderous lead-black sky.

'What do you think you're doing?' I demanded, coming round the car to confront them. They turned to face me.

'She's a thieving gypo!' one of the boys said.

'Has she stolen something from you?'

'No,' he said. 'But she was gonna. They're all the same.'

'My da' says they caused the crash at Appleby, because they were playing on the line. It was in the papers.'

'I think you'll find the crash is still under investigation, boys,' I said. 'And you should leave this little girl alone.' They stood looking at me, a bunch of wet, wretched children, stupid with second-hand rage. 'Go on, off with you. You'll all catch your death of cold in this weather. Go on, go off home.'

'Why should we?' asked one cheeky chap, who was probably no older than ten. 'Who do you think you are?'

'It doesn't matter who I am, young man. You should have some respect for your elders, and for a poor little girl.'

'She's a dirty gypo!' said the boy, rain-spray splashing up around his feet.

'Do you have a sister?' I asked.

'Yes.'

'Well, you'd do well to remember that this little girl might be your sister.'

'Your sister's a gypo!' cried another of the boys.

'No she's not!'

'Yes she is!'

This caused general merriment, and then the boys started to fight among themselves.

'Boys!' I said. 'Boys!' It was pointless reasoning with them in this diabolic weather, and, besides, Miriam had by this time got out of the Lagonda.

'Boys!' she said, in her deepest tones. They turned, took one look at her, in her wet silken clothes, her hair slick, her make-up running down her face, like an Electra or a wraith summoned up out of the storm, and they ran off screaming down the street.

Back in the Lagonda, Naughty was perched next to Morley. He had wrapped her in the car blanket and was saying something to her in his rough-and-ready Romani.

'Now what, Father?'

'I said we'd take her home.'

'All the way back to Egremont?'

'No, no,' said Morley. 'Apparently the gypsies are on the move.'

CHAPTER 14

GAVVER-MUSH

WE DROVE FOR NO MORE than five minutes outside the town but suddenly we had escaped the squall. The rain simply stopped and we found ourselves looking back at black skies from under a bright sun. Westmorland was divided: here, new and fresh; there, foul and dark. Naughty directed us to turn left down a narrow lane, and then right, and left again, and then we parked and were off on a nature walk, our wet clothes sultry and steaming in the sunshine. The rain had brought down scuds of autumn leaves, which now lay in drifts like piles of copper pennies.

'This way!' cried Naughty. 'This way! This way!'

'English weather, eh!' exclaimed Morley. 'Hearty and unpredictable.' He could have been describing himself.

When Naughty grew tired I picked her up and carried her on my shoulders, wrapped in the blanket. Miriam was smoking, for the warmth, producing her own little smoke-clouds in the clear blue air, and Morley was picking grasses and flowers.

'The mighty *capsella bursa pastoris*. They eat it in China, you know.'

'Really?' said Miriam, with a shiver. 'Is it far to your mummy and daddy?' she asked Naughty again. We were all wet and cold. 'Honestly,' she muttered to me. 'I feel about as dismal as a cold wet dog on a cold wet night.'

'Not far! Not far!' cried Naughty.

'I had it fried once,' said Morley. 'Terribly good. I've no idea why we don't use it for culinary purposes ourselves. Very advanced in that sense, the Chinese. Though our gypsy friends use it in childbirth, I believe. It has wonderful healing properties.'

We were going to need it.

We were walking down a grassy avenue towards a river when in the distance a woman stepped out of a glade of sheltering trees to our left, took one look at us, laid down the heavy wicker basket she was carrying, and came charging towards us, her broad bright skirts a-flapping like a peacock in full plumage, screeching like a banshee.

'You put my daughter down!' she screamed at me. 'You put her down, now! Do you hear me!'

I did as I was told and Naughty ran off towards her.

'Mummy!' she cried. 'Mummy! The nice man brought me home. Some boys were chasing me.'

'I told you not to go into the town!' said the woman. 'You mustn't go into the towns by yourself. It's not safe. Are you OK? You're soaking wet. Did you get caught in the storm? Who are these people?' She looked up at us. Which is when I recognised her: she was the gypsy woman from the Egremont Fair, the woman who had offered to tell us our fortunes. She had not, it seemed, foreseen any of this.

'It's you?' she said accusingly, at Miriam. 'You were at Egremont.'

'That's right,' said Miriam, doing her best to appear authoritative and haughty, all appearances to the contrary.

'What are you doing with my daughter?'

'Saving her skin, actually,' said Miriam. 'Thank *you* very much. You really shouldn't let her out of your sight. She's far too young.'

'And what would you know about it?' said the gypsy woman. 'You haven't got children.'

'How do you know I haven't got children?' asked Miriam.

'Anyway, she's safe now,' said Morley. 'That's the main thing.'

'Thank goodness,' said the woman. 'Come on, Naughty.'

'The boys said we caused a crash, Mummy! They called me names.'

'Don't listen to the gorgio,' said the woman. 'You know what they're like. They tell all sorts of lies.' She turned towards us. 'Thank you for bringing her back. But you can go now.' She unwrapped Naughty from her blanket and tossed it at Miriam. 'Yours? You look like you might need it.'

'The nice man gave it to me, Mummy,' said Naughty.

'Well, thank you,' said the woman thanklessly, taking Naughty's hand. And then she turned and began walking away, down towards the river.

'We're friends of your husband, actually,' Morley called after her.

'I'm sure you are,' said the woman, calling back.

'Noname. We know Noname.'

'Do you now?' said the woman, half turning her head.

'Yes, I'm Swanton Morley.'

The gypsy woman stopped in her tracks and turned fully around to look at Morley.

'*You're* Swanton Morley?'

'That's correct.'

'You were with him in Egremont?'

'That's right.'

'He's told me about you.'

'I wonder if we might have a word with Noname, to say goodbye?'

'Daddy loves Swanton Morley!' said Naughty. 'Daddy reads to me from the book! *Morley's Book for Boys*! He's teaching me to read! Can you read?' she asked Morley.

'Yes,' he said. 'I can.'

'I can read some words.'

'That's good,' he said. 'And I know your daddy is a very good reader. I'd very much like to see him,' said Morley.

'Can he, Mummy? Can he?'

'Well,' said the woman. 'I don't know. We're very busy.'

'Please, please, please, Mummy. Please, please, please.'

In *The Parenting Paradox* (1928) Morley describes the relationship between parents and children as a classic version of the omnipotence paradox: the irresistible force meeting the immovable object. On this occasion the irresistible force proved to be overwhelming.

'I suppose it mightn't do any harm,' said the gypsy woman. 'Five minutes. Come on. Follow me.'

She led us down through the meadow towards the river, where there was an ancient copse of trees. We saw the smoke from the fire before we saw the encampment. And then we heard shouting.

'Gavver-mush! Gavver-mush!'

By the river

There was a rattling crash and a yell. The gypsy woman turned to us, panic-stricken. She pointed at Miriam. 'You look after her.'

'But—'

And then she began to run.

Morley and I followed.

'Stay here,' I shouted back to Miriam, who had scooped up Naughty.

'Now, we're playing a game,' said Miriam, thinking on her feet. 'We're going to play hide and seek. You stay here with me and we're going to count to one hundred.'

We made it to the campsite – if you could call it a campsite. It was a clearing by the river, approached by a number of pathways through the copse, and there was a campfire, and Noname's vardo, and another caravan and a tent – and all hell breaking loose.

Noname was thrashing around, being held by no fewer than four policemen.

'I'll have you!' he was yelling. 'I'll have you!'

'And we'll stitch you up!' shouted a policeman in response. 'You bastard!' They had Noname in a headlock, and an armlock, and one man was holding him from behind, and another from the front. Noname was certainly putting up a fight. Another gypsy, owner of the other vardo, I assumed, was being held by four more policemen: he was even more ferocious. It was a scene of total confrontation: the old gypsy woman from Egremont, Noname's mother, was screaming at our old friend the chief inspector, who was also having to do his best to fend off Noname's lurcher, which was snarling in a way that suggested imminent attack.

'What on earth is the meaning of all this?' demanded

Morley, striding straight into the centre of things. 'Rusty!' he said to the dog. 'Come on, boy, here. Heel. Good boy.' The dog came over to his side. 'Good boy.' He gave the dog a treat from his pocket: he always kept dog treats. 'You never know when you'll need to treat a dog, Sefton,' he liked to say. 'And one day you might be glad of a treat yourself.' His presence had an immediately calming effect.

'What on earth are you doing here?' asked the chief inspector.

'They say that I killed that woman, Mr Morley!' said Noname.

'Maisie Taylor?' said Morley.

'I didn't touch her!'

'I'm sure you didn't,' said Morley.

'Did you hear him?' shouted the gypsy woman, who had now joined her mother-in-law and stood directly in front of the chief inspector, her hands on her hips. 'Now get away and leave us alone!'

'Are you arresting this man?' asked Morley.

'Not that it's any of your business, Mr Morley.'

'I'm a friend,' said Morley.

'Are you now? That would make sense. Well, he's just accompanying us to the station. We've got a few questions for him.'

'Questions about what?'

'We've had a tip-off about your friend here.'

'A tip-off?'

'Yes. These folks made their way from Egremont late last night, apparently, having attempted and failed to sell a bicycle at the fair.'

'A bicycle?'

The chief inspector removed his pipe from his mouth and used it to point towards a bicycle which was being held by another policeman. It sported a big wicker basket on the front.

'I wanted to sell the bike to buy a horse!' said Noname. 'Ask Mr Morley. I just wanted to buy a horse!'

'It's not illegal to sell a bicycle, is it?' asked Morley.

'Well, that rather depends whether the bicycle is yours to sell, Mr Morley, doesn't it?'

'And who does this bicycle belong to?' asked Morley.

'It's Maisie Taylor's bicycle,' said the chief inspector.

'Are you sure?'

The policeman holding the bicycle turned the handlebars to face us. On the front of the wicker basket, painted in bold black, were the words 'TAYLOR'S PHARMACY'.

'What were you doing with Maisie's bicycle?' Morley asked Noname.

But before Noname could answer Naughty came running into the clearing and threw herself around his legs.

'Daddy! Daddy!' She was crying.

Miriam followed behind.

'I told you to keep her away!' shouted the gypsy woman.

'She escaped!' said Miriam. 'She bit me, the little beast!'

'Daddy! Daddy!' cried Naughty, hanging on to Noname's legs.

'It's all right,' said Noname. 'I'm just going to talk to these men about something. Emerald,' he called over to the gypsy woman, 'you pack up here with Job. Everything'll be OK. I'll sort things out and then we'll be on our way again.' He had ceased struggling with the policemen. 'I'll not cause no more trouble.'

'That's better,' said the chief inspector. He wandered over towards Noname. He had removed his pipe from his mouth and pocketed it. I thought for a moment he was going to strike Noname. But instead he patted him on the back and put his arm around his shoulder, as if they were long-lost friends. 'Much better. See? There's no need for all this fuss. We all behave like gentlemen and we'll have this cleared up in no time.' He gave a nod, and the policemen released the other man, Job, who had also given up the struggle. 'My colleagues here'll escort you to the station, sir, and we can resolve matters amicably there, eh?'

'Noname!' called Emerald.

'It's all right,' said Noname. 'You just look after Naughty and the baby and we'll soon be on our way again. Job, you take care of Mr Morley. Naughty, you look after your little sister.' Then we all stood and watched as he allowed himself to be led away by the police down one of the pathways out of the copse. One of the officers wheeled away the bicycle, and Noname's lurcher hirpled alongside. It was an odd, pathetic procession, like watching the capture and surrender of some great general – a general who'd gone to war on a bicycle, accompanied by his dog.

The clearing was suddenly quiet except for the sounds of the birds and the river rushing by.

'Well, this is unfortunate, Mr Morley,' said the chief inspector.

'Indeed it is,' said Morley. 'Very unfortunate.'

'I'm afraid you and your companions have rather tried my patience, sir.'

'I'm terribly sorry if that's the case.'

'If you wouldn't mind reporting to the station this evening I'd finally like to take a statement from all of you.'

'Very well, Officer.'

'Including you, Mr Sefton.' The chief inspector spoke directly to me. 'We've not been able to have our little conversation about the crash yet, have we?'

'No,' I said.

'Matters seem to continue to keep arising, don't they?' He pushed his shoulders back. 'And once we've all had our discussions this evening I'm going to have to ask you to leave.'

'Leave?' said Morley. 'Leave the Tufton Arms, do you mean?'

'Leave Westmorland, Mr Morley. I think you've caused quite enough trouble here, don't you?' With which he turned and walked away, before any of us could respond.

'What have *you* done?' Emerald asked.

'Nothing,' said Morley truthfully.

I didn't speak.

'Oh, Father!' said Miriam. 'Honestly! This is absolutely . . .' But she said no more. Her teeth were chattering – the sun was out, but so was the wind, and the clearing offered no shelter. Miriam's fine silk dress offered little protection.

'You look cold, miss,' said Emerald.

'Yes, I suppose,' Miriam agreed reluctantly, wrapping her arms around herself. She was always reluctant to admit to any weakness. 'A little. I'm afraid I didn't really come out prepared for this sort of . . . adventure.'

Emerald spoke to Naughty in Romani and the little girl ran off.

'Well, come and warm yourselves by the fire a minute.'

I was certainly glad to do so – my clothes were beginning to feel increasingly like I was in a Turkish bath – and I was all the more glad when Naughty reappeared with her baby sister under one arm and some fine Scotch blankets for us to wear under the other.

'One good turn,' said Emerald, handing round the blankets and taking her baby.

'Thank you,' said Miriam. 'Much appreciated.'

We wrapped ourselves in the blankets and stared blankly into the fire, composing ourselves after the chaos of the police raid. Or at least Miriam and I wrapped ourselves in the blankets and composed ourselves. Morley decided to use his blanket as a towel – 'Would you mind?' he asked – and stripped off down to his vest and long johns, pegging out his trusty tweeds on a line above the fire to dry. He was fascinated by the campsite, asking all sorts of questions – how did they choose the spot, where did they draw fresh water – and paying particular attention to the big old Dutch oven with a ventilator on top that sat shuddering at the centre of the fire, threatening at any moment to explode, and also to Emerald, who was breastfeeding her baby. This was by no means a common sight at the time in the towns and villages of England, among any kinds or any classes. Indeed, it was the only time I witnessed the practice during all my time with Morley. There were wet-nurses, of course, and women must have fed their babies, but it was not a public spectacle. With Morley stripped down to his scanties and Emerald feeding the baby, and Miriam and I clad in blankets thick with woodsmoke, we might as well have been some primitive tribe. I was worried that Morley was going to ask me to take notes – or, worse, a photograph.

'That's quite a contraption,' he said.

'The oven, you mean, Father?' said Miriam.

'Yes, yes, the oven,' said Morley.

'Noname made it,' said Emerald. 'He can turn his hand to anything.'

'I'm sure he can,' said Morley. 'It's for—'

'Cooking, isn't it?' said Miriam.

'You can roast beef in it, if you can get your hands on it,' said Emerald. 'Or make a nice frying-pan cake, at least.'

The other gypsy, Job, who was a man of few words, was busy noisily collapsing the tent, which he soon had strapped up under his wagon.

'So,' said Morley eventually, having exhausted all his other questions. 'Do you want to tell us exactly what you think has happened here, my dear?'

'I don't know,' said Emerald. 'You've as much idea as me, sir. Everything was fine when I went looking for Naughty and then—'

'Can you read your book to me, Swanton Morley,' said Naughty, running up to Morley with his *Book for Boys*.

'Not now,' said Emerald. 'Let Mr Morley get himself dried here first, and then we'll read to you, OK?'

'When is Daddy coming back?'

'Very soon,' said Emerald. 'Very soon.'

Naughty went to play and Emerald resumed, transferring the baby to her other breast.

'I do know there's no way Noname has anything to do with this dead woman, whoever she is. He wouldn't have anything to do with a gorgio. Not after what his father did.'

'What did his father do?' asked Morley. He wasn't one to miss a good story – relevant or not.

Emerald looked at the old woman. 'Do you want to tell him?'

The old woman shook her head, but then added, with a rasp, 'You tell them.'

Emerald adjusted the feeding position of the baby. 'Sol was a respected man,' she said.

'Sol?'

'Noname's father.'

'My husband,' said the old woman.

'Noname idolised him. But Sol had a . . . weakness.'

'What sort of weakness?' asked Morley.

Emerald looked towards the old woman, who nodded.

'He got involved with a woman. This was many years ago. At the Appleby Fair.'

'Oh dear,' said Morley. 'Involved?'

'Very involved,' said Emerald.

'Ah. Yes, I'm afraid some men are like that,' said Morley. 'A terrible weakness.'

'She was a townswoman,' said Emerald. 'He couldn't help himself.'

'I see,' said Morley.

'Anyway, this townswoman had a child. Sol's child. And Sol wouldn't leave her. He felt more for her and her child than he did for his own wife – and for Noname.'

'I'm so sorry,' said Morley. 'Then what happened?'

'He was cast out,' said Emerald.

'Marime,' said the old woman.

'Marine?' said Miriam.

'Marime,' repeated the woman, as if Miriam were stupid.

'To be made marime is to be no longer one of us,' explained Emerald. 'It's our laws and our judgements.'

'Yes, yes, I've read about this. To be cast out is a terrible fate, is it not?' said Morley.

'It is, and Noname – he suffered because of it. To have a father or a husband who goes to be with the gorgio . . . When he died Noname couldn't even mourn his father properly or bury his body.'

'That's terrible,' said Morley.

'Yes. It changes you. Even now, we mostly make our own way without the others.'

'Outcasts among outcasts,' said Morley.

'That's right.'

'Well, that is terribly sad,' said Morley.

'That's how I know Noname would never have had anything to do with a gorgio woman. He'd never risk anything to lose his own daughters, like he lost his father. He just wouldn't.'

'He'll be able to explain that to the police, then,' said Morley.

'Ha!' Emerald's laugh was bitter. 'And you think they'd be interested?'

'But what about the bicycle?' asked Miriam. 'That *was* Maisie's bicycle, wasn't it?'

'I don't know anything about the bicycle,' said Emerald.

'You don't know where it came from?' asked Morley.

'We're magpies, sir. We collect things. The things you discard. Noname must have picked it up somewhere along the way.'

The old woman said something in Romani.

'I'm sorry,' said Morley, 'I didn't catch that.'

'She says maybe the gorgio gave him the bicycle, as a trap,' said Emerald.

'Surely not?' said Morley.

'People always try to blame us for everything,' added Emerald. 'Something gets stolen. Somebody gets hurt—'

'A train crashes,' said Morley.

'That's right. What's the first thing that happens? They blame us.'

'I'm not sure that's entirely true, is it?' said Miriam.

'It's just what happens, miss. It's easier for you to blame us than to look for the answers among yourselves.'

'Hmm,' said Morley, carefully considering Emerald's words. 'There is certainly a terrible prejudice against your people.'

'And getting worse,' said Emerald.

'Yes,' said Morley. 'And no. All sorts of terrible prejudices are being stirred up everywhere at the moment, granted, but I fear 'twas ever thus. Which English king was it who passed the law that gypsies should be branded, Sefton?'

'I don't know, Mr Morley, was it—'

'Edward VI, I think you'll find it was,' said Morley, answering his own question. 'Many years ago. Utter barbarism. Even Cromwell executed gypsies for the crime of being gypsies. I'm afraid the history of the persecution of your people is a long and ignoble one, my dear.'

As the conversation took this darker turn, the other gypsy, Job, sidled over to the fire, keen to keep an eye on things. He was a weasel-faced fellow with what one might describe as a miner's build: thick, strong arms and legs, with a thick, knobbly, muscly neck. He looked like he'd make a good Westmorland wrestler.

'This is my brother, Job,' said Emerald.

'Satismos,' said Morley.

Job spoke to Emerald in Romani.

'He asked if you really speak Romani,' said Emerald.

'Only a very little,' said Morley.

Job said something else: 'Gadje Gadjensa, Rom Romensa.'

'What was that?' asked Morley.

'He was just saying, he's . . .' She looked at Job and he looked at her, threateningly, unpleasant. 'He's absolutely delighted that a gorgio can speak Romani.' His facial expression seemed to suggest the exact opposite.

The old woman, who had been tending to a pot on the fire, interrupted, saying something to Emerald.

'A little jogray?' asked Emerald.

'Stew?' said Morley.

'That's right,' said Emerald.

Job grunted, unimpressed, and then slipped away.

'We call it greasy water stew,' said Emerald.

'Mmm,' said Miriam. 'Sounds delicious.'

'But Mother's thrown in a few other bits and pieces. Do you want some?'

'Well,' said Miriam. 'When in Rome, I suppose.' You could never say that Miriam wasn't up for a challenge – whatever the challenge.

The old woman spooned out a large helping of the stew into an enamel mug.

'The Wedgwood's away at the moment, I'm afraid,' said Emerald.

'No, this is perfect,' said Miriam, taking the mug. 'Thank you.' Emerald and the old woman were watching her closely for her reaction. There was no knife or fork forthcoming. She took a deep breath and then took a glug from the mug and began to chew. 'Do you know . . . It's . . . rather tasty, actually,' she said. 'Is it . . . venison?'

Emerald translated for the old woman, who burst out laughing – and not, I have to say, in a nice way. If one were permitted to describe an old woman's laugh as a 'cackle' then on this occasion – at risk of offence, but for the simple purpose of accuracy – one might perhaps be permitted to do so. She jabbed a sharp finger at Miriam.

'Hotchiwitchi!' she said. 'Hotchiwitchi!'

'Hedgehog,' translated Emerald.

'Yes, I know what it is,' said Miriam. 'Thank you.' I thought for a moment that she was going to be sick. But she wasn't. She stared at the old woman, grinned widely, and choked down another mouthful. And another. And another. And when she finished she banged down the enamel mug in triumph.

'Delicious!' she pronounced, glaring.

This seemed to win over the old woman, who whooped with laughter and said something to Emerald.

'What did she say?' asked Miriam.

'It's a saying we have,' explained Emerald. '"A good daughter-in-law is one who eats unsalted food and says that it is salted."'

'I think she likes you, Miriam.' Morley laughed.

I think he was right. The old woman presumably recognised in Miriam a kindred spirit: headstrong, mischievous, unbeatable. Miriam's consumption of the stew certainly brought about a warming of relations. While Emerald laid the baby down for a nap in the vardo, the old woman – at Morley's prompting – agreed to reveal to us some of her 'traditional' food preparation methods. She led us over to a line strung up between Noname's vardo and a tree. I thought at first that what was on the line were drying socks, but as she began unhooking an item to show us I realised that they weren't in fact socks, nor indeed any other item of clothing. They were hedgehogs. Morley of course was delighted. As we learned from the old woman, through a process of complex hand gestures, and Emerald's translations – and as Morley later explained in detail in his book, *Morley's Backwoods Cooking* (1938) – the best way to cook a hedgehog, contrary to popular myth, is not to bake it in clay, but simply to catch it, nick it on its underbelly, blow it up, peel off the prickles, peg it out, soak it in salted water, and hang it out to dry, before frying. It's not a technique I have myself bothered to try. The old woman also kindly showed Morley how to hoick out snails from a tree stump, how to boil them in a bucket, and how best to eat them (with a good clean nail, eyes closed, and dipped in salt).

After what seemed like hours of demonstration and instruction we parted with Emerald and the old woman on the best of terms. Morley read to Naughty from the *Book for Boys*, Miriam swapped her ruined silk dress with Emerald for one of her embroidered blouses and billowing skirts, and I was offered a bottle of Noname's home-brewed spirits by the old woman. (It tasted rather like sloe gin, without the gin and the sloes, and there was a strong aftertaste of turnip.) Job had disappeared to I know not where.

As we left, Morley gave Emerald a solemn promise.

'I give you my word, madam, that I will do everything in my power to ensure that your husband, if innocent, returns to you as soon as possible.'

It was typical Morley: intrepid, keen, well-meaning and utterly reckless.

When we returned to the Lagonda to make our way back to Appleby we found that someone had let down the tyres.

Morley suspected the boys from Kirkby Stephen. Miriam suspected the police. I rather suspected Job.

I rather suspected Job

CHAPTER 15

A 22-LEVER MIDLAND TUMBLER

WE WERE ARGUING, as usual, in the Lagonda. It was the site of many an argument – a kind of four-wheeled debating chamber in many ways, a small mobile contested territory of endless dispute. During the course of our travels I came to think of the Lagonda almost as a kind of province unto itself, an honorary county almost: 'Visit Lagonda, the County of Argument and Debate'. (Interestingly, in *Morley's Atlas of Imaginary Places* (1922), an utterly bizarre collection of essays, privately printed and hand illustrated by Fred Adlington, and now very much a collector's item, Morley writes with tremendous and utterly disproportionate fondness for L. Frank Baum's Land of Oz, as if it were an *actual* place, inhabited by *actual* people. He claims indeed to have visited the land himself – ! – and to have spent time in Rigamarole Town, in Merryland, in Thumbumbia and Squeedonia, and all the other ludicrous made-up places. He always had a tendency to confuse categories. Sometimes I wondered if his England was an entire invention, a dream kingdom, an intellectual curiosity rather than a real place.)

I had pumped up the tyres using a foot-pump, which took quite some time, giving us ample opportunity to go over what had just happened with the gypsies, as well as reviewing the likely guilt or innocence of Noname, of Gerald Taylor and of Professor Jenkins. I had long since withdrawn my claim that Nancy might have been romantically involved with Maisie and was in some way involved with her death. It was a ridiculous suggestion, made only to counter Miriam's equally ridiculous suggestion that Gerald's sister had been involved in Maisie's murder, on the basis that she was a bit of a shrew. For his part, Morley was beginning to come round to the idea that Gerald Taylor may have murdered his wife, and was absolutely adamant that Noname was innocent.

'I have given my word,' he said, 'that I will do everything to assist the poor gypsies.'

'Well, I do wish you wouldn't be giving your word here, there and everywhere, Father, and making these ridiculous promises that you can't possibly keep,' said Miriam. 'I really can't see what you can do to help.' Her borrowed gypsy clothes rather suited her, I have to say. She looked and sounded like a fearsome Kalderash – a gypsy played by Garbo in a film by Cecil B. DeMille. I, meanwhile, was still dressed in the ridiculous squire's outfit that Morley had procured for me in Appleby's gentleman's outfitters. 'I do feel very sorry for the poor man, but the police clearly want us out of the county, and I personally would be very happy to go. This entire trip's been nothing but an absolute disaster from the moment we left London.' Or in my case, from before we left London.

'I'm afraid I can't see what we can do either,' I added.

Morley wasn't listening. He had produced the paper bag of boiled eggs from the Tufton Arms, and a flask of tea.

'Egg?' he offered me.

'No, thank you,' I said.

'Miriam?'

'Thank you, Father.'

He peeled a boiled egg slowly and carefully, as if unwrapping a precious jewel.

'*Ab ovo usque ad mala*,' he said.

'I can't see that Horace can help on this occasion,' said Miriam, peeling her own egg.

'From the egg to the apple,' said Morley.

'Yes?' said Miriam. 'And?'

'From the beginning to the end.'

'Yes?' repeated Miriam.

'I mean, I think we need to think more like archaeologists,' said Morley. 'Like Jenkins. We need to crack through the layers, as it were, the outer surface, in order to get at the truth buried beneath.'

'Mmm?' said Miriam, through a mouthful of boiled egg.

'We need to go back to where this all began,' said Morley, holding a shiny white egg aloft.

'Back to the site of the crash?' I said.

'Precisely!' said Morley, popping the egg entire into his mouth. 'Shall we?'

We parked at Appleby Station. It was unsettling to be back at the site of so much recent sorrow and pain – like picking at an unhealed wound. The station itself was locked and there were signs everywhere saying that the line was closed until further notice and indeed that the entire area was closed to the public. It gave the place a rather forbidding aspect. But this was no deterrent to Morley, of course, or indeed presumably to anyone else: we simply wandered round the station and onto the platform. It had turned into a bleak afternoon, with clouds forming again, and everywhere was wet and slippery from the earlier showers. I found myself growing more and more anxious with every step and Miriam seemed equally uncomfortable. Morley seemed to have no plan other than to go back to the beginning, which was not a place either of us was particularly interested in visiting.

The platform was being used temporarily to store big black sleepers and all sorts of track-laying tools and equipment, vast and gnarly, but set out neatly, like a giant's torture equipment. In the distance down to the right there were gangs of men working away on the line, dozens of them shovelling ballast, and laying iron, and doing whatever else it takes to remake a railway line. But instead of going down towards the scene of this activity, towards the crash site – which is why I thought we were there – Morley started making his way in the other direction, up the line towards the signal box.

'Father!' called Miriam. 'Father? You can't just . . . Shouldn't we—'

'Shall we leave him?' I said. 'He'll probably just wander back in a minute.'

'Have you met my father?' asked Miriam. 'He doesn't wander back. He wanders off.'

She was right. He didn't wander back. He walked along

the line towards the signal box and bent over to scoop up a handful of dirt, which he carefully pocketed.

'What's he doing?' I said.

'Goodness only knows,' said Miriam. 'Panning for gold?'

He then continued walking further into the distance and up the steep steps into the signal box. Before we could call out again he had disappeared inside.

By the time we got up there Morley had already made himself at home and was happily chatting away and drinking a cup of tea. This was surprising – though it would probably have been more surprising if he was alone. He was not alone, because there in the signal box – inevitably – was the signalman, George Wilson, the man we had last met in the bar of the Tufton Arms on the evening of the crash and who had been less than impressed with Morley's analysis of his moral and ethical dilemmas. He and Morley seemed to have overcome their differences and were deep in conversation.

'You couldn't have chosen better,' George was saying. 'She's the finest line in England.'

'Indeed she is, indeed she is. There are few journeys to rival it. Ah!' said Morley, as Miriam and I entered. 'This is my daughter, Miriam, and my assistant, Stephen Sefton. You remember George, of course? Mr Wilson? I was just telling George here about my book on the Settle–Carlisle line.'

'I hadn't realised it was him that had written it. It's a classic,' said George. 'I've had it out the library two or three times m'self. I think they've more than one copy, so many of the lads want to read it.'

(Morley's fame often preceded him and made smooth his path, though at other times it caused unnecessary obstacles and complications. I never envied him his fame. 'Fame,' he writes, in *Close-Up with Swanton Morley* (1935), one of his endless books of rambling asides and observations and *obiter dicta*, 'is neither a blessing nor a curse. It is simply a means of travel. In the future everyone will be famous, and all of us will be everywhere.' I had no idea what he meant then, but I have a better idea now.)

'You'll have a drop of the chatter watter?' asked George. Miriam looked at me. I looked at her. George looked at the teapot on the little stove in the corner.

'Ah!' said Miriam. 'Tea. No, thank you.' I also declined. 'You've got it set up here very nicely,' said Miriam.

'Yes, I was just saying to George,' said Morley, 'that this is an exceptionally fine example of Midland Railway architecture.'

'Home from home,' said George.

'I'm considering in the second edition of the book including much more detail about the buildings along the line,' said Morley.

'Fascinating,' said Miriam.

'There's plenty of them anyway,' said George. 'Keep you busy. As well as the stations and t'signal boxes you've got all the buildings along line where the gangers and t'platelayers put up.'

'Yes, of course,' said Morley.

'There's the workman's coach on the siding down at Horton, and then there's the cabins the gangs sleep in during the summer – Tom's cabin, Ted's cabin. They're basic all right, but some of them are done up nice, with the old plum and straw paint and all. Just a stove and a few benches inside, but they does the job.'

'I had no idea,' said Morley. 'Did you, Sefton?'

'No,' I said.

'Folk don't realise how much it takes to keep t'railway running, sir. There's the slip and drainage gang, and the relaying gang, and the ballast gang – we've dozens and dozens of lads on this stretch alone.'

'So you certainly don't get lonely up here then?' said Morley.

'No, not at all, sir. There's plenty to keep me occupied. Fourteen hours a day I'm here most days.'

'Well,' said Morley. 'It's a very fine workplace, sir.'

'Thank you.'

'I wonder if I might take a few notes, if I may, while I'm here.'

'I'd be honoured, sir. There's no trains running, but I wanted to be here anyway, just in case, like.'

'Yes, of course,' said Morley. 'Once a signalman, always a signalman.'

'Exactly, sir. A man has to take pride in his work, or what's he got? And where else would I be? My wife wouldn't want me under her feet all day.'

'Dora?'

'You've met my wife, sir?'

Morley nodded. 'Yes, we certainly have. We were lucky enough to sample some of her hospitality over at the archaeological dig at Shap.'

'Ah, yes, of course.'

'*Dora's Station Café and Outside Catering – Catering For All Tastes.* Quite a little business she's got herself.'

'She is a remarkable woman,' said George.

'Quite so,' said Morley, 'quite so.'

'And a marvellous mother to our boys.'

'Good, good,' said Morley. 'Glad to hear it. A woman who can combine her role as a mother while running her own café – quite an example, eh, Miriam?'

'Indeed, Father.'

'Are you married yourself?' asked George, rather hesitantly, of Miriam.

'No,' said Miriam.

'I just wondered,' he said. 'Because you're . . .' He nodded towards Miriam's gypsy get-up. 'Are you a . . . travelling woman?'

'Oh no,' said Miriam. 'No, no, no. I'm just borrowing these clothes from a friend.'

'Ah,' said George. 'Only my wife's some gypsy blood in her, you see.'

'Dora?' said Morley.

'That's right, sir.'

'I see,' said Morley. 'Is that common, round here?'

'I don't know,' said George. 'Not as far as I know.'

'Hmm,' said Morley. 'I wonder if . . .' He started smoothing out his moustache – a sure sign that he was onto something. 'I wonder . . .'

'Father?' said Miriam.

'Yes?'

'You were just wondering about something?'

'Ah, yes, yes. I was just wondering what . . . have you got here then, Mr Wilson, your lever system?'

'This?' said George, indicating the long row of important-looking signal levers, which stretched the width of the box and which stood tall and straight beneath an even more important-looking row of instruments, which included a bell, buttons, a telegraph and a telephone.

'What is it,' asked Morley, 'a twenty-lever Midland tumbler?'

'Twenty-two,' said George. 'There was levers added for the creamery.'

'It is a beautiful frame,' said Morley.

'Thank you, sir.'

'And what's that distinctive smell in here?' asked Morley. We all sniffed. I couldn't smell anything.

'It's probably the polish, sir,' said George. 'We have to keep the levers perfect, you see. You only ever touch 'em with a cloth.'

'Of course,' said Morley. 'Yes, yes, it probably is the smell of polish . . . And just remind me, how does the system work? I must add some more details for the next edition of the book.'

'It'd take me more than a while to explain it, sir.'

'I'm sure it would, but Miriam and Sefton here would doubtless be very interested to know the basic working of the system, wouldn't you?'

Miriam was too busy coughing to reply. She'd clearly caught a chill, and anyway I doubted she was very much interested in the basic working of the lever system in the Appleby signal box.

'Here, miss,' said George, indicating that Miriam should sit herself down in the armchair by the stove.

'Thank you,' said Miriam.

'Do go on, though,' said Morley, who was not always entirely attentive to the needs of others. I was ready to go on myself.

'I might just take a walk here, Mr Morley,' I said, 'warm myself up a bit.' My clothes were still damp from earlier.

'You'd want to hear how the system works though, Sefton, wouldn't you?' This was not a question. It was an instruction. 'It's basically a block working system, isn't it?' Morley spoke to George, and my eyes began to glaze over.

'That's right, sir. The line's divided into sections or blocks, and when a man has a train he wants to despatch to a section—'

'A signalman, you mean?' said Morley.

'That's right, he requests from the next signalman whether he can send her forward.'

'And he requests it how?'

'Using the Morse tapper here' – he indicated his Morse tapper – 'which rings a bell code in the next signal box.'

'So you're sending codes both ways up and down the line, is that right?'

'That's it, in summary, sir.'

'And what would the code be for all-clear, say, to allow a passenger train through to the next section?'

'That's a 3pause1, sir.'

'And that must have been the signal you sent on that fateful day last week then, before you saw the gypsy children?'

I began to see why Morley was so interested in the working of the system.

'That's right, sir. I've been over it all a thousand times in my mind.'

'I'm sure you have.'

'I'm sure I did the right thing, at the time.'

'I'm sure you did.'

'I've not been sleeping right, actually,' said George. 'For a railwayman, it's the baddest thing that could have happen't.'

'Of course it is,' said Morley.

'And a tragedy for the town, like. All the people who are employed on the railway. The goods office, porters, maintenance. Everyone's been affected. I feel bad for them.'

'Not to mention the family of the little girl who died,' I said.

'Of course,' said George.

'You must feel very guilty,' I said.

Morley looked at me harshly. He was never a man to rush to condemnation.

'So just tell me exactly what happened,' said Morley. 'On the day of the crash.'

'I saw the children—' said George.

'The gypsy children?'

'That's right, on my last check and so I rang once to call attention, and then I put the near signal to danger. I didn't have time to change the distant signal. I was acting on pure instinct, sir. As a railwayman. I knew I had to change the points, or the children would . . .'

'Yes, that would have been a terrible tragedy, of course. And would you have had gypsy children on the line at other times?'

'Not as far as I'm aware, sir.'

'Because you'd have reported it, of course.'

'Of course.'

'And have you had trouble with the gypsies generally?'

'Folk in t'town complain around the time of the fair, of course, but I haven't got a bad word to say against them myself.'

'No,' said Morley. 'I suppose, with Dora—'

'That's right. I haven't had no troubles with them. Sometimes they come and take a few tatties or what have you that's been spilled when the wagons are loading, or they come selling rabbits, but apart from that, no.'

'Never on the line?'

'I've had lads in the summer, during the fair, who get up to mischief, trying to go swimming in the tank house by the stables, but never on the line, no.'

'And when do you think the track will be open again?'

'It'll be a day or two yet.'

'I think I'll just go out for a smoke,' I said.

'That's fine,' said Morley. Apparently I had heard everything he wanted me to hear, and so I left Morley quizzing George more about signalling practices, and Miriam warming herself by the stove.

'You just mind the steps there,' called George, as I opened the door of the signal box. 'They're more steep than you think.'

It was a perilous descent.

I wandered down to the scene of the crash.

It was a mistake.

The workmen had lit lamps against the early evening gloom and they continued to work with their shovels and lifting equipment, heaving and heaving and dragging, like miners of the surface of the earth. A man who I assumed was the gangmaster – a man dressed in a grubby Midland Railways uniform, with a neckerchief – called out at me as I approached.

'What do you want?'

'I was in the crash,' I said. 'I just . . .'

'Sorry, sir. Closed to the public. This is a dangerous area. You need to move on.'

I stood and looked at the spot where our carriage had

lain, and beyond that towards the field where Lucy had died. Everything had been cleared and everything was empty, but memories of the crash came back sharp and unexpected, like stabbing pains, or the sudden sound of incoming shells overhead in Spain: the jerking and shuddering of the carriage; the look of pain and fear on Lucy's mother's face, and the sound of the baby crying, and Lucy somehow not there; and the walking wounded dragging themselves away. I was about to walk away myself when I thought I saw something in the embankment, something familiar, something glittering in the workmen's lights. It seemed to be calling out to me, beckoning me towards it. I walked straight past the gangmaster.

'Hey, hey! What do you think you're doing? Hey!'

A man raised a shovel to bar my way, but I dodged round him, only realising then what I had seen.

It was my camera – buried in the weeds and the rubble. The Leica. I had at least managed to recover something from the crash.

CHAPTER 16

THE HANGING ROOM

IT WAS GETTING ON for six o'clock by the time we left Appleby Station and drove directly to the other Appleby station, the police station – a journey of just a few minutes. Morley was delighted that I had recovered the camera, and his conversation with the signalman seemed to have filled him with renewed confidence and vigour, something to do with the thrill of talking about levers and signals, no doubt. The rain and the clouds had returned, but Morley's curiosity and enthusiasm – as always – blazed on. He launched into song.

> *A la porte du corps de garde,*
> *Pour tuer le temps,*
> *On fume, on jase, l'on regarde*
> *Passer les passants.*

'Miriam?'
'*Carmen*,' she said.
'Correct!' said Morley. 'Poor old Bizet. Anyway, look at

this! What do you think? Old gaol and courthouse, would you say, Miriam?'

'Possibly, Father.'

'Late 1800s, Sefton?'

'Yes, Mr Morley,' I said. 'Definitely.'

'Hipped roof, two storeys, centre doorway with rec-tangular fanlight.'

'And some rather lovely quoins,' said Miriam.

'Indeed, lovely quoins,' agreed Morley. He loved a lovely quoin. 'Single-storey wing on either side, segmented-arched passageway in front, courtyard enclosed with low parapet wall. Four-square solid market-town Georgian. Very nice indeed, isn't it? Very nice.'

'For a place of imprisonment and punishment,' I said sarcastically, and regretted it immediately. (Morley was not a great fan of sarcasm, 'that unreal, cruel and transitory mirth, as the crackling of thorns under a pot', as he puts it in *Morley's False and Unreasonable Arguments and Other Enemies of Reason* (1924), a book consisting largely of arguments that are themselves false and unreasonable.)

'Is there any reason why a place of imprisonment and punishment *shouldn't* be architecturally interesting, Sefton?'

'Well, I . . .'

'Indeed, couldn't we learn rather more about the for-mation and *deformation* of human history from a study of gaols and garrisons and fortifications than from a study of, I don't know – say – palaces and pleasure houses?'

'Yes, Mr Morley,' I agreed.

'Law courts, lunatic asylums – the great emblems of state power. One might write a rather interesting book, mightn't one, analysing and describing the changing architecture of discipline and punishment?'

'No. No one would be interested, Father,' said Miriam. She helped Morley from the car and we all stood for a moment under a large umbrella, admiring Appleby's own little emblem of state power.

'Reminds me rather of a place in Bohemia I visited once, fortified town, most peculiar. And another place near Antwerp, deserted fort – name escapes me – but these sorts of places are literally littered across the European landscape, Sefton—'

'Literally?' said Miriam.

'Literally,' insisted Morley. 'Littered like tombs and grave-yards and burial pits, ready at any moment to be forced into service as human pens and charnel houses by some diseased state or diabolical despot. These buildings, Sefton, these temples of the state, are terrible evidence of mankind's desperate need to protect itself from the imagined other, from the enemy, the felon, the outcast. This is what this building represents, Sefton, in this place, in this town, in this nation, in this Europe!'

'Oh, please!' said Miriam. 'It's a police station, Father. And we're late.'

We were interviewed in the station one by one: Miriam first, Morley, and then it was my turn.

'You're up in the hanging room,' said Morley, when he was escorted back by a policeman, and I was being led away.

'The hanging room?'

'It's where the executions used to be held, apparently. Absolutely fascinating – ask the chief inspector. Place of private hanging. At one time they'd have done it out in the open, of course, in the yard, I suppose. Represents a change in how society views the criminal, eh? Wouldn't fancy it either way, would you?'

I swallowed hard. 'No, Mr Morley,' I said.

'If you wouldn't mind coming with me, Mr Sefton,' said the policeman.

'We'll see you back at the Tufton Arms, shall we?' said Morley. 'Much to discuss! Much to debate!'

It was a long, narrow room with a single window looking out across the town. The chief inspector sat facing me with another policeman next to him taking notes. I took a deep breath. I had been interviewed before. I would be interviewed again. This was not – I told myself – something to worry about.

'Stephen Sefton,' said the chief inspector, when I sat down. 'Stephen. Sefton.'

'That's me,' I agreed.

He had disassembled his pipe, which sat before him on the desk. During the course of our conversation he slowly and deliberately cleaned it, dislodging all the unpleasant pieces of coagulated tobacco, and put it back together.

'Pretty handy in a fight, aren't we, Mr Sefton?'

'Am I?' I said. I immediately started to worry.

'You certainly put up a good show at the wrestling.'

Ah, the wrestling. Not Marlborough Street.

'I suppose.'

'You suppose?' The chief inspector nodded and made

a long face. 'You suppose. Not sure, eh? It was a famous victory, Mr Sefton! A famous victory! There was big Gerald Taylor, undefeated for many years in these parts, champion at Grasmere, and yet you came sidling along, half his size, and floored him just like that. Very impressive. Very impressive.'

I made no reply. He did something with a pipe cleaner.

'How do you explain that, then, Mr Sefton?'

'Beginner's luck?'

'Really? Beginner's luck. Nothing to do at all with you being in Spain and fighting with the Republicans then? Hand to hand, was it?'

'How do you know I was in Spain?'

'We have our methods, Mr Sefton. It's not only you and your friend Mr Morley who like to go around asking questions – it's my job.'

'Of course.'

'And let's just say I had a feeling about you, when I met you.'

'Really?'

'Yes. Not a good feeling.'

I gulped nervously.

'You see there are certain people, Mr Sefton, who seem to get . . . nervous around the police.'

'Are there?' I was doing my best to stay calm.

'Yes, and when you've been in the job as long as me you learn to be able to identify them, and then you start to ask questions about them. That's the nature of police work. Preemptive police work, I call it. Knowing who to look for, and what to look for.'

'I see.'

'And I just got that sense around you, Mr Sefton, that sense that you are . . . a little nervous, shall we say. Which is strange. Educated man, like yourself. Everything going for you. Assistant to a famous writer. So I just started wondering if there was anything you'd have to be nervous about. And . . .' He sat back in his chair and crossed his arms. 'But I shouldn't be doing all the talking, should I?'

I was very happy for him to be doing all the talking.

There was a long silence. If this room wasn't the hanging room then it was certainly a place of great discomfort.

'Well?' said the chief inspector.

'Well what?'

'Is there anything you want to tell me about, Mr Sefton?'

'I don't think so, no.'

'You might find it a relief to be able to tell someone about it.'

'About what?'

'I don't know, Mr Sefton.'

'I don't think there's anything I want to tell you about.' I didn't even want to tell him that I didn't want to tell him anything.

'You see,' said the chief inspector, looking very pleased with himself, having finally put his pipe back together, and leaning forward in his chair again. 'You see, that's what I thought you'd say. So I took the liberty of calling Scotland Yard, to see if we could find out anything about you. And lo and behold it seems you are a member of the Communist Party, is that right?' The pipe was lit and resumed its rightful place back in his mouth.

'Was a member,' I said. 'Which is not illegal, is it, as far as I'm aware?'

'No, no, that's not illegal at all. Not at all. It's just what being a member of the Communist Party might . . . lead you into.'

'I'm not aware that it led me into anything.'

'Apart from going to Spain?'

'I rather regret going to Spain,' I said.

'Regret it? Really? And why's that?'

'For a number of reasons.'

'Kill anybody out there, while you were there?'

'It was a war,' I said. 'And in a war people get hurt.'

'And did you find you got a taste for hurting people, Mr Sefton?'

'No,' I said. 'On the contrary.'

I was terrified that at any moment he might start asking me about my whereabouts on the night a man was found beaten to death outside Marlborough Street Magistrates' Court.

'Can I just ask what this has to do with the train crash, or the death of Maisie Taylor?'

'I don't know. You tell me,' said the chief inspector.

'As far as I'm aware my membership of the Communist Party has nothing to do with the murder of Maisie Taylor, or the train crash.'

'Well, that's good then, isn't it? Because if I were to find out that there were any connection between you . . . and the crash . . . and the death of Maisie Taylor, or if there were *anything* you knew about and had failed to tell me about, even though I had given you ample opportunity to speak to me about it, then I think you would understand that I would be very disappointed. And so would a court of law, should it come to that.'

'Again, there's nothing I can think of that might be of interest to you in your investigations.'

'Quite sure?'

'Yes.'

'That's fine, then, Mr Sefton. Fine.'

He leaned back again in his chair and dismissed the policeman who had been taking notes, who left the room. Only the two of us remained.

'You might just want to think about it overnight – and then you could always come and see me in the morning, after you check out of your hotel.'

'Check out?'

'That's right. As I explained to Mr Morley earlier, and as I pointed out to his charming daughter, and as I believe I may have already explained to you, I'm expecting all of you to be leaving Westmorland tomorrow. I've asked the hotel to let me know when you're on your way.'

'And if we're not?'

'If you're not I'm afraid I shall be charging you all with obstructing a police investigation and you will find not only that you and your friends are not welcome in Westmorland, sir, you will find that you are not welcome in Lancashire, Yorkshire, Suffolk, Surrey, or indeed the Outer Hebrides – indeed everywhere on these islands where there's a police station or a policeman. Policing is a family, you see, Mr Sefton. And if you upset one member of a family you upset them all. Do you understand?'

'Yes,' I said.

'Good. In which case, I think our business here is done. Thank you for your time.'

As I came out of the hanging room and down the stone

steps I tripped and nearly fell in the dark passage. I maintain what I said about the architecture of imprisonment and punishment: there is nothing good or noteworthy about it. I walked away from Appleby's lovely Georgian police station as quickly as possible in the pouring rain, and across the bridge, past St Lawrence's Church at the bottom of Boroughgate and up to the Tufton Arms. I needed a drink. As far as I was concerned we couldn't get out of Westmorland fast enough.

CHAPTER 17

EJECTA, REJECTA, DEJECTA

SITTING IN THE LOUNGE of the Tufton Arms was Nancy. As always she seemed perkish, alert, and yet also somehow menacing. With her big round eyes, her sleek hair and a dark grey mannish suit matched with a bright white shirt, she looked as though at any moment she might pounce, a cat waiting by a mouse hole. She glanced up as I entered.

'Nancy,' I said.

'You,' she replied, disappointed. A cat who had caught the wrong mouse. 'Have you seen Miriam?'

'No,' I lied. 'Why?'

'Just because. I've been kicked out of my digs. I expect Jenkins had a hand in it.'

'Jenkins? Isn't he still helping police with their enquiries?'

'Not any more. They released him this morning.' Her perky good looks deserted her for a moment and her face turned bitter and scornful; the face she'd grow into, I thought, with age. 'He's off the hook and back at the dig – and absolutely furious.'

The Tufton Arms

'I never really thought he had anything to do with Maisie's murder,' I said.

'Well,' said Nancy. 'Of course it doesn't mean he had nothing to do with it. It just means there's no evidence at the moment. Men like Jenkins. All men, in fact, they . . .' She thought better of whatever she was about to say.

'Anyway,' I said.

'If you see Miriam, can you tell her I'm here? I was hoping I might be able to catch her.'

'I'll certainly do my best. Where are you staying?'

'Well.' She laughed. She had that habit – shared only by the very confident and the terribly shy – of laughing at things that weren't obviously or necessarily funny. 'The thing is, I haven't quite got that sorted yet. I was hoping maybe to talk to Miriam about it.'

'You know we're leaving tomorrow?'

'No?' She looked absolutely crestfallen – her features again crumpled. 'Why?'

'We have a book to write,' I said, not entirely untruthfully, though even I realised that *The County Guides: Westmorland* was now far behind schedule. 'If I see her tonight I'll tell her you were looking for her.' I had absolutely no intention of doing so.

But I did think I should probably let Morley know that Jenkins had been released without charge, so I went upstairs and knocked on his door. He opened it quickly: he was always able to move swiftly and silently, like a tweedy ghoul or a brogue-footed deer in a forest. He glided and shimmered, in fact – like a Jeeves. This could be enormously disconcerting. He seemed to be expecting me.

'Sefton! At last! Come in, come in, come in.'

His room had been arranged, as always, perfectly to his liking. We could have been in any room in any hotel on any of our journeys: the whole country was his study, and his study was always the same. The window was wide open ('Air, Sefton! Wild air! Fresh air! Thought-nestling air! A man needs air to think!'). The bed had been moved under the open window ('Sleep should be a ventilation of body and of mind, Sefton! Not a clam-like closing up!'). And up against the wall stood a desk arrayed – from left to right – with a writing slope, a typewriter, a set of boxes and cabinets full of writing requisites, piles of paper, an expanding bookrest filled with reference works, the egg-timer, a tumbler and a jug of barley water. This was of no particular interest: this was the way it always was. There was something else, though, something urgent that he wanted to show me.

'Look!' he said, pointing with both hands to his little bedside table. 'What do you think of those?'

Those appeared to be two small piles of camel-coloured dirt, like two tiny crumbled pyramids set upon the glass-topped table.

'Erm.' Animal deposits? Sand? Soot? Some sort of fine powder? Paint? Human remains?

'Do they look the same to you?'

'Yes,' I said.

'Come on! Look carefully, Sefton! You haven't looked properly at all! Go on, go on! Have a closer look.'

I leaned over the table and looked down.

'Closer!' said Morley. 'Inspect them! Interrogate them!'

I wasn't entirely sure how I was supposed to interrogate two small piles of similar-looking camel-coloured dirt, but anyway I knelt down and examined them at eye level. After a thorough inspection I confirmed that they did indeed appear to be . . . two small piles of similar-looking camel-coloured dirt.

'You're sure they look the same?'

'I think so, yes.'

'OK. Good. Now have a quick sniff.'

'A sniff?'

'Don't inhale though.'

This was turning into a scene from one of Delaney's Soho clubs.

'Go on! Go on! Quick sniff, just.'

I took a little sniff, first of one pile, then the other.

'Smell the same?' asked Morley.

'Yes,' I said hesitantly. They smelled to me – approximately – of absolutely nothing.

'Good. Now, have a taste.'

'A taste?' Some sort of spices perhaps?

'Yes, go ahead. Just dip your finger in.'

'What is this stuff?'

'Just . . . try it, Sefton. I'd be interested to know your opinion. Go on.'

I dipped my finger in the pile of dust on the left.

'Lick your finger first, man! You won't get anything otherwise.'

I licked my finger and dipped it again.

'Good! Go on then. Taste it.'

I tasted it.

'It tastes like brown-coloured dirt,' I said.

'Good! Now try this one.'

'What is it?'

'Just try it.'

I tried the other one.

'It also tastes like brown-coloured dirt,' I said.

'Well,' said Morley triumphantly, as if we had just discovered the secret of the universe itself. 'You will be delighted to hear, Sefton, that it is brown-coloured dirt!'

'Right.'

'Yes! Marvellous, isn't it?'

It may have been marvellous. I could not tell, though I could see that it was Morley's sort of thing: ejecta, rejecta, dejecta; dirt. Right up his proverbial street. ('Every drop of water, every speck of dirt, every grain of sand, is as full of stories as a Dickens novel,' he claims, in *Morley's Answers to Questions of Natural History* (1935), part of his popular Morley's Answers to Questions of . . . series, books that often raised as many questions as they answered.)

'And they definitely taste the same, do you think, both piles?'

'Yes,' I said. Tasteless brown dirt.

He dipped his own finger in one pile, tasted the dirt, savoured it, and then tasted the other.

'Mmm,' he said, chewing. 'They really do, don't they? That's excellent, Sefton. Excellent.'

I was struggling to see exactly what was excellent.

'Would you describe it as a sort of . . .' He rubbed his fingers together. 'A sort of salty, churchyardy sort of taste, would you say, with a hint of bone, perhaps?'

'I'm not a great connoisseur of dirt flavours, Mr Morley.'

'Obviously not, Sefton,' he said. 'Obviously not. Me neither. And we'd need to get these into a laboratory to test them properly – it's just a shame I haven't brought my microscope with me – but our senses certainly give us something to go on, don't they?'

'Yes,' I agreed.

I thought it was probably time to tell him the reason I was there, since it seemed rather more significant than his eccentric dirt-tasting experiment, whatever it might tell us about the smell and the taste of brown powders.

'You know that Jenkins has been released without charge?'

'Yes, yes, I know.'

'And the chief inspector wants us out.'

'Yes, that's right,' said Morley. He wasn't listening.

'He's absolutely adamant.'

'Yes, he is, isn't he? Anyway, as I was saying, Sefton, we'd need to get these samples tested properly, but I think we might be onto something here.'

'Onto what, exactly, Mr Morley?'

'The sample on the left here is from Maisie Taylor's shoe, when we found her in the souterrain, do you remember?'

'Yes,' I said. How could I forget?

'And the sample on the right here is from outside the signal box at Appleby.'

'Right. That's why you were pocketing handfuls of dirt when were at the station?'

'Exactly. And both samples seem to be red sandstone; laboratory tests to confirm, obviously, but they certainly look the same, smell the same and taste the same, isn't that right? We're agreed?'

'Yes,' I said. Though I probably would have agreed if he'd suggested the opposite.

'The soil around Shap, however, is largely carboniferous limestone.'

'Right.'

'So it seems likely that Maisie wasn't killed there, at the dig, and furthermore that she might have been killed somewhere in the vicinity of the railway station! The train crash in fact could have merely been a distraction created by the murderer!'

'A distraction? A train crash?'

For all his reputation as a man of reason, Morley often made these ludicrous leaps in logic. His peculiar range of knowledge meant that he was always making strange connections and drawing ridiculous conclusions.

'It is indeed unlikely, Sefton, and I haven't quite worked out the details yet, but I think you'll agree that unless Noname can be proved to have been around Appleby Station on the day of the crash then it may be unlikely that he's guilty of Maisie's murder!'

'I'm not sure that that's *absolutely* conclusive, Mr Morley.'

'Perhaps, perhaps not,' said Morley. 'But it's a start, eh?'

'And didn't the signalman say that there were gypsy children on the line? Which is what caused the crash, which surely makes it more than possible that Noname was indeed in the vicinity of the railway station?'

'What, just because he's a gypsy?'

'Well, yes,' I said.

'And what if there were a murder or a crime involving a white middle-class Englishman, Sefton, a member of the Communist Party and a veteran of the Spanish Civil War, would that necessarily mean that you were a suspect?'

'No, of course not, not . . . necessarily.'

Morley didn't notice my nervous cough.

'Anyway, as I say. I haven't quite worked out the details yet. I think I might skip supper, if that's all right with you, Sefton? There's clearly more work to be done here.'

'Indeed,' I said.

And he happily returned to contemplating his little world of dirt.

I dined alone that evening – Miriam did not appear at dinner either – and eventually retired early to my room.

I lay down on my bed and closed my eyes, pressing my fingertips hard against my weary lids. I needed to sleep but instead I lay and smoked cigarette after cigarette, staring at the ceiling, going through all the events of the past few days, following each train of thought with every long slow exhalation. The room filled with smoke and in this cloud of my own making, raised above myself, I was able to view everything that had happened, going backward and forward, all the way back to the start and back again: to my night out in Soho, to the card game at Delaney's, to Marlborough Street, to Euston, to King's Cross, and on the train with Lucy and her mother, taking photographs all the way up to Appleby – or almost up to Appleby.

I leapt off the bed. It was an Archimedes moment. (Morley, though easily the most intuitive and instinctive thinker I have ever known, always claimed to distrust accounts of sudden inspiration and insight: for him, the Archimedes moment made sense only in the context of an Archimedean lifetime.) There was no point involving Morley: he was clearly obsessed with his little piles of dirt and with clearing Noname. I was left with little alternative. I had no other ally. I quietly crept out of my room and knocked on Miriam's door. It was around midnight: dim lights in the corridor, and horrible smells from the day's cooking.

At first there was no answer, so I continued knocking and then started softly calling her name.

'Miriam? Miriam?'

'Sefton?' she answered immediately, from the other side. Clearly she hadn't been asleep. 'Is it you?'

'Yes.'

'Thank goodness,' she whispered.

She opened her door. She was wearing a light blue silk embroidered dressing gown which featured desperate-looking bees suckling flowers across the chest and butterflies flying high upon the shoulders. It was an exquisite item, the sort of thing one sees in the window of Selfridges, and on the fashion plates of ladies' magazines. It would have cost more than I was earning in a month. Beneath it Miriam wore a dark blue camisole – deep indigo – that covered very little but would doubtless have cost me even more.

'You didn't bring me any supper, by any chance?' she asked.

'No. Why? Are you unwell?'

'I think I picked up a chill from being out in the rain earlier, but I'm fine, just a bit of a fever. The real trouble is that woman . . .' She lowered her voice and glanced nervously up and down the corridor.

'What woman?'

'Nancy, she keeps pestering me. I was going to go down for supper but I simply couldn't face her. And then she came and knocked on my door! Honestly! I had to pretend I was asleep! I've been holed up here all night by myself. I think she thinks I'm . . .'

'What?'

She lowered her voice again. 'Interested.'

'Interested in what?'

'Her.'

'Well . . .'

'You don't think I am?'

'No. But . . .'

'What?' said Miriam.

'Well, perhaps you're sending out the wrong signals,' I suggested.

'The wrong signals, Sefton? What on earth do you mean?'

'You went to the dance with her last night.'

'It was just a dance, for goodness sake! What's wrong with you people!'

At that moment Nancy appeared at the end of the corridor. She must have been waiting, out of sight – sitting at the top of the stairs? With the dim lights, and in her dark suit, she resembled Garbo slinking onto the set of some film noir.

'Miriam!' she said. 'I was waiting for you downstairs.'

Miriam stared horrorstruck, first at Nancy and then at me and then – in a blatant attempt to send out a different sort of signal – she pulled me close to her and cried, 'Come here, darling! Kiss me!'

Her skin was hot to the touch and her mouth burning. I responded as any man might, and before she tugged me into her room I saw Nancy out of the corner of my eye: she looked disgusted as she turned and walked away. The whole thing was over in seconds.

'Thank goodness,' said Miriam, slamming her door behind us. 'That should do the trick, shouldn't it?'

I stepped back into the room and stared at her.

'Don't,' I said.

'What?'

'Don't play with me, Miriam.'

'I'm not playing with you, Sefton.' She reached up and ran her fingers through her hair. 'You'd know it if I was playing with you. That was just . . . necessary, that's all. That beastly woman.'

I couldn't make up my mind what to say or do. There she was. There was the door. And behind me was the bed. The room was the opposite of Morley's but again entirely typical: where Morley had made his room into an outpost of order, Miriam's was in total disarray. There were clothes and scarves and books and make-up and newspapers and magazines scattered everywhere.

'Anyway,' said Miriam, walking over to her bedside table and tugging her dressing gown protectively around her.

'Anyway,' I said. 'I helped you get out of a spot. So now I need you to help me.'

'Really? Is that what you wanted? Is that why you were knocking?'

'Yes.'

She lit a cigarette and inhaled, taking a long deep breath before exhaling slowly, allowing the smoke to swirl around her.

'You know you're so predictable, Sefton.'

I ignored her and continued. 'I found my camera earlier.'

'So?'

'And I've been going back over in my mind everything that happened on the day of the crash.'

'Really?' She sat down on the edge of the bed and crossed her legs, the silk robe falling away to reveal her legs.

'And I remembered we were taking photographs—'

'We?'

'Lucy and I. The little girl.'

'Ah.'

'Of the railway line and the station at Appleby as we were approaching. And Lucy was . . . leaning out of the train.' It wasn't easy to concentrate, but I pressed on. 'So I just wondered if I was able to examine the photographs, they might be able to tell us something about the moments before the . . .'

Miriam breathed smoke through her nostrils, stroked her lips with her thumb and smiled.

'Mmm,' she said.

'It's just, I don't know where we'd be able to develop the photographs. We need a darkroom and chemicals and—'

'Well, maybe I can help. But first . . .'

She stood up, undid her robe at the waist and allowed it to fall to the floor, revealing her naked shoulders and arms, and much else beneath the camisole.

'I said don't play games with me, Miriam.'

'And I said I wasn't playing games with you, Sefton.'

'Then what are you doing?'

'What does it look like? I'm getting dressed.'

'Dressed? Or undressed?'

'One usually precedes the other, Sefton, unless one sleeps naked? Do you sleep naked?'

There was no answer to that.

'Give me five minutes to get ready. And go and get your camera.'

CHAPTER 18

SOME PHOTOGRAPHIC TECHNIQUES

IT WAS GONE MIDNIGHT by the time we arrived at Taylor's Pharmacy in Kirkby Stephen. The town lay in complete darkness; even the usual faint light from the stars and moon was entirely muffled and obscured by cloud. It was steely cold and the streets were tarnished with wet. I was reminded of Spain: it felt like a night for the settling of scores. We parked the Lagonda some distance away from the pharmacy and made our way on foot around the back.

'I'm not sure about this,' I said.

'Oh come on, Sefton,' whispered Miriam. 'What's the matter with you?'

'What if someone's there?'

'Didn't Gerald's sister say he was going to stay with her? It'll be fine. There's no one here.'

'But what if there is?'

'If there is,' said Miriam, her voice hoarse with the cold, 'we'll deal with them.' She could say things like that: she had no idea of what it might mean. I knew from experience that it paid to be cautious and to avoid any kind of harm. 'Anyway, we'll be in and out in no time.'

The back door – of course – was locked.

'So what's the plan?' whispered Miriam.

I didn't have a plan. Thinking about the photographs was as far ahead – and as far back – as I had gone.

'We could smash the window,' I said.

'And wake everybody up?'

'We could try and do it quietly.'

'Are you mad, Sefton?'

'Well, we're never going to be able to pick the lock,' I said. 'Morley couldn't do it.'

'No, but Father didn't have this, did he?'

Miriam removed the long elaborate orange scarf from around her neck – in later years she became a fanatical collector of Hermès, at considerable cost and inconvenience – and from it took a brooch. She showed me the brooch – or, rather, its long thin bent pin.

'You're going to pick the lock?' I said.

'No, actually. I'm going to rake the lock.'

'Rake it?'

'Rake it, Sefton, yes. *Rake* it. Quite different.' She inserted the brooch pin into the lock. 'Father makes everything so complicated, you see. Sometimes you just have to' – she forced the pin in and rattled it around – 'be a little resourceful and a little . . . rough, with it.' And just as quickly as she had inserted the pin she pulled it back. 'Though it takes a woman, Sefton, to know exactly how much force is necessary.'

She pulled the door open.

'Where on earth did you learn to do that?'

'One picks these things up as one goes along, doesn't one? And don't forget, Father taught me at home for years – all sorts of useful skills.' She was whispering with her mouth up to my ear, her body pressing close.

'Indeed.'

'I can also fix pocket-watches, sharpen razors, restore paintings, raise hothouse fruits and vegetables, *and* I offer very competitive rates on fine carpentry and marquetry work, if you're interested.' She held the door open. 'I can turn my hand to most things, in fact, Sefton. If I care to.' She pulled away. 'After you,' she said.

At the back of the pharmacy was where all the chemicals were kept – all the good stuff. There were wooden shelves with bottles and tubs containing every imaginable chemical and compound. It was a mirror image of the front of the shop: smelling salt bottles; boxes of cosmetics; and lipsticks; and rouge; and important-looking jars with important-looking labels. In the middle of the room was a large wooden table set with areas of marble and zinc for preparing medicines. By the back door was a sink. Another set of shelves contained rows of empty cough mixture bottles, and beneath them gallon-drum containers of rosehip oil, dried concentrated orange juice, butterscotch flavour malt, and cod liver oil emulsion.

'Wow,' said Miriam. We were both impressed. 'Look at all this, Sefton. I could do with a dose of something myself.'

'Quite,' I agreed.

She smiled at me sarcastically. 'Shame we're not shopping. Anyway, I got you in, but now it's up to you. Where do we start?'

'Give me your scarf,' I said.

'Why do you want my scarf? Whatever are you thinking of, Sefton?' She looked at me coquettishly and handed the scarf to me. 'What do you want me to do?'

'Nothing,' I said, climbing onto the table and reaching up on tiptoes to wrap the scarf around the central light as best I could. I then jumped down and switched it on. Thank goodness Gerald had installed electricity. The room became lit with a soft electric amber glow.

'Good.'

'Nice,' said Miriam. 'Very classy. Rather like a tart's boudoir.'

'Now, I need to make three baths.'

'Three baths?'

'The developer . . . the stop bath . . . and a fixer – though we could probably do without the fixer.'

'No idea what you're talking about,' said Miriam. 'Modern technology. Layman's language, please, Sefton.'

'Just a tray will do,' I said, looking around. There was fortunately a tray on a shelf, filled with prescription pads and pens and pencils, which I emptied out onto the table. There was also a bucket serving as a bin by the back door, and then there was the sink. So we had all the necessary receptacles.

'Measuring jug?' I said.

'Here,' said Miriam, fetching an enamel jug from a shelf.

'Great. Now, what else do we need?' I was talking to myself, trying to remember.

'Are you sure you know what you're doing, Sefton?'

'Not really,' I said. 'I've read about it. Your father's keen to set up a darkroom at St George's and I've been doing some research, though after Devon . . .' But the less said about Devon the better.

I clicked my fingers, trying to recall. 'We could just look at the negative, but we're going to need a print for evidence. So. We will probably need some . . . rubbing alcohol, or vinegar. Lemon juice?'

'Are we making cocktails?'

'For the stop bath,' I said.

'Anyway.' Miriam pulled a bottle containing rubbing alcohol from a shelf. 'There you are.'

'Good. Sodium sulphite. Potassium carbonate.'

'Are they all going to be here?' she asked.

'I've no idea,' I said. 'Let's hope so.'

'Sodium sulphite!' Miriam pulled down another big brown bottle.

'I'll also need some lithium hydroxide.'

'Slow down!' said Miriam. 'What was the one before that?'

'Potassium carbonate.'

'And then?'

'Lithium hydroxide.'

Within minutes we had found everything we needed – and not a moment too soon.

I thought I heard a door creak open upstairs.

'Did you hear something?' I whispered.

'I don't think so.'

We paused in silence. Nothing.

'It's your imagination,' said Miriam. 'Now, is that it? Is that everything?'

'Well, if we're going to print we need some photographic paper, I suppose. I hadn't really thought about that.'

'You hadn't really thought about it?'

'No.'

'For goodness sake, Sefton!'

'I'm just making it up as I go along,' I protested. 'I didn't have it all planned out in advance!'

'Why not? You know what Father says. Perfect preparation prevents poor performance.'

'Well, I hadn't planned on developing and printing film in the middle of the night in a chemist's shop in the middle of nowhere, had I?'

'Clearly not. Can't we just use ordinary paper?'

'No, no. It's special paper that's light sensitive. We could probably make some if we could find—'

Miriam opened a cupboard that stood by the door into the front of the shop.

'Would Kodak photographic paper do the job?'

'Perfect!' I said.

'Is that it now?' said Miriam.

'Almost. I just need something we could use as an enlarger.'

'Again, no idea what you're talking about. In plain English – we need?'

'A lamp maybe? With a lens. Or in fact we could do without the lens. Just a light source that we can . . .'

Miriam opened the back door, went outside and reappeared moments later with an old carbide bicycle lamp.

'Will this do?' asked Miriam.

It would, and it did; and so I can safely say that my first ever attempt at developing and printing photographs was in Taylor's Pharmacy in Kirkby Stephen, some time late at night in September 1937, using a bicycle lamp, rubbing alcohol, lemon juice and whatever other chemicals were to hand.

I have to admit that it was not an entirely successful experiment. Trying to remember the process, I sometimes became confused, though somehow – more by luck than judgement – I managed to mix and warm the chemicals to make a serviceable developer. (The ideal warmth for the developing solution is about 68 degrees – Fahrenheit, obviously – and the proportions of activating agent to restraining agent and preservative should always be carefully calculated, though what temperature we achieved that night warming the enamel tray over the gas ring by the sink I have no idea, and as for our proportions – they were entirely hit and miss. For an easy-to-follow step-by-step guide to developing and printing photographs, see *Morley's Big Book of Photographic Techniques* (1939). This book earned me my one and only co-writing credit: 'By Swanton Morley. Technical Adviser: Stephen Sefton'. My technical advice, for what it's worth, is this: if at all possible use a professional photographic laboratory.) I managed to get the film from the camera without exposing it and into the developer, and then it was just a matter of time before placing it in the fixer that I had mixed in the bucket and the stop bath in the sink.

'So, what do we do now?' asked Miriam.

'We have to get the timing right,' I said. 'It can't be for too long, or too short.'

'Well, how do you know how long is long enough?'

'I don't know,' I said. 'We'll try about five or six or . . . ten minutes. Fifteen? Twenty?'

'Accurate, huh?' said Miriam. 'So what do we do for five or six or ten minutes? Or twenty?' She leaned in closely towards me.

'Nothing,' I said.

'Nothing?'

'We just wait,' I said, moving away and leaning up against the far end of the table.

'I don't like to just wait, Sefton,' said Miriam, moving round towards me.

I edged slightly away – and she edged closer.

'I told you earlier not to play with me, Miriam.'

'I'm not playing with you, Sefton.' She *was* playing with me. 'Do you not believe in making the most of every opportunity?'

'I . . .'

'Do you really not like me, Sefton?'

'I don't not like you, Miriam, no.'

'Is that a yes or a no?'

'It's not a question I can answer here and now.'

'Why not?'

'Because.'

She was up against me now, nestling against me, whispering in my ear. I found myself turning involuntarily towards her.

'Tell me honestly,' she said, 'did you enjoy it when I kissed you earlier? Were you *very* excited? I know you were excited, Sefton.'

Not as excited as I was at that moment – when the door from the pharmacy was flung open and there was Gerald's sister, her hair in curlers, wrapped in a thick black overcoat and with an umbrella in hand. She screamed with all the force and fury of a woman being attacked by a mob, bellowing like some workhouse mistress who had discovered her unruly orphans stealing food. Goodness only knows what the scene appeared to be to her: the shaded light; the stench of the chemicals. Miriam screamed back, I yelled, 'Get out!' And Gerald's sister, having taken a breath, screamed again. Miriam bolted for the back door. I grabbed the chemical tray and brandished it as Gerald's sister came lunging towards me with her umbrella.

'Don't come any closer!' I said.

'What is the meaning of this?' she yelled. 'You . . . ungodly fornicators!'

'Don't come any closer!' I threatened again.

But she did, and so I had no choice. I flung the chemical tray at her – and in the moment before doing so, as the tray and the chemicals and the film left my hands, I caught sight of the photographs that were developing. What I saw were not clear images, and they were tiny images. But in that instant, as the tiny photographs unspooled in the orange light, I saw the end of my journey with Lucy on the train, reversed, and in black and white: the dark outline of the signal box and at the bottom of the steps a bright white bicycle with a large wicker basket.

By the time I made it outside, the police had arrived. Miriam, thank God, had made it away in the Lagonda, and I surrendered without a fuss. There was no point in arguing. As I was led away I noticed a group of onlookers who had come out of their houses to see what was happening. Among them – though it was difficult to see in the darkness, and I had to look hard two or three times in order to be sure – I saw Nancy. There was a look of pure animal delight on her face: she might almost have been a cat who'd caught a mouse.

CHAPTER 19

A TOTALLY DIFFERENT COMPLEXION

I WAS RELEASED AROUND DAWN. I do not know and cannot confirm if – as Morley suggests in *The County Guides* – the cells at Appleby police station are haunted by the ghosts of those long ago held and tried and executed at the county gaol and assizes. (Morley claimed he was not a super-naturalist but I can confirm absolutely that he did believe in ghosts. The contradictions in his thinking covered quite a range: naturalist/supernaturalist, sceptic/believer, socialist/conservative, lowbrow/highbrow, man of the people and lord of his own manor.) I saw nothing in the cell – no float-ing apparition, no chain-rattling phantom. But I was awake all night listening to the sounds: footsteps, dragging noises, crunches, knocking, the nearby rustle of clothes. Strange smells came and went: something was burning, something was wet, the smell of rope and metal. At one point I thought I heard the voice of a child calling my name and the hair on my head stood on end and my skin went icy cold; it was as if someone held me in a vicelike grip. But then I woke. It was a dream. I know nothing about psychic phenomena but I know that a man might drive himself mad from memory and imagination alone.

Morley was standing outside. Miriam was parked in the Lagonda.

'Get in,' said Morley.

I climbed in. Everything was packed. It looked like we were ready to leave.

'Midnight flit?' I said.

No one said anything. The atmosphere, frankly, was cell-like. Miriam reached over and handed me a cigarette. I was about to light it.

'Must you?' said Morley.

I didn't light it.

'Well?' he continued. 'What have the pair of you got to say for yourselves?'

'I explained; we were just trying to help, Father!' said Miriam.

'Help? Help!?'

'Sefton found his camera and we thought—'

'I know what you thought, Miriam! But a thought's no good without a second thought and an afterthought, and everything that makes thought thoughtful! How many times have I explained? What you did was totally unacceptable. Breaking into the pharmacy!'

'But you'd tried breaking in the other day,' said Miriam, 'when—'

'In the dead of night? With a poor defenceless woman there? The distress you've caused poor Miss Taylor at this difficult time! You should be totally ashamed of yourselves. You're just lucky she's decided not to press charges.'

'Why?' I asked.

'She's Gerald to look after.'

'He's been released,' explained Miriam. 'There's no evidence to link him to the murder of his wife.'

'And Noname's out, thank goodness,' said Morley.

'They're charging him with the possession of stolen goods,' said Miriam.

'The bicycle?' I asked.

'Precisely,' said Morley. 'And Jenkins is already back on his dig. So they've exhausted all their current lines of enquiry and unfortunately the chief inspector's not interested in my theories connecting the dirt from Shap with the dirt at the station. He wants us out of the county. He says we're wasting police time – and frankly I agree.'

'But Mr Morley—' I said.

'I gave them my word we'd be back on the Great North Road and heading south by breakfast.'

'What?'

'We have to check in at various police stations along our route.' He looked at one of his watches. 'Which means time is no longer our own, I'm afraid. You two have *cheated* us of time.'

'But—'

'And if we don't check in at the agreed hours then I'm afraid the pair of you will be brought in again for questioning.'

'But that's—'

'Which means we have to leave . . .' He checked another watch. 'Precisely . . . now. Miriam?'

'But what about Maisie Taylor?' I said. 'And the investigation into the crash. Lucy?'

'It's none of our business, Sefton,' said Morley. 'We came here to write a book, plain and simple. We should never have got involved.'

'But we are involved!' I said. 'And it is our business: it's my business. I was there when Lucy . . . And we discovered Maisie's body. It's you who insisted that we stay and become involved! I was ready to leave! I put myself in danger so we could stay and work on the book!'

'You put yourself in danger?' said Miriam.

'I mean . . . We can't just drive away now as if nothing's happened, just because some policeman tells us to!'

'First, Sefton,' said Morley, 'the law of the land is the law of the land. And if a policeman instructs us to leave, we leave.'

'You don't believe that!'

'Second, we drive away when I say we drive away. And third – and perhaps most importantly – as long as you're in my employ, sir, your business is *my* decision. While you were languishing in your cell, I might point out, I spent the night talking to the police and to Gerald's sister, doing my level best to prevent charges being brought against both of you in relation to your idiotic escapade! How do you think your latest fiancé's going to react when you find yourself in court, Miriam? Your reputation!'

Miriam made no answer.

'And as for you, Sefton, the police already have you marked down as a troublemaker and so you would be well advised to start behaving like an exemplary citizen – immediately! I have made a decision on all our behalf that we should leave, and we are leaving! Do I make myself entirely clear?'

Silence descended. It was rare for Morley to lose his temper but when he did his face became flushed and his fists clenched, his voice raised in pitch. 'Do I make myself clear?'

'Entirely,' I said.

'Miriam?'

'Entirely,' she agreed.

A thin mist was rising from the ground as the sun began to break through overhead and we began our journey out of Appleby. I was exhausted – but I had absolutely no intention of leaving. There was one sure way to keep Morley on the case.

'I saw some photographs,' I said.

Morley said nothing.

'In the pharmacy. Before Gerald's sister arrived, we were developing the photographs. I saw them.'

'Well, that's marvellous!' said Miriam. 'Isn't it, Father?'

'I think one of them may have shown where Maisie was shortly before she died,' I said.

'Where?' asked Miriam.

'At the signal box,' I said.

'The signal box?' said Miriam. 'Really? Well, wouldn't that mean—'

'Stop the car!' said Morley. 'Miriam! Stop the car! Now!'

Miriam pulled over and stopped the car.

'Say that again,' he said.

'Say what again?' I asked.

'Where do you think Maisie was shortly before she died?'

'At the signal box,' I said.

'At the signal box?'

'Yes, I saw a photograph. Lucy must have taken it moments before the crash.'

'And the photograph shows?'

'It shows Maisie Taylor's bicycle parked by the rails near the signal box.'

'And how can you be sure it was Maisie's bicycle?'

'It was the Taylor's Pharmacy bicycle with—'

'The wicker basket?'

'Yes.'

'You couldn't have made a mistake?'

'Definitely not.'

'You're absolutely sure?'

'I'm certain.'

There was silence again in the car, and then Morley exploded with rage. (He did not of course approve of the phrase 'exploded with rage'. 'Bombs explode,' he writes in *Morley's Handbook for Editors and Journalists* (1921). 'Men are not explosive devices and should not be compared to such. The predominance of the machine should be resisted in our speech, as in our thinking. A man may become enraged or impassioned; he cannot and will not explode, unless, alas, exposed to battle.') He became enraged.

'Well, why the hell didn't you say so before, man?'

'Because you were insisting that we had to leave and—'

'This puts a totally different complexion on matters, though, does it not?'

'It does?' said Miriam.

'A *totally* different complexion.' Morley consulted all his watches. 'Good Gordon Highlanders, Sefton! Did you tell the police?'

'I wanted to tell you first.'

'Hmm . . . Well. In fairness, good thinking, Sefton.' He looked at his watches again. 'OK. I think perhaps we have a few minutes to spare before we hotfoot it out of here. It does however put us rather at risk of missing our appointments with His Majesty's constabulary along the way. Is that a risk you're willing to take, Miriam?'

'Yes, Father.'

'And you, Sefton?'

I didn't even have time to reply before Morley had instructed Miriam to swing the car around and we had turned left and then right and had parked along a terrace of railway workers' cottages only a few minutes' walk from Appleby Station.

'Come on,' said Morley. 'No time to lose.' He jumped out and was banging on the door of a mid-terrace house by the time I joined him.

George Wilson the signalman opened the door. He was wearing shirtsleeves and a waistcoat: it was the first time I'd ever seen him without his uniform.

'Good morning,' said Morley.

George was taken aback. 'It's seven o'clock in the morning,' he said.

'Yes, I'm sorry it's so early. Is Dora not here?'

'She's up at the station, sir. They've cleared the line. The first trains'll be running again shortly. It's an early start, at the café.'

'Of course. I wonder, would you mind if we had a quick word?'

'I've the boys to get away to school here.'

'It won't take a minute. We're just on our way, you see, and there were some things I forgot to ask you about the railway.'

I could see – and hear – three boisterous young boys playing in the room behind him.

'I don't know. Could you come back later?'

'As I say, unfortunately we are on our way – and not really able to alter our arrangements.' Morley squeezed his way past George into the room, calling out to Miriam over his shoulder.

'Miriam, perhaps you'd like to help the boys get ready for school, while Sefton and I have a little chat with Mr Wilson here?'

Miriam glanced at me. She looked appalled.

'Of course!' she said, smiling. 'Absolutely! It would be a pleasure. Come along, boys! Shall we play?'

George had no choice but to allow Morley to make himself at home. It was a sad, sulky, sparsely furnished place. We sat by the window at a square table set with an oilcloth, spread out with some meagre breakfast things: a pint of milk, a teapot in an old brown knitted tea cosy, four enamel mugs half full and the remains of a loaf of bread and a butter dish scraped clean. By the table were three pairs of shoes, lined up ready to be polished. The room looked out over a small grey sorry-looking yard.

'I really am terribly sorry to disturb you,' said Morley, 'but it's just . . . I've been thinking about what happened. And – well, I have come up with a little theory and I wondered what you might make of it?'

'About what happened? What do you mean?'

'On the day of the crash.'

'I've spoken to the police and the investigator about all that.'

'Yes, of course. It's just – as you know – I am some-thing of a railway enthusiast, so I wanted to be clear in my own mind. It may have some bearing on what I write in the second edition of my book about the Settle–Carlisle line. If you could help me and my readers understand the workings of the railways I'm sure we'd all be very grateful.'

'Well,' said George. 'If you put it like that.' Morley always knew how to put it like that. 'I could make some more tea, if you'd like.'

'No, no, thank you,' said Morley. 'That's very kind. We are in a bit of a hurry. But I do wonder . . .' He bent over and picked up a wooden toy train from the floor. 'Might I? It might help me get clear in my mind exactly what hap-pened.'

'Be my guest.'

'Very fine thing,' said Morley, admiring the toy train. It was painted in a bold purple and gold. 'Very fine thing indeed. Did you make it?'

'I think it was something Dora picked up from some-where.'

'Anyway. As I understand it, the train was approaching the station and the signal was in the all-clear position. Is that right?' Morley ran the little wooden train across the oilcloth towards one of the enamel mugs.

'That's right.'

'But you changed the points at the last moment, without warning, because there were gypsy children on the line?'

'That's right.'

'And the train ran on into the creamery.' Morley changed the direction of the train towards the milk bottle, smashing the train into it, knocking it over and spilling milk over the oilcloth. 'Oops,' he said. 'Sorry about that.'

'That's all right.' George mopped up the milk with the tea cosy.

'But that's what happened?'

'That's about it, yes.'

'So that's what led to the death of the little girl and the injuries of many others.'

'Unfortunately, yes.'

'Indeed. Good. Just so I'm clear. Anyway, I wondered if there might perhaps be an alternative explanation?'

George made a face. 'I'm not sure what you mean, sir.'

Morley set down the wooden train, drummed his fingers on the table and then stretched out his hands, as though he were a pianist preparing to play.

'Well, I wondered,' he said, 'and this is just me imagining now, remember, I'm hardly an expert!'

'Granted,' said George.

'I wondered, if it might be possible – under certain circumstances – for a signalman to become distracted?'

'Distracted?'

'Yes. I mean, let's imagine you or some other signalman were entertaining a visitor, for example.'

'A visitor?'

'That's right. Someone . . . I don't know. Someone *vivacious*, shall we say. Someone like . . . Maisie Taylor?'

'Maisie Taylor?'

'That's right. We know in fact that Maisie was out on the day of the crash delivering prescriptions and I suppose I just wondered if she could have been delivering a little something for you?'

'At the signal box? I don't understand.'

'Well, let me be clear,' said Morley. 'And as I say, please forgive me if this is entirely wrong, it's just me trying to work all this out in my head!' He tapped his head with both index fingers, as if awakening some hidden, latent powers of thought. 'So . . . when I was wondering about what might have happened I started to wonder whether a man might possibly become so caught up in his . . . attentions to an attractive young lady, like Maisie Taylor, that he might neglect to perform his professional duties.'

George remained silent.

Morley continued. 'One might easily imagine – might one not? – a man caught in, shall we say, an intimate embrace, which might cause him to fail to switch the points as he should have done, and fail to send a signal, meaning that the driver carried along towards the creamery at perilous speed, derailing a train.'

'You can imagine all you like, sir, but I'm afraid that's not right. Maisie was never in my signal box.'

'Ah,' said Morley. 'Was she not?'

'No.'

'That's strange, you see, because I have some soil samples that would most definitely connect Maisie to the area around the signal box on the day of her death.'

'I don't know anything about soil samples,' said George.

'Right. No, of course not.' Morley paused for effect. 'Oh! And we also have the photographs to prove Maisie was there,' he added.

This was not entirely true. We didn't have the photographs, unfortunately: the film was presumably utterly ruined and overexposed back at Taylor's Pharmacy. But I had seen the photographs, just as I now saw a look of absolute terror flash across George's face.

Morley had seen it too.

'You see, my assistant here,' he continued, pressing home his advantage, 'was on the train, taking photographs with the young girl who tragically died in the crash . . .'

George shifted in his seat.

'. . . and so, with the photographs and the soil samples, having pieced these various things together, I wondered if what actually happened – contrary to what you've been saying – was something more like this. You and Maisie were enjoying your fun, as it were, and the train crashed' – Morley was illustrating all this for George's benefit with his hands running around the oilcloth – 'you rushed down to the scene of the crash, realised you were in terrible trouble and came back to the signal box to find Maisie distraught, perhaps hysterical. Does that sound about right?'

George again made no comment.

'Anyway, now is when it gets really interesting.' He smoothed his moustache and again held out his hands. 'I'm guessing it went something like this. You probably couldn't have trusted Maisie to keep quiet – quite the chatterbox, wasn't she? A garrulous sort of soul? But if it had got out that you had been negligent in the performance of your duties it would surely have cost you your job, not to mention your marriage and goodness knows what else. And so – reluctantly, *of course*, with no malice aforethought – you made up your story about the gypsy children on the line, and then made sure that Maisie wouldn't be telling anyone anything. You then disposed of her body under cover of night, hauling her up to the dig at Shap. Possibly? Probably? What do you think?'

It was an astonishing accusation. If Morley was right, George was responsible for the death of little Lucy. I could have reached out there and then and choked the life out of him. I could feel myself tensing. I could hear Miriam upstairs, reading to the boys.

'Who have you told?' asked George.

'Who have I told? You, Mr Wilson. And you alone.'

'The police?'

'Not yet. I think it would probably stand in your favour for you to go and confess directly to them, don't you?'

George sat looking at the spilled milk and at the toy train on the oilcloth.

'Will you, Mr Wilson? Will you go and confess?'

'I'll confess to messing up the signals, and failing to secure the points, but I won't confess to murdering Maisie, because I didn't.'

'You didn't?'

'I'm happy to take the blame for what was my fault – it had to come out in the end. But I'm not to blame for Maisie. As soon as it happened I told her to sit tight and then I ran down onto the track, which is when I saw you, sir.' He nodded towards me.

'And when you returned to the signal box?' asked Morley.

'She was gone.'

'Gone where?'

'I don't know. It was . . . Everything was confused. I wasn't thinking straight. And it was just as if she'd disappeared.'

'Just as if she'd disappeared,' repeated Morley.

'Yes. Like she'd never been there.'

Miriam entered the room with the three boys looking spruce – hair combed and ready for school.

'How are we getting on then?' she asked.

'We're all done here, I think,' said Morley.

'Can we play with the trains before school, Daddy?'

'It's probably time to go,' said George.

'Yes, time for us to leave as well,' said Morley. 'And you'll definitely do as we agreed?'

'I'll get the boys off to school first.'

'Very good,' said Morley. 'Yes. That's the right thing to do.'

CHAPTER 20

DORA'S STATION CAFÉ

'Now what?' asked Miriam as we left the house, Morley having explained Mr Wilson's confession to her.

Morley checked a watch. 'Time for breakfast, I think.'

'Breakfast, Father? How can you even think of breakfast?'

(Morley was a man with Victorian energies, Edwardian tastes, and eccentric tendencies, so he thought a lot about breakfast, but his thoughts could be rather peculiar. See 'The Breakfast in History', for example, in the *Ladies' Home Journal* (1935), a short but commanding survey of the subject in which he recommends that the housewives of Britain adopt foreign and Oriental breakfast practices. Back in Norfolk, at St George's, I was occasionally subject to some of his own outlandish breakfast experiments: spicy fish with mustard and Gentleman's Relish, devilled eggs with bean curd, sour lassis, and all sorts of strange fermented concoctions.)

'Shouldn't we be going to the police?' I said.

'Mr Wilson will be going to the police himself, Sefton.'

'Are you sure?'

'The crash investigators would be on to him soon enough anyway,' said Morley. 'We've just speeded up the process.'

'But what about Maisie Taylor then?' asked Miriam. 'You say he claims he didn't kill her.'

'Yes,' said Morley. '"Just as if she'd disappeared," he said, Sefton, didn't he?'

'That's right,' I agreed.

'"Like she'd never been there?"'

'Yes.'

'That is admittedly a problem.'

'Admittedly!?' said Miriam.

'There's something not quite right about it.'

'To say the least,' I said.

'Anyway, a cup of tea and a bun might help, I think.' (For all his more exotic proclivities he was partial to a railway bun for breakfast.) He checked a watch again. 'Or coffee and cigarettes, obviously, in your case, Sefton. Come on. We've probably got time.'

We walked the few hundred yards up to Appleby Station and to Dora's Station Café. We'd almost made the door when a voice called out behind us.

'Miriam!'

It was Nancy.

'Miriam!'

'Oh drat,' said Miriam.

'I'll go on ahead here,' said Morley. 'If you don't mind.'

'Stay with me,' Miriam whispered, tugging at my arm. 'Please. No games this time, Sefton, I promise.'

'Miriam? Yoo-hoo? It's me.'

Morley went into the café and Miriam and I turned to face Nancy.

With her suitcase and beret, and dressed in a light travelling suit, she reminded me of a young Brigader setting off to Spain.

'You're leaving?' said Miriam.

'Yes,' said Nancy. 'I'm not welcome on the dig any more, and I heard the trains are running again. So I'm heading down to London.'

'Right, well, goodbye then!' said Miriam, turning to go into the café.

'Miriam? Don't go! I've got a little something for you.'

Miriam turned back. She looked alarmed. I leaned up against the wall of the station and lit a cigarette. I was intrigued. This could be interesting.

'It's a little gift,' said Nancy.

'It's not my birthday,' said Miriam.

'No. But I wanted to apologise.'

'Apologise for what?' asked Miriam, rather nervously. She looked over towards me. 'Really, you have nothing to apologise for.'

'Oh, but I do,' said Nancy. 'I . . . wanted to apologise for . . . ringing the police last night.'

'What?' said Miriam. 'You rang the police?'

'Yes, it was me, I'm afraid.' Nancy didn't seem that apologetic, I have to say. But it made perfect sense. That's why she was outside the pharmacy.

'You?' said Miriam.

'Yes. I saw you breaking in with . . . him.'

She gave me a feline glance and I raised my eyebrows in what I hoped was a sign of detached curiosity.

'You followed us?' said Miriam.

'I couldn't help myself. After I'd seen you in the hotel, I

was just so . . . Anyway.' She knelt down and opened her suit-case. 'Here you are.' She thrust a carefully wrapped parcel at Miriam. It was thick, round, cylindrical. A jar of something? Some sort of strange electrode? A large artillery shell? 'I was going to send it. You can open it if you like.'

'Thank you but no thank you,' said Miriam. 'I can't accept it, Nancy, sorry.' She offered it back. 'I'm sure you can under-stand why.'

'Please,' said Nancy. 'I'm . . . You should understand . . . Sometimes I get so lonely and I thought you might be a friend, because . . . Please. I made a mistake. And . . .'

It seemed very likely that Nancy was about to cry. I knew there was no way that Miriam was going to put up with that and if preventing tears meant accepting the damned present . . . Miriam straightened herself up.

'Well, that's really very kind of you, thank you.' She took the proffered package. 'Perhaps we'll run into one another in London.'

'I'd like that,' said Nancy.

'Yes,' said Miriam. Meaning – clearly – no.

Nancy walked round the station onto the platform and over the bridge to wait for the train.

'Well!' said Miriam, as we entered Dora's Station Café. 'The cheek of her! At least we avoided tears.'

She spoke too soon.

The café was deserted. It was a determinedly bright sort of place, though rather muggy with ancient tea and coffee fumes lingering beneath the sharp stinging rinse of recent disinfectant. Pot plants and vases and displays and posters advertising Wyman cigars and Capstan cigarettes obscured the autumn light at the windows. Rows of shiny tin teapots and thick white china were lined up behind a counter on narrow shelves, the clinically clean counter itself being framed by deep red damask curtains, giving the whole place the feeling of an intimate theatre or a fairground sideshow – or perhaps a rather opulent operating theatre providing tea, coffee, sandwiches, cakes and 'quick lunches'.

Morley was sitting at a corner table with Dora. She was dressed in a pinny with her wild hair up tucked up under a scarf, but with a blood-red blouse and a blazing silver locket around her neck she still looked as though she might at any moment burst into her habanera, were it not for the fact that she was silently weeping. Morley held her silver-ringed and braceleted hand and was offering her his handkerchief.

'Oh, for goodness sake!' said Miriam.

We approached the table.

'Father?' said Miriam. 'Is everything OK?'

'Yes, I was just talking to Dora here, about her husband.'

'I see,' said Miriam.

'Sefton, I wonder if you would you be so kind as to change the sign on the door?' asked Morley. 'We don't want any customers coming in and finding Dora like this, do we?'

'Thank you, Mr Morley,' said Dora, through her tears. 'Thank you.'

I walked over and flipped the cardboard sign. Dora's Station Café was now officially closed.

Miriam and I pulled up two chairs and joined Morley and Dora at the table.

'I didn't know anything about her, Mr Morley,' said Dora. Her mascara had run: in her bright red lipstick and red blouse she looked rather grubby and menacing. 'Honestly. Not until after the crash.'

'When did he tell you?'

'Maybe the day after – when her body was discovered. He was acting so strange, you see. And at first I thought it was just the shock of the crash . . . But, I don't know, a woman somehow knows these things, Mr Morley.'

'Female intuition?'

'That's right. You just . . . know when something's not right between you. And George is usually such a good man and a loving husband, he's . . . He probably went with her more out of politeness than anything.'

'Out of politeness?' said Miriam.

'You know what men are like, miss. They're such silly buggers. They're like children.'

'Mmm,' agreed Miriam.

'But he claims he didn't kill her,' said Morley.

'She was on at him to own up because of the crash,' said Dora. 'He knew he'd lose everything. His job. Everything. So he panicked. He was thinking of me and the kids. He didn't want us to lose everything—'

'He told you all this?' I asked.

'And so then he took the body and buried it at the dig.'

'As I thought,' said Morley. 'You poor thing.'

'How did he know where to take her body?' I asked.

'He heard me talking about the dig, I suppose. He must have thought it was as good a place as any.'

'Where there were lots of people digging? Why would he bury her there? A bit risky, wasn't it?'

'Go easy there, Sefton,' said Morley. 'Dora's upset.'

'It's OK, Mr Morley,' said Dora. 'I'm not saying it was clever of him. George is a signalman, he's not an archaeologist.'

'And how did he get her to Shap?' I asked.

'I don't know. I can't say any more.'

'That's enough, Sefton,' said Morley. 'You really don't deserve any of this, Dora.'

There were people banging on the door of the café, keen for a cup of tea and a bun.

'Thank you for coming, Mr Morley,' said Dora, sniffing and wiping her eyes. 'I appreciate you coming but I probably have to get on here. This is my livelihood, and if George is going to . . .'

Morley stood and put a hand on her shoulder. 'You're being very brave, Dora. Thank you.'

'Thank you, Mr Morley,' she said. 'You're a good man.'

CHAPTER 21

THE END OF THE STORY?

WE WALKED BACK DOWN the terraced street and towards the Lagonda. Miriam climbed in and ostentatiously slammed the door behind her. She was of course incapable of un-ostentatiously slamming a door, but there is ostentation and there is fabulous ostentation, and Miriam was a fabulously ostentatious door-slammer. Net curtains shivered all the way along the railway workers' terrace. I imagined the trembling of marmalade as far away as Milburn and the quivering of sausages in Swindale.

Morley tapped on the window. 'Miriam?' he said. 'Is everything OK?'

'No, it is not, Father!'

Clearly.

'Why, what's wrong?'

Miriam wound down the window. 'What's wrong? Really? You embarrass me sometimes. Flirting with that . . . woman!'

'Flirting?' said Morley, taken aback. 'I wasn't flirting, was I? I'm not aware of ever having flirted with anyone in my whole life.'

'Oh really! "You don't deserve any of this, Dora"? "You poor thing"? "Female intuition"? Do you really think it's appropriate behaviour?'

'Appropriate?'

'I mean what would Mummy think? Hmm? She's only been . . .' Miriam coughed. I rather feared that she was going to burst into tears.

'Well,' said Morley, who was also now clearly upset and embarrassed. 'She would . . . I don't think it's . . .'

Morley and I were standing awkwardly at the side of the road. Men and women were beginning to emerge from their houses, either on their way to work, to clean their doorsteps or – more likely – simply to get a better look at what was happening. We were rather conspicuous.

'Your mother was – is – irreplaceable, Miriam. She—'

'Oh, just get in the car!' said Miriam. 'You stupid fool.'

We both climbed in. Miriam threw the gift from Nancy onto the back seat towards us.

'What's this?' asked Morley.

'Don't ask!' she said. 'Some silly gift. Right. Now where?'

'Well, aren't you going to open it?' asked Morley.

'Just put it away, Father. It's nothing.'

'I wonder what it is?' asked Morley. He shook it: it rattled.

'Open it if you want,' said Miriam. 'I don't care. Let's just get out of here. I hate it here! I hate it!' She stamped her feet on the floor and opened the window to address the women who stood on their doorsteps, watching us. 'Yes, ladies, I said I hate it here! Now run along!'

Morley, oblivious to this little tantrum but inquisitive as always, opened the parcel. It was a candle in a jam-jar holder, with a little metal handle soldered around the top.

'It's rather pretty actually,' said Morley. 'Quite ingenious. Who gave it to you?'

'Wait a minute,' I said. 'Isn't that exactly like the one that was next to Maisie's body, in the souterrain?'

Morley held up the jam jar. 'Do you know, I think you're right, Sefton. Who gave it to you, Miriam?'

'Nancy,' said Miriam bitterly. 'And before you speak, Sefton' – she held up a forbidding finger – 'I do hope you're not going to suggest again that Nancy was the person who killed Maisie. Because it's quite ridiculous. The poor girl's clearly confused, but she's not a murderess.'

'No,' I said. 'I wasn't going to suggest that she was a murderess, actually.'

'Clearly not,' said Morley. 'But I think I know who is.'

'Yes, we already know who is,' said Miriam. 'George.' She nodded towards his house. 'We've been through all that, Father.'

'Do you know, I fear we have been barking up the wrong tree,' said Morley. 'And I think perhaps you're right, Miriam. I may have been rather a fool as far as your mother is concerned. I—'

Miriam held up a hand. 'We're not talking about it now, Father. I'm sorry. I just get upset sometimes when I think about her.'

'I know,' said Morley. 'And I think my judgement may have been clouded by the very same thoughts. You may have saved things in the nick of time, Miriam!'

'Really?'

'Yes, yes! I think you've given me a wake-up call!'

'I have?'

'You have indeed! Fire her up, my dear! Come on. As fast as she'll go!'

Miriam revved the engine like she was starting in the Gordon Bennett Cup.

'Goody!' she said. 'Where to?'

'I think we need a last word with the gypsies.'

We sped out of the terrace, Miriam tooting the horn in farewell to our onlookers, and out of Appleby and made it to Kirkby Stephen in record time.

Naughty ran up to meet us as we approached the gypsy encampment down by the river.

'Mr Morley! Mr Morley!' she cried. 'Can you read to me, Mr Morley?'

'In a moment, my dear,' said Morley. 'In a moment. I just want a quick word with your daddy first.'

The vardos were packed and ready to go. There was nothing left at the site, no evidence that the gypsies had ever been there but for the dying embers of a fire.

'Mr Morley,' said Noname, as we approached. He stood by the fire with Job, a hand-rolled cigarette clutched tightly in his fingers. Job made it perfectly clear we were not welcome. He ignored us and went to harness his horse. Noname was hardly more welcoming.

'You're moving on then?' asked Morley.

Noname looked around him, surveying the scene, which was a perfect idyll, the sort of thing a Constable might paint on a Lakeland holiday.

'This is a terrible ole place to bide in,' he said.

'I thought it was quite beautiful,' said Morley.

'Not if you're us,' said Noname.

'And where are you planning on going?'

'Devon, Somerset. Before the snow. People say there's places down there no one know about that you can bide till you'm grey-headed. Not like here. And plenty of winter work. Hedge-laying, cutting logs.'

'The police released you without charge?' said Morley.

'They charged me with handling stolen goods is all,' said Noname. He pinched out the remains of his cigarette and pocketed it. 'The girl's bicycle.'

'Yes,' said Morley. 'I wanted to ask you about that.'

Emerald emerged out of the vardo. She did not look in the mood to be trifled with.

'Ah, Emerald my dear, good morning,' said Morley.

'He didn't have anything to do with the murder of that young woman,' she said.

'No. I know he didn't.'

'So what do you want?' asked Emerald, hands on hips. 'As you can see – if you've eyes in your head – we've things to do.'

'I just wanted to ask Noname a few questions,' said Morley.

'Oh no. No more questions,' said Emerald. 'He's answered all the questions he'll be answering, to you or anybody else.'

'That's quite understandable,' said Morley.

'On your way then,' said Emerald.

Morley turned to Noname. 'You enjoyed my stories when you were a boy, didn't you?'

'I did, Mr Morley. And I do so still today.'

'Well, rather than asking you any questions perhaps you'd

allow me to tell you a story and you can tell me what you think of it?'

Noname looked towards Emerald. She shook her head.

'I can't see as it can do any harm,' he said.

'Good!' said Morley. 'It concerns your father.'

'My father?'

'Emerald told us about him the last time we saw her.'

'You said we could trust him,' said Emerald to Noname.

'And you can,' said Morley. 'You can. I was very sad to hear about the troubles that you went through because of your father. His being banished from his own people because he pursued a relationship with a gorgio. You must have felt the pain of that terribly.'

'I did, Mr Morley. Yes, I did.'

'And every year when you came back to Appleby to the fair it must have been worse. Did you see him?'

Noname's mother now appeared beside Emerald at the door of the vardo. She was holding the baby in her arms and looked even less in the mood to be trifled with than Emerald. She glared suspiciously at Morley, but even more suspiciously at Noname.

'Did you?' asked Morley.

'Once or twice, yes,' said Noname. 'But no more than that.'

'Dordi, dordi,' said the old woman. 'Dordi, dordi, dordi.' And then she went back inside the caravan.

'He was my father,' said Noname. 'I did nothing wrong, seeing him.'

'No, of course not,' said Morley. 'But it wasn't only him you saw, was it?'

Noname looked at him a moment in astonishment and then shook his head.

'Your father had a child with his new wife, didn't he? A daughter. Your half-sister. And you saw her too, didn't you? You loved her as your own kin, even though she was a gorgio.'

'She has Rom blood in her veins, the same as me,' said Noname.

'What are you talking about?' demanded Emerald. 'Noname?'

'Brother and sister,' said Morley. 'And right from those early summers when you were children playing together did you swear never to desert one another?'

'What is this? Is it true?' said Emerald.

'So when she came and asked you for help you could not refuse her, could you?'

Naughty came charging over, chasing the dog.

'Can you read to us now, Mr Morley?'

'In a moment,' said Morley. 'We're nearly done here.'

Noname stroked Naughty's head and kissed her on the forehead and spoke softly to her in Romani and told her to go and play – which she did.

'I didn't kill Maisie Taylor, Mr Morley.'

'I know you didn't,' said Morley. 'But you took her body, didn't you? You put it in your wagon and buried it near the dig. You did it for your sister.'

'How did you know?'

'I didn't. Not until less than half an hour ago. It took me a long time to work it out. You covered Maisie's face – a gypsy burial rite – and then you placed a candle beside her in one of these.' He produced the jam-jar candle-holder given to Miriam by Nancy. 'To light her way in the next world.'

'But why?' asked Miriam. She and I had stood by silently

[285]

during the previous exchange. It hadn't been clear to me initially why we were there. But it was pretty clear now. 'Why would he do that?'

'Because it seemed like the right thing to do,' said Morley. 'Didn't it, Noname? Maisie Taylor had done no wrong to you. You wanted to afford her a safe passage.'

'That's right.'

'That is right. And it is morally right, spiritually right. But under the law . . . I'm afraid it makes you an accessory to murder.'

'What?' said Emerald.

'Which I'm afraid is a serious crime.'

'Get away from us!' shouted Emerald, who had realised the implications of what Morley was saying. 'Do you hear me? Get away! You've brought us nothing but trouble, even though you said you'd help us!'

Naughty came running over. Noname's mother appeared again at the door of the caravan with the baby.

'It's OK,' said Noname.

Job came sauntering over too.

'What are you going to do now, Mr Morley?' asked Noname.

We were faced with six pairs of eyes fixed upon us.

'Do now? I'm not going to do anything. It's up to you and your conscience, Noname. It's not up to me. I didn't come here to judge. I just came to tell you a story. It's up to you to work out the moral of the story. Do you remember what I wrote on the last page of *Morley's Book for Boys*?'

'I'm not sure I do, Mr Morley, no.'

Morley spoke to Naughty. 'Could you fetch your father's book now? I'd like him to read from it with you.'

Naughty climbed up into the caravan to fetch the book while we all waited in silence and then she came and sat on Noname's lap.

'Are you going to read with me, Daddy?'

'Yes I am,' said Noname.

'Just the very last words,' said Morley. 'On the last page.'

Noname opened the book and started to read, Naughty perched happily in his lap.

'"Boys,"' he read, '"as you grow older you will face ever greater challenges and . . ." I can't . . . I don't know that word.'

'Preoccupations,' prompted Morley.

'. . . "preoccupations. I hope that the lessons you have learned from this book might stand you in good stead for those challenges to come, and that one day, if you are lucky enough to have sons and daughters of your own, that you might share these simple life lessons with them so that others might benefit from the knowledge that takes us beyond ourselves to understand and appreciate others."'

'It's boring, Daddy!' said Naughty. 'Can we read one of the proper stories? Is that the end of the story?'

'That's the end of all the stories,' said Morley.

'Let's start again,' said Naughty. 'Daddy, let's start again!'

All that was left for us was to see to the murderer.

CHAPTER 22

OPEN TO CLOSED

WE PARKED AT THE STATION, next to the big Excelsior motorbike and the Steib sidecar with its proud purple and gold lettering announcing DORA'S STATION CAFE AND OUTSIDE CATERING – CATERING FOR ALL TASTES.

Inside the café, Dora was bustling about. She spotted us immediately.

'Mr Morley! Back again! What a nice surprise! Do take a seat. I'll be with you in two minutes. I just need to sort these people out.'

An elderly gentleman slowly counted out pennies to pay for his tea at the counter, and then another elderly gentleman put in an order for one of Dora's Herdwick lamb and juniper pies – he had his son and his family visiting at the weekend. He and Dora swapped local news and gossip. He lingered, and lingered, but finally he left and we were then the only customers. Dora came over to the table, grinning, and Morley solemnly nodded to me. I knew what to do. I went over to the door, turned the key in the lock and flipped the sign from OPEN to CLOSED.

'No, no need!' said Dora brightly. 'It's fine. I'm fine now. We'll not need it closed. Don't you worry, Mr Morley.' She laughed. 'I'm not going to get upset again.' She was wrong.

'Take a seat, Dora,' said Morley.

'Why, what's all this about then?' asked Dora. 'Have you not given me enough to worry about today, Mr Morley?'

'I'm sorry,' said Morley.

'You're all right,' said Dora. 'I was upset earlier, that was all. You can understand that.'

'I can, yes,' said Morley.

'What is this about then? Someone's not been complaining about the food, I hope?'

'No, Dora. We just saw your brother,' said Morley.

Dora didn't skip a beat. 'But I haven't got a brother, Mr Morley.'

Morley looked at me and Miriam, disappointed.

'Noname,' he said. 'Dora, we've just come from talking to Noname.'

I had no idea how she'd react.

She stared at him, pursed her lips and let out a long low sigh, as if having been holding her breath for a very long time.

'How did you know?'

This was a question I often asked myself. I have often tried to reconstruct the ways in which Morley solved a crime or a puzzle. In a way it's become my job. But it's not always easy. It often feels like reaching the end of one of his beloved Ellery Queen thrillers, to find all the evidence set out before one, and yet still being incapable of solving the mystery. On this occasion, however, Morley was kind enough to explain everything to Dora. It went something like this.

He explained first that when he had met her at the dig at Shap he had been immediately impressed by the ingenuity of her sidecar hotbox – a great work of homespun art and engineering, the kind of thing that could only have been created by a blacksmith. And then of course the sidecar was painted that distinctive purple and gold – the very colours of a handsome Tom Tongs vardo. And then he had noticed her silver locket – a silver locket in the shape of a horseshoe.

'Your family emblem?' he asked.

Dora nodded.

And there was more – much more. The solving of a puzzle requires so many pieces. (For Morley's thoughts on solving *actual* puzzles see his perennially popular compendium of games, *Morley's Big Book of Puzzles* (1933), and its even more popular companion volume, *Morley's Puzzle-Solver* (1934), a book I have open before me now, and which begins, rather grandiloquently for a book of crossword tips and handy hints on domino stacking, jigsaws and word games: 'All true progress of mind begins with the arrangement and resolution of complex objects and ideas into their component parts.')

'I was very taken with you when I first met you, Dora,' he explained. 'My daughter here subsequently pointed it out to me and I must admit I felt a little ashamed; but then I realised that it wasn't you I was attracted to.'

'It wasn't?' said Miriam.

'No,' said Morley. 'It was the smell.'

'The smell?' said Dora.

'Arpège by Lanvin. Your perfume?'

Dora's eyes widened.

'My wife's perfume also, you see,' said Morley. 'I must have smelled it on you when we first met and then I smelled a hint of it again in George's signal box. Top notes of polish and oil but base notes of Arpège by Lanvin. You'd been in the signal box?'

'Of course I'd been in the signal box! I'm his wife. He forgets his lunch all the time. Men!' She appealed rather pathetically, I thought, to Miriam, who did not respond or smile.

'Had he forgotten his lunch that day?' asked Morley.

'Which day?'

'The day of the crash?'

'I don't know what you're talking about,' said Dora.

Morley then began to build on his evidence. ('Anticipations and calculations will take a man so far in solving a puzzle,' he writes in the *Puzzle-Solver*, 'but at a certain point one must rely upon vision and imagination. Puzzle-solving is a painstaking business. It also involves the art of risk.')

'Did you perhaps arrive to find a bicycle leaning up against the railings by the signal box? Had you already had your suspicions?'

Dora's face revealed nothing.

'Your father was a weak man, Dora. Perhaps you were disappointed in yourself that you had chosen another weak man as a husband?'

Again, Dora remained tight-lipped.

'Dora?' prompted Miriam.

'You wouldn't understand.'

'We might,' said Morley. 'You might try us?'

'I was furious,' said Dora. 'Furious with him. Furious with her. I knew he was up to something. People had been talking. But I had to have proof. I needed to see it with my own eyes. I knew I'd catch them.'

'So what happened?' asked Morley.

'I didn't mean to hurt her. I just burst in to the signal box and there she was. And the door was open and . . .'

'She fell down the steps of the signal box?' said Morley.

'That's right,' said Dora.

'She wasn't pushed?' I asked. 'You didn't push her?'

'Sefton!' said Morley.

Dora said nothing.

'If she fell down the stairs, why didn't you simply confess?' asked Miriam. 'Go to the police?'

Dora went to speak – but seemed unable to find the words.

'Because that's not all you did, is it, Dora?' said Morley.

Dora looked at Morley as a condemned man might look into the eyes of a sentencing judge, begging for mercy.

He continued. 'When did the train crash? At that very moment? A few minutes later? Was it you who sent him off down the tracks with his concocted story?'

'I didn't tell him to say it was gypsy kids on the line,' said Dora. 'I told him to say there were kids, that's all.'

'And then you hid the body?'

'It was chaos everywhere. George was taken to the station to talk to the police, I hid the body under the signal box and then . . .'

'And then?' said Morley.

'I went to Noname. I knew he'd help me.'

'And he did help you?'

'We put her in the back of the vardo at night and took the ancient way up to Shap.'

'And you told him where to bury her?'

'We both knew about the underground pit.'

'How?'

'This is where we're from, Mr Morley. We know all the secrets and hiding places, from when we're children – not like Jenkins and his stupid dig.'

'And you were happy to see Professor Jenkins framed for Maisie's murder?'

'He wasn't framed,' said Dora.

'And Gerald Taylor?'

'I wasn't thinking. It all got out of control. I didn't think she'd be found. I just wanted to get rid of her.'

'Like she was never there?'

A blustery wind had picked up outside the station and the door, though locked, rattled on its hinges.

'Did you ever tell your husband about your father, Dora?' asked Morley. 'Did you tell him your father was a gypsy?'

Dora shook her head.

'I've never told anyone.'

'But he knew,' said Morley. 'He told us. He must have known there was something different about you.'

'He might have guessed, I suppose,' said Dora. 'But I never told him. I never told anyone. Not even when I was a kid.'

'Why?' asked Miriam.

'You wouldn't be able to understand,' said Dora. 'Woman like you.'

'And what became of your father?' asked Morley.

'He never got over losing his family and his people.'

'Being made marime?'

'That's right. He'd drunk himself to death by the time I was ten years old.'

'So Noname lost him and then you lost him too?'

Dora looked at Morley, at Miriam and me, and began sobbing – but this time none of us offered her a handkerchief.

'And every year you saw Noname at the Appleby Fair,' continued Morley. 'Brother and sister, united in your loss.'

'It was me who made him do it. It's not his fault.'

'I know,' said Morley.

'I always knew it would end like this.'

'What would end like this?'

'Me, living a lie. Not one thing or another, half gypsy, half gorgio, not fully accepted in either world. That's the trouble with this place—'

'Which place, Dora?'

'This town, this place, this country. If you don't fit in it's like . . .'

'It's like you're not there?' said Morley. 'And that's why you had to work so hard to prove yourself. *Dora's Station Café and Outside Catering – Catering For All Tastes.*'

'Will I go to prison?' asked Dora.

Morley sat back in his chair and relaxed his shoulders. It had been an extraordinarily tense and difficult conversation.

'I don't see why you should,' he said. 'If Maisie Taylor tripped down the stairs, as you say. Plus, you're a mother, well-respected in the local community – no right-thinking judge would send you to prison, Dora. At worst, you were guilty of a crime of passion.'

There was a banging on the door.

The banging grew louder. Dora turned to see who was there.

'It's George,' she said.

'Well,' said Morley. 'You two will doubtless have much to talk about. Perhaps we should take our leave.'

'We're just going to leave them?' said Miriam.

'That's right, Miriam,' said Morley. 'We're just going to leave them. There's nothing more we can do here. Thank you for your time, Dora.'

∽ ∾

We continued our discussion outside the station, by the Lagonda.

Miriam was absolutely furious. I was none too happy with the outcome either. Dora and her conspiring husband disgusted me. But I could see at the same time how events had conspired against them.

'We should at least escort them to the police station!' said Miriam.

'We're not their gaolers, my dear. And the police station is . . .' He pointed off to his left, down the hill past the railway workers' cottages to a building no more than half a mile away. 'What? There. A five-minute walk away?'

'But what if they run away?'

'I don't think they will, do you? Where would they run to? This is their home, isn't it?' He looked down over the town of Appleby. 'Or where they live – which is as close a place to home as any of us ever have. And anyway they'd be caught sooner or later, if they ran.'

'They might not,' said Miriam.

'No one can hide for ever,' said Morley. 'Not in England. You'd have to be on the move the whole time, wouldn't you?'

'Do you think she killed Maisie, Mr Morley?' I asked. 'Do you think she pushed her?'

'Perhaps only she will ever know,' said Morley. 'But perhaps that's enough. Living a lie is a terrible thing – it eats away at your soul.'

'They're responsible also for the death of the little girl,' I said.

'I know,' said Morley. 'Which must be a terrible burden.'

Miriam lit a cigarette. 'You know your trouble, Father?'

'No,' said Morley. 'But I have a bad feeling you are about to tell me.'

'Your trouble is you can always find something to like in people.'

'We all have redeeming qualities, Miriam, don't we? Even those with the darkest hearts and those who have committed the most heinous crimes – and I hardly count Dora and her husband in that category.'

'Well, I strongly disagree,' said Miriam.

'Why am I not surprised?' said Morley.

'Not everyone has redeeming qualities. Do they, Sefton? Do you believe that?'

'I don't know,' I said.

'Well, personally, I know I could never find anything to like in a murderer.'

'Not in any murderer?' asked Morley. 'Really? King David? Moses? Samson?'

'That's different, Father.'

'I don't see why.'

'Because,' said Miriam.

'Because what?' said Morley.

'Because it was a long time ago! I'd like to think we're rather more civilised now.'

'Yes, well, I'd like to think so too,' said Morley.

We fell silent all at once as the sound of a train could be heard in the distance, drawing into the station.

'Listen!' said Morley. 'Wonderful sound, eh? They really are running again. Life goes on, as it always must. And we have work to do! Much left for us to do in Westmorland alone!'

'What about the chief inspector?' said Miriam. 'I thought we had to check in at police stations all the way along the Great North Road?'

'I don't think that'll be much of a problem now, do you, my dear? Besides, there's this place, Mardale Green – a village that was submerged by the Manchester Corporation a couple of years ago when they raised the level of Haweswater to form a reservoir and the whole village simply disappeared. Worth a visit, eh? Bit of a metaphor, what? And then there's—'

'Is that the London train, do you think?' I interrupted.

'Leeds, then London, yes, I would have thought so,' said Morley. 'Why?'

'It's just, I thought perhaps I might—'

'Ah, yes, good thinking, Sefton! Still thinking about the book, eh? Trying to get it back on track? The Settle–Carlisle line, in reverse?'

'That's right,' I agreed.

'Good, good.'

Miriam looked suspiciously at me.

'We'll see you back in Norfolk, then, shall we?' said Morley. 'What, tomorrow?'

'Yes,' I said. 'Absolutely. Definitely.'

'You're not coming with us then?' said Miriam.

'No, I don't think so,' I said.

'Well, really, I thought I could rely on you, Sefton.'

'He'll be back tomorrow, Miriam,' said Morley.

'Will you?' asked Miriam, giving me her sternest gaze. 'You're not thinking of deserting us?'

'I'm—'

'Leave the poor chap alone, Miriam!' said Morley, who had climbed into the back seat of the Lagonda. 'Can you come and get the typewriter fixed? We really have to get on here.'

Miriam ground out her cigarette underfoot and leaned to-wards me – I thought to kiss me goodbye.

'You'd better be back in Norfolk with us tomorrow,' she whispered. 'Or I'll come looking for you. Do you under-stand? My life is moving on, Sefton. I have things to do. Plans to make.'

'Wedding plans?'

'All sorts of plans. And you're looking after Father now.'

'Miriam, come on!' called Morley.

As the train pulled in, and just as the doors were opening, I bought a newspaper from the vendor on the platform. Turning to get into the carriage I saw – to my horror, but also to my relief – Lucy's mother, with her baby, struggling to climb aboard. I quickly went to assist. I wanted to say something. But she stopped me with a stare. In her eyes all I could see was hate.

Finding a seat in the corner of a carriage, I opened the paper and found what I had been dreading at the bottom of the front page, an article entitled 'MARLBOROUGH STREET MURDER?' A man who had been found beaten outside Marlborough Street Magistrates' Court the week previously had died in hospital. Police were treating the death as suspicious and were appealing for anyone with information to come forward.

I had enough cigarettes to last me till London and a pocketful of Delaney's powders. The train pulled out of the station.

ACKNOWLEDGEMENTS

For previous acknowledgements see *The Truth About Babies* (Granta Books, 2002), *Ring Road* (Fourth Estate, 2004), *The Mobile Library: The Case of the Missing Books* (Harper Perennial, 2006), *The Mobile Library: Mr Dixon Disappears* (Harper Perennial, 2006), *The Mobile Library: The Delegates' Choice* (Harper Perennial, 2008), *The Mobile Library: The Bad Book Affair* (Harper Perennial, 2010), *Paper: An Elegy* (Fourth Estate, 2012), *The Norfolk Mystery* (Fourth Estate, 2013), *Death in Devon* (Fourth Estate, 2015). These stand, with exceptions. In addition I would like to thank the following. (The previous terms and conditions apply: some of them are dead; most of them are strangers; the famous are not friends; none of them bears any responsibility.)

Toluwalope Alabi, Hannia Amir, Aubrey Anderson-Emmons, Jennifer Andrews, Sophie Asty, Andreas Avraam, Emma Axelsson, Hugo Ball, Kanika Banwait, Hope Barker, Sarah Batty, Julie Bowen, Monica Boyajiev, Amy Brandis, Benjamin Bryant, Ty Burrell, Sarah Wayne Callies, Cassandra Cooper-Bagnall, Hannah Cooperwaite, Coppi (Belfast), Benjamin Creeth, Thomas Crompton, Owen Davies, Abigail

Day, Daniel Day, Will Dove, Melissa Edmunds, Martin Edwards, Laura Elliston, Lorayn Emterby, the English Library (Alassio), Established Coffee (Belfast), James Reese Europe, Rhiannan Falshaw-Skelly, Jesse Tyler Ferguson, Scott Flanigan, Hannah Froggatt, Samuel Fry, Pascal Garnier, Nolan Gould, Roseanna Gray, Alice Griggs, Hackney Colliery Band, Nichola Harding, Jamie Hardwick, Zoe Harrington, Eleanor Hastings, Hebe Hewitt, Ellen Hiller, Jaden Hiller, The Hop House (Bangor), Elizabeth Hurst, Sarah Hyland, Alex Jago, Aamir Kapasi, Rebecca Kelley, Samantha Kelly, Ming Yi Koh, Sohini Kumar, Vicky Lai, Emily Lambi, Ellen Lavelle, Anna Lodwick, Jessica Lowe, Mica Lowe, Carmella Lowkis, John Lynas, Nicholas Makinen, Jean-Patrick Man-chette, Alick McCallum, Lucy McCarthy, Cathy McKenna, James McKenna, Olivia McNeilis, Annmarie McQueen, Wentworth Miller, Samuel Mitchell, Steven Moore, Abigail Neale, Charlotte Newbury, Yvonne Okey-Udah, Ed O'Neill, Morfudd Owen, Alex Payne, Mrs Peabody, Brogan Pierce, Andrey Platonov, Alexandra Prew, Olive Higgins Prouty, April Roach, Katyana Rocker-Cook, Rico Rodriguez, Kent Russell, Colin Sackett, Joshua Saffold-Geri, Simran Sandhu, Joanne Sarginson, Allegra Scales, Paul Scheuring, Sophia Schoepfer, John Servante, Jimi Sharpe, Alex Smith, Brillia Soh, Maaike Spiekerman, Oliver Stockley, Eric Stonestreet, Mark Storey, Patrick Symmons-Roberts, Hu Ting Tan, David Taylor, Anne-Marie Thomas, Lewis Thomas, Michel Thomas, Josephine Throup, Kate Tolley, Sofía Vergara, Jonella Vidal, Matthew Walpole, Gabriella Watt, Robert W. Weisberg, Ariel Winter, Dahmicca Wright, Cheuk Ling Ann Yip.

The next of

THE COUNTY GUIDES

ESSEX POISON

The county is their oyster . . .

October 1937. Stephen Sefton is sliding deeper
into depression and despair. His employer, Swanton
Morley, shows no signs of letting up in his quest to
write a guide to every county in England – despite
the disasters that seem to follow him. And Morley's
daughter, Miriam, continues to cause chaos.

The trio set off to Essex when Morley is
invited as an honorary guest at the Colchester
Oyster Festival. But when the mayor dies suddenly
at the civic reception, suspicion falls on his fellow
councillors. Is it a case of food poisoning?
Or could it be . . . murder?

PICTURE CREDITS

THE NORFOLK MYSTERY

IAN SANSOM

The first of

THE COUNTY GUIDES

Quaint villages, eccentric locals – and murder!

Professor Swanton Morley needs help writing a history of England, county by county. His assistant must be able to tolerate his eccentricities – and withstand the attentions of his beguiling daughter, Miriam. Stephen Sefton is broke and looking for an adventure.

The trio begin the project in Norfolk, but when a vicar is found hanging from Blakeney church's bell rope, they find themselves drawn into a fiendish plot. Did the Reverend really take his own life, or was it . . . murder?

DEATH IN DEVON

IAN SANSOM

The second of

THE COUNTY GUIDES

Cream teas, school dinners and satanic surfers!

When Swanton Morley is invited to give a speech
at Rousdon school, he, his daughter and his assistant
pack up the Lagonda for a trip to the English Riviera.
But when the trio arrive they discover that a boy
has died in mysterious circumstances . . .

Join Morley, Sefton and Miriam on another
adventure into the dark heart of 1930s England,
as they follow up a Norfolk mystery with a
bad case of . . . death in Devon.